Call

Me

Cy

Robert Barton

Call Me Cy is a work of fiction.
Any similarity regarding names, characters,
or incidents is entirely coincidental.

Published in the United States by Kalinowski & Martin
Publishing, Whitman, Massachusetts.

Hardback ISBN: 979-8-9899316-0-6
Paperback ISBN: 979-8-9899316-1-3
Epub ISBN: 979-8-9899316-2-0

Printed in the United States of America

Front Cover Artwork: majivecka

Edited by Christopher E. Blackman

Designed by Riverhaven Books
Whitman, MA

This book is dedicated to
Reese, Lilian, and Eloise,
the lights of my heart.

Prologue:

Shadows, being creatures of darkness, dread the night. For when it comes, they cannot see the edges of themselves.
And no longer know who they are – or even if they are.
Becoming lost in the dark where no one hears their cries…

One: Who do you think you are?

"Hmph!"The shadow fled before him along the red clay road as if trying to escape his anger, with its little book bundle hanging from its left hand, its lunch pail hanging from its right hand, and its shoes tied together and hanging from its shoulder. It looked like a good little shadow schoolboy. A drumbeat to his anger came from the steady sound of bare feet slapping on the dusty, hard-packed clay this shadow often traveled – dust had covered his well-tanned feet and turned them red, and one little red foot would come into view with each step – left, right, left, right.

"Who do you think you are, little boy?' Who d' I think I am? WHO d' I think I am? I know who I am! I know right well who I am! Y' mean ol' school teacher! I am Cyril William Ledbetter, but people call me Cy, and my daddy's named William, and my mama is Ida. I know who I am! 'At's what I should o' told her. I'm 'onna say it next time. And I ain't no little boy neither; I'm ten years old – 'at's big enough to help my daddy on the farm and t' run to the general store for my Mama when she needs somethin'. Who are you anyway, Miss Bevis? Ain't got no husband – pro'bly can't keep one inna cage. Betcha can't even cook an' 'at's why you ain't never found a man 'at'll have y'. Ain't got no kids of y' own t' be mean to so y' gotta be a school teacher so you can be mean t' other folks' kids. I'm tired o' you – y' ole biddy. 'At's what I shoulda told her – Imma tell her 'at next time."

"Hey Cyril – Cyril slow down," came a little boy's voice. "Hold up, Cyril; I wanna ask y' somethin'."

The shadow never broke stride as the little boy called back over his shoulder. "You askin' to get y' nose broke, Billy – I told y' don't call me Cyril."

The angry little boy watched as two more shadows ran up from behind and joined on either side of the one ahead of him. One shadow was the same size as his own, and the other was a little smaller and wearing a shadow dress.

"But yo' name is Cyril," came a little girl's voice.

The angry shadow froze and planted its feet as the other two shadows went forward another step before they stopped and turned.

"I told y'all to call me Cy," said Cyril.

"Ok, Cyr… um Cy," the little girl's voice replied. "Are you gonna break my nose if I forget?"

Cyril responded, "No, Norma Jean, I ain't gonna hit no girl. I'll tell y' what though, I'll hit yo' brother if y' forget."

A smiling little freckled face looked up as she rocked on her feet, "ok Cyyyyril, I'll try to remember not never to call you Cyyyril again.

Cyril looked over at his friend with an evil grin. "Hey Billy, c'mere."

"Y'all ain't funny, y'all ain't funny at all," responded Billy. "Norma Jean, y' run on home now. We gonna go down to the creek and swim."

Wrinkling her brow, she answered. "I wanna go swimmin' too."

"You ain't old enough t' go swimmin' with us," said Billy. "B'sides y'd hafta go swimmin' with the girls anyways. So you run on home now – and be shore to put y' bonnet back on, or granny gonna make y' scrub yo' face with buttermilk t' git rid o' them freckles."

Norma Jean pursed her lips and stomped her foot. "I'm 'onna tell Mama."

"What you gonna tell Mama?" The older brother asked.

"Im 'onna…. I'm 'onna tell her somethin'," she said with an angry squeak.

"Yea, and I'm 'onna tell granny you runnin' round hye with yo' sleeves up and yo' bonnet off," threatened Billy.

The little girl yelled back, "It's hot – an' it's nineteen twenty-one. Some folks don't even wear bonnets no more."

Billy said, "Well, while y' telling thangs t' Mama, y' be shore t' tell granny about it bein' nineteen twenty-one an' see what y' git. Now run along."

The little girl huffed and turned to stomp off back toward town.

Billy turned to Cyril and shook his head, "Boy, young 'uns is irritatin'. Why you so mad anyway?"

"That damn school teacher, 'at's why," came the answer.

Billy sucked his teeth, "She ain't gonna call you anythang but Cyril. And if y' Mama hear you cussin' like 'at, she gonna wear y' like a shoe."

Cyril took off running toward the creek and called back over his shoulder, "Race y' there, slowpoke."

Billy ran after Cyril, yelling, "That ain't fair; how come y' always cheat?"

Later that afternoon, Cyril had just run up the lane and through the back door. He remembered too late that he should catch the screen door before it slammed, and he heard the loud crack just as he spun to grab the door's wooden frame.

"Cyril!" He was startled at his mother's voice calling from the kitchen.

"Sorry, Mama," the boy responded.

"And what did you forget?" Ida asked from the kitchen.

The boy stood there on the screened-in back porch and took stock of everything that he had with him. He remembered to put all his clothes back on after swimming; he had his lunch pail and book bundle, and shoes hanging from his shoulder. "I don't, um … I do not know, Mama."

3

His mother stepped into view inside the door from the porch to the kitchen. She was tall, with her dark brown hair pulled back into the tight bun that farmers' wives wore during the day. She stood ramrod straight as she looked down at her son, lifting her eyebrows in a way that caused her brown eyes to flash expectantly as she waited for his memory. "What was the last thing I said to you this morning as you left here for school?"

"I, I don't, um, I do not recall Mama," the boy stammered.

"You do not recall that you were told to come home straight away after school in order to go into town and pick up a few things from the general store?" Her voice came in the clear, clipped words that made her sound a little more formal than the other ladies. "Who do you think that you are? Do you think you are someone special who can ignore his mother?"

The boy shook his head, "No, ma'am, I just plain ol' forgot Mama, and I'm sorry."

The woman said, "Well, tomorrow is Saturday, and you can go first thing in the morning to get what we need, and you can have extra chores to help train your memory. Your feet are filthy, and I would not have you feed dogs with hands that dirty. Put your lunch pail in the kitchen, your shoes by the door and go outside to the pump and clean yourself up – with soap. Supper is almost on the table, and I will not have your father wait for you, so if you wish to eat, you will be ready before he says grace."

"Yes, ma'am," the boy responded.

It was only eight o'clock the next morning, and the red clay road was already heating up from the sun. Cyril could feel it warming his bare feet as he ran into town with his Mama's list in one hand and his shirt in the other hand and wearing a pair of old denim overalls that his mama had cut short after the knees had worn out. He was headed to the general store and wanted to get there and back home as fast as his feet could carry him. He knew that the longer he took on this

4

mission, the more extra chores his Mama would have time to consider adding to her list. And he aimed to keep that list of tasks as short as possible.

He felt his feet hit the wooden porch of the store. He headed into the door, but going from the bright sunlight to the relative darkness inside left his eyes trying to adjust. Before he could see anything, he heard the storekeeper's voice, Mr. Dawson, already yelling at him, "Stop right there, boy! You can't come in here right now."

Cyril blinked against the darkness to get his eyes to work as he responded to the familiar voice. "Why not, you open ain't y'?" He said between breaths as he panted from his run. "An' why you always yellin' at me?"

"Yes, we are open, but it's Saturday morning," said the man. "And if you knew how to listen to folks, they wouldn't have to yell."

The little boy's eyes adjusted to the darkness but still looked confused as he faced the man. "I know, it's Saturday mornin' – I was s'posed to come by hye yesterday after school to get some thangs for my Mama, but I forgot, and she ain't too happy with me right now. If'n y' gimme ever'thang on this hye list, I'll git right back outta your store for the rest of the day."

The man looked thoughtful. "As tempting as getting rid of you sounds, you cannot come in here right now. You will have to wait until ten o'clock before you are allowed in the store."

"Ten o'clock?" The boy shouted in a panicked voice. "I can't wait till then. My Mama told me 'at she knows how long it takes me to run into town and git back and how long it'll take you t' git her list together an' 'at I best get back directly. If I gotta wait till ten o'clock, my Mama gonna be Old Testament angry, and I 'on't wanna die." In the store, he heard a chorus of feminine snickers around him, but he was too intently focused on Mr. Dawson to look around.

"Old Testament angry, is it? Like the plagues of Egypt?" The man asked.

"Yes, sir, just like that. Big ol' swarms o' fleas and yellajackets," the boy responded.

The man said, "There were not any fleas and yellow jackets in the plagues of Moses."

The little boy shook his head. "No, sir, but that was Egypt. This hye is Alabama, and y' know if they was plagues in Alabama, it'd be fleas an' yella'jackets – and prob'ly some rattlesnakes too." Another chorus of laughter from inside the store.

The man sighed. "You all, please don't laugh at him. It just eggs him on, and that little boy would argue with a stump to get it to move out of his way rather than walk around it like he has any sense." The man looked at the little boy in the doorway. "Your mother is a fine upstanding lady, and her temper is not that bad."

"I'll be sure t' tell her you said that," the little boy responded. "Then you can talk t' her about when we see y' at church tomorra'."

The man pointed toward the back of the store. "Boy, one of these days, I am going to take down one of them there brand new razor straps and wear it out on your behind. Wear your britches out too. And then I'll make you pay for the strap and new britches."

"There y' go wantin' t' beat me," the boy said. "Why does ev'rybody wanna beat me? You wanna beat me; my Mama wanna beat me; the teacher wanna beat me, ev'rybody."

The man shook his head. "Well, you are the common denominator in all of those equations. "

The boy looked confused again. "What d' y' mean?"

Another sigh from the man. "It's you. You argue with everyone. Your single mouth outworks both of your ears. God gave you one mouth and two ears, and you ought to use them in those proportions."

"I don't argue with my Mama," the boy said.

"Nobody argues with your mother," the man said.

"Are you scared o' her too?" The boy asked.

"I am not afraid of anybody but God," said the man. "Your mother is a lady, and I don't argue with ladies."

The boy shook his head. "I ain't seen God get mad, but I seen my Mama get mad, and I know who I better be scared of."

The man couldn't help a tiny smile as he nodded toward the door. "Now, you go on back outside, and I will see you at ten o'clock, and you better have that shirt on – there are ladies shopping in this store."

His voice sounding frustrated, the boy said. "But y' still ain't told me why I gotta wait 'til ten o'clock."

In an equally frustrated tone, the man explained. "Boy, I do not know how you can be nine years old and from Bratton, Alabama, and still not know how things work here. Every Saturday morning from eight until ten is the colored hours when the colored folks can come in the store to shop. The rest of the time, the white folks can come in. But right now, it is colored only."

The little boy finally looked around at the other people in the store, and he saw a half dozen somewhat familiar local female faces in various shades of brown looking at him and a very light-skinned unfamiliar man standing at the counter. He realized that he had never seen a Black person in the store before and had never been to the store early on a Saturday. And then he piped right up. "Well, I don't mind."

"You don't mind? YOU don't mind. Aren't you the privileged little prince? Well, maybe they mind. Maybe they don't want to be in the store with some stinky little white boy who needs a bath. Maybe they want to shop in peace. Maybe I will not allow any improper mixing of the races in my store. Maybe other folks mind. But it is just fine because you don't mind. Boy, sometimes you are like a shadow after the sun goes down – you do not know the edge of yourself."

With an indignant expression, the boy said. "I 'on't stink; I went swimmin' in the creek yesterd'y after school – so I 'on't stink. Besides, you white an' you in the store."

The man's voice hardened. "I am the shopkeeper, so I have to do the math. And you have an hour and a half until ten o'clock, so you go on back down to the creek and rinse that smell off because you didn't get it all the first time."

Mr. Dawson turned to the light-skinned man in front of the counter and said, "that is why I do not have any children."

Cyril heard this as he walked out of the store, and he called back over his shoulder, "And I thought it was 'cause you can't find a wife – an' I'm ten years old, by the way."

The man raised his voice to call out to the boy. "Who do you think you are speaking to me that way? Ten years old? Then you are all the more ignorant, and you should keep your mouth shut until someone puts a plate in front of it. You will be lucky if I let you back in this store at ten o'clock."

Cyril found himself standing on the store's porch with more than an hour to kill, so he just moved away from the door and sat down on a little barrel on the porch right outside the open window of the store. He could hear the voices inside but was paying them little attention.

Two: Sharing Things

The storekeeper was finally able to concentrate on the customer in front of his counter. Standing across the counter was a well-dressed light-skinned Black man. The gentleman was about average height with a light build. His weathered but self-respecting look indicated he was somewhere close to sixty years old. Mr. Dawson glanced down at the man's hands as was his custom. As a storekeeper, he liked to figure out as much as he could about a new customer, and he could tell a lot about a man's profession from his hands – and what he saw surprised him. There were no scars or calluses from decades of heavy work outdoors. They were instead the hands of someone who makes his living with his mind rather than his back. "I do not recognize you. Are you just visiting here in town or maybe passing through?" As the store clerk spoke, he continued to study the man before him. He noticed that the man wore good solid shoes and his pants were not those of a farmer, and his shirt and suspenders were good quality with the sleeve cuffs neatly folded up three turns for the heat outside. They were standing inside, so the man held his well-brushed hat in his hand. The storekeeper noted that every item of clothing on this new customer was comfortably worn in but of good quality and higher on the price scale. Almost enough to be uppity, but not quite.

"Actually, I have newly arrived here in town," answered the man.

"I retired recently and decided to move here from Tennessee. I purchased a house a few doors down from the train station."

The storekeeper looked quizzically at his new customer. "The old Dempsey house was down there – did you buy the old Dempsey house?"

"That I did," the man responded. "And it requires some serious attention. I have a carpenter set up to start with repairs on Monday morning. And I have a list of paint, lumber, and supplies that he and his men will need in order to get started." He pushed a sheet of paper across the counter toward the shopkeeper, who looked it over.

"This is quite a list," said the white man. "This is going to be fairly expensive. Are you aware that I don't extend any credit accounts? We are strictly cash on the barrel head here."

The man nodded. "Oh, that is fine. I will pay for everything now in cash – and if I may, I would like to leave thirty dollars with you on an account. That way, as Mr. Fletcher needs incidental supplies or equipment, he can just send one of his men down to pick it up."

"Thirty dollars – on an account?" The shopkeeper was visibly taken aback. "We can certainly do that. Isaac Fletcher is the best carpenter in Alabama. Not going to lie. He did my porch steps and my roof last year. I know all the boys that work with him, so you just send one down for anything you need. They all know to talk to Jeremiah around back. Jeremiah is my boy around there; takes care of the lumber yard and supplies, makes some deliveries, and gets everything from the train station when the stock comes in. And during the week, if you need anything, he can get it for you. You'll meet him after we settle up here. You can take your wagon around back, and he will get you loaded right up. Let me tot all this up real quick." The man picked up a pencil and rapidly scratched numbers onto the page. "Going to have to order these tin shingles; we don't keep them in stock – most folks can't afford them. Tell Isaac to plan on doing the roof last to wait for them shingles to get here."

"I will be sure to pass that along to Mr. Fletcher," the Black man responded.

The storekeeper continued to talk as he calculated. "So you said that you are retired. What kind of work did you do up there in Tennessee?"

"Over thirty years as an attorney in Memphis," responded the customer.

The shopkeeper stopped and looked up with surprise on his face. "A lawyer – you were a lawyer? Boy howdy, I have never seen a colored lawyer before. I guess that if we can have a colored doctor, we can have colored lawyers. Have you met the doctor down there on that side of town? Jonathan is the only colored doctor in this part of Alabama – maybe anywhere outside of Birmingham. And he's pretty young too. Not sure what would bother me more, but we got old Doc Harrison up on this side of town anyway."

"I have an appointment to meet Dr. Barnes Monday morning just before lunch," the man answered.

"I hear that he is a good doctor. Back during the influenza, when Dr. Harrison got sick, he sent for Jonathan to come and take care of him. Dr. Harrison said that he was as good as any white doctor. Well, here is the total." The white man slid the paper across the counter for his new customer. "That's a pretty big number. If you want, I can ask Sarah Stiles over there by the notions to take a quick look at it. She works as a calculator over at the bank, and she is quick with numbers."

The Black man looked in the direction the storekeeper had indicated and saw a young dark-skinned woman looking in their direction, having heard her name. The two customers exchanged polite smiles and nods, and then the man turned back to the counter and said. "That will be fine; I can look it over." The man quickly scanned the column of numbers as he slid his finger down the paper. "Everything looks to be in order." He reached into his pocket for his billfold and began to lay crisp cash on the counter. "I hired a wagon over at the livery, so I will go pick that up now, and you said that I should take it around to the lumber yard in back and ask for Mister … ? Forgive me, what was his name again?"

The storekeeper smiled. "Just ask for Jeremiah is all – he's the only one around there anyways."

After he finished paying, the man thanked the storekeeper and turned to leave, and as he reached the door, he heard the white man's voice behind him. "I didn't get your name."

The Black man turned back and responded. "Bratton, Cyril Bratton." The man noted a slight, startled wave sweep across the face of the clerk, and he felt several other sets of eyes turn to look at him.

"Cyril?" The shopkeeper asked loudly. "I have only heard that name on one person here lately – that irritating little boy that was in here earlier."

Meanwhile, young Cy was sitting there, not paying attention to the sounds coming out of the store, until he heard the shopkeeper call out his name. He jumped up and zipped quickly through the door, squeezing passed the man who was exiting. He looked at Mr. Dawson and asked. "Did y' call me? Can I come in a get my Mama's thangs now?"

Anger swept across the face of the man. "No, I did not call you, and no, you cannot come in here yet." He pointed back behind the child. "That boy that just left here – his name is Cyril too. So all you heard was me saying his name."

"His name is Cyril?" Asked the boy excitedly. "I ain't never met nobody with my same name before." The child spun around and rushed out of the door, calling. "Hey!"

The clerk shook his head and said out loud to no one in particular. "Maybe that'll get that itchy little boy out of my hair." And then he turned to tend to a middle-aged lady who was approaching the counter with a basket of goods. "Hello, Missy. Did you find everything that you need?"

Cy called again, "Hey!" The man heard the voice of the boy so he stopped and turned. "Can I talk t' you?"

The man resumed walking. "If you can walk and talk, you may – I have an appointment behind the store, and I need to go get a wagon."

"Are you really named Cyril?" The boy questioned as he fell in beside the walking man. "I ain't never met n'body with my name before. I'm Cyril too. But ev'rybody calls me Cy."

"Your name?" The man asked. "I have had this name fifty years longer than you have been alive. I think that you have my name. Cy, is it? Why Cy instead of Cyril?"

"Oh, I reckon that it was your name first. Ah, Cyril is just a queersome name – just too strange. You don't never hear 'bout people named Cyril 'cept for folks what's been dead for a while. Was you named after somebody? My Mama says that she named me after my granddaddy. But I ain't never met him before. He lives too far away, is what she says. And between you and me, I don't think that he and my Mama were too awfully friendly about her marrying my daddy."

"Is that so? Named for your grandfather," the man responded. "Well, I was named after my father, and he was named after his. But you prefer to be called Cy? How do you spell that?"

The excited boy continued. "Like Cyril but without the ril. What's your last name? Because my last name is Ledbetter."

"My surname is Bratton," answered the man.

"Bratton?" The boy asked. "Like the town?"

"Yes, just like the town," said the man.

"Huh. Have you ever been to Bratton before?" Asked the child. "You know the town was named after a family what used t' own most of the land around here on their plantation, way back when?"

The man nodded. "Actually, I was born on that plantation. 'Way back when.' But my mother and I moved away when I was very young, though I did come back here to visit once as a young man – and to see my father."

"I hope 'at you 'on't mind me sharing yo' name wi' y'," the boy said. "Kinda nice knowin' somebody who shares my same name."

The boy noticed the man stop, so he stopped and looked up at the man who was smiling down at him. "Yes, young man, sharing a name with someone is nice. Proud to meet you, Cyril."

The boy said, "Nice to meet you too. But ev'rybody calls me Cy."

The man started walking again and asked. "Did you ask your mother to call you Cy?"

The boy's eyes got big, and he responded. "Noooo, tha's as bad as a day could get."

"Old Testament bad?" The man asked.

"At least." The boy responded.

The boy was watching the two shadows on the ground as they walked, and he stopped just after the shadows scooted over the train tracks that divided the main street – and the town. "I ain't never been on this side o' town before. Is we going t' yo' house t' git yo' wagon?"

The man responded. "I imagine you have never needed to be on this side of the train tracks before. And no, we are not going to my house; I do not own a wagon. We are going to the livery, where I have arranged to hire a wagon for the day. I have also hired some young men to unload it at my house." The man began to walk again.

"No wagon?" The boy asked incredulously. "Ev'rybody has a wagon. How d' y' git around with no wagon?"

The man stopped in front of a barn-sized building where a wagon and mule waited for him. "Well, I can walk anywhere here in town. The train station is right there if I need to take a long trip. And for anything else, I have an automobile."

"An automobile?" The boy shouted as he became excited. "Can I see it? I wanna see it. An automobile; don't nobody around here have an automobile 'cept Judge Haines an' the Doctor. An' 'ey don't hardly never take 'em out. An' 'ey won't let me just come an' see 'em. I want an automobile when I'm grown. I'm 'onna have me one too."

The boy was interrupted by a booming voice, and he quickly looked up to see a tall, dark-skinned Black man in his forties affixing a hat to his head with one hand while pointing at the mule. "He's all hitched for you, Mr. Bratton; his name is Sally."

"His name is Sally?" The elder Cyril asked.

The livery owner answered. "Named all my mules Sally after my first wife left. Got three females and two geldings – all named Sally. Woman's still here in town, and it makes her mad as a wet hen, but pretty much everything does – just like a mule."

The lawyer laughed. "Well. I hope that the second Misses Stone worked out better."

The darker man smiled. "Oh yes, she was like seeing an orchid flower for the first time – so beautiful that it hurts. And she never changes and never ages."

The elder Cyril showed a quick flash of pain across his face which then resolved to a haunted smile. "I know the feeling."

The liveryman said, "Then we are two lucky men." After a pause, he continued. "Now I can send my sons up there to the lumber yard to load everything for you."

The older man answered. "No thank you, just send them across the way to my house in an hour. I am told that there is a man in the lumberyard to load the wagon."

The liveryman answered. "That there is. My sons will see you in an hour, and they can just bring Sally and the wagon back with them."

"Very good, thank you, Mr. Stone," the older man said as he climbed onto the wagon seat.

The boy looked up at the man. "Can I ride back t' the store wi' you?"

The man nodded toward the empty side of the seat, and the boy scrambled up beside the man. As the elder Cyril took the brake off, but just before he started the mule moving, he called to the liveryman who was walking back into the stable. "Mr. Stone, could you tell me the name of the man who works loading wagons at the lumberyard behind the store?"

The younger man stopped. "That'd be Jeremiah, Jeremiah Dawson. Just like the name on the store. Always been a Dawson who owns the store and always been a Dawson loading the wagons."

The older man nodded his appreciation as he snapped the reins and clicked his tongue to get the mule moving.

The little boy said, "That's a funny coincidence how they both got the same last name. Dawson – make it sound almost like they family or somethin' like that. I reckon they both inherited their jobs; one owns the store like his daddy, and the other works there like his daddy did. I reckon that a lot of thangs run in families."

"Yes, they do, Cyril," the man agreed.

"Ever'body calls me Cy." The boy corrected.

"Except your mother," said the man.

The boy nodded. "Except my Mama and the school teacher – but she's just mean."

"I am sure that the school teacher has your best interests at heart," the man said.

"I 'on't thank she has a heart," said the boy half to himself.

The man chuckled.

"What kinda work do you do?" Asked the boy.

"For over thirty years, I was a lawyer in Memphis, but I am retired now," answered the man.

The boy asked. "Was yo' daddy a lawyer too? Does that run in your family?"

"No, he was not." Responded the man.

"Oh, that's right, Y' said that y' was borned on the old plantation. So was yo' daddy one o' the farmers on the plantation?"

The man glanced down at the boy sitting beside him. "Something like that."

The boy continued. "I on't want t' be a farmer like my daddy. I mean to say, I love 'im – he's my daddy. But I jus' 'on't wanna be a farmer. They have t' work so hard ever' day."

"So what would you like to be then?" The man asked.

"I 'on't know," the boy responded. "Maybe I'll be a lawyer like you."

"You will have to study hard. And improve your English," the man said.

"What's wrong with m' English?" The boy asked.

The man continued, "Let me ask you this. The way that you have been speaking this morning. Is that the way that you speak in front of your mother?"

"Oh, I see." The boy responded.

The man motioned ahead. "Here we are." He pulled the mule to a stop and then reached down and set the brake. Mr. Bratton immediately started climbing down. The boy jumped down from the wagon on the other side.

"You must be here to pick up this long list of supplies." Came a disembodied voice from within the darkness of a long shed. A medium-brown-skinned man quickly followed the sound, wearing well-worn overalls. He was tall, looked about forty, and walked with a slight limp.

"That I am," responded the older man. "You must be Mr. Dawson."

"I am he," said the man in overalls. "Gave me the list, but he didn't tell me your name."

"Cyril, Cyril Bratton." The older man held out his hand.

The younger man reached out to shake hands while giving the older man a studied look. "Haven't heard that name in a long time. Like out at the old plantation?"

"Yes. Like out at the old plantation. I was born there – before the war," said the older man.

The younger man nodded. "My father was born before the war, too, not twenty feet from here. There used to be some quarters back here behind the store, but they're gone now – knocked the cabin down to expand the lumber yard and shed. Some of the buildings are still standing out there near the old plantation house if you ever want to go out and see 'em. That place out there has been abandoned for thirty years now since old man Bratton died. His wife couldn't have children, so there wasn't anyone to take over the place. But he had sold most of the land off before he died anyway."

The older man shook his head slightly, saying, "No, thank you, I left there as a boy and went back once as a young man. I have seen everything that I need to see out there."

Mr. Dawson looked thoughtful and nodded. "Maybe there's not anything out there for anybody anymore." Then after a pause, he clapped his hands to dispel the moment and said, "Welp, let's get this wagon loaded." He motioned toward the boy and said, "Looks like you got a puppy following you, Mr. Bratton."

"He is just waiting for his turn in the store," said the older man.

The two men headed into the large shed to get the things on the list, and the boy followed.

Mr. Dawson called to the boy, "If a puppy comes in here, puppy's gonna work; you go over there and start grabbin' gallons of white paint and totin' 'em out to that wagon. There are ten gallons on the list. And one gallon of green."

The boy looked indignant and said, "At's yo' job; I ain't here t' work."

Mr. Dawson looked at the boy and said, "You can stand outside with your mouth closed, or you can come in here, but in here, you gotta work. Besides that, the ground knows how to hold itself down, and bein' useful might do you some good."

The boy said, "I am useful."

The man shook his head and said, "Not at the moment; you're not."

With a huff, the boy headed over and picked up the first gallon bucket of paint to carry to the wagon. He asked, "Are you gonna show me that automobile today?"

The older man responded, "I don't think you will have sufficient time to see my automobile today. I understood that your mother was waiting for her goods from the store and that as soon as you can get in there, you will be heading home to face her anger – her 'Old Testament' anger, I believe you called it."

Mr. Dawson said, "If you waitin' for your turn in the store, it's nigh on ten o'clock now. I can attest that a woman will just get more angry the longer you keep her waiting – nobody wants to go home to a wrathful woman."

The eyes of the boy opened big as he remembered what he was supposed to be doing, and he nodded and said, "I gotta go." He put the bucket of paint he was carrying next to the wagon and then started to undo his overalls to get his shirt on before running around to the front of the store.

The two men watched the boy as he ran.

Three: Family Time

"Met me a man today that has the same name as me," Cyril said to his parents as they sat at the supper table.

"I met a man today," Ida Ledbetter corrected her son.

"Yes, ma'am," the boy responded as he glanced up to see his father give him a subtle smile and wink.

"Is something amiss with your eye Mr. Ledbetter?" Ida asked her husband from across the table.

William Ledbetter looked across at his wife and let his smile broaden as he gave his wife a heated look. "Not at all; these eyes are working just fine."

Ida sat up just a bit taller, and with a mock scolding tone, she said, "We are at the table."

"For now," the man responded with a tilt of his head.

"William Ledbetter!" Ida sounded disapproving, but she looked the man in the eye with her own slight smile.

The boy just put his head down and tended to his plate. He hated it when his parents spoke to one another like this. He hated it when he knew that they were saying many things that were not in the words that he was hearing. The things that people hate hearing the most are the things that they have decided that they do not want to know. And Cyril most definitely did not want to know THIS. Having a room next to his parents was bad enough; hearing it was bad enough, but hearing about it was just too much. He couldn't help but feel like there were always two conversations going at once. He could feel his cheeks warming up and knew his face must be red like a beet.

Then he heard his father's voice. "What's a matter, boy? Your face is red as a smacked backside. You ought t' be happy your parents love one another."

"That will be enough of that, Mr. Ledbetter," said Ida.

"For now," William once again answered.

"For a good long time if you are not careful," said Ida

Cyril, wondered if his parents would even notice if he just sank out of his chair and hid under the table. He felt relieved when he heard his father speak next.

"So tell me about this man you met today," said William. "This man that's got your same name."

Cyril said, "Well, he said that he reckons that it was his name long before it was my name, so I got his name instead of him havin' my name. Anyways, he just moved into town – he bought that house that the old crazy lady used to live in, down just the other side of the tracks."

"Cyril William Ledbetter!" His mother's voice snapped like a whip. "I will not have you showing disrespect to the dead or your elders. Do you understand me?"

"Yes, ma'am," the boy answered. "I am sorry, Mama. It was just what I heard someone say about her at the barbershop. A white woman livin' on the south side of the tracks beside the colored folks."

"Boy, you probably shouldn't repeat what you hear at a barbershop," said his father.

"Or maybe you shouldn't hear what men are saying at a barbershop, and I should just keep you home and cut your hair myself next time your father goes there. My mother always said that children don't belong in a barbershop listening to what men will say in a room

21

with no Bible present." Ida was glaring right at her husband.

William took a breath and continued. "She wasn't crazy. She was born in that house a long time ago – that's where her family lived. She was supposed to get married, but he was killed in the war, so she stayed a maiden lady all her life. She was the last of the Dempseys, and she died in that house. But she was a good Christian woman, and nobody should speak ill of her. My Aunt Jess knew her well – they were good friends. Now the Dempsey house used to be the only house on that side of the town as the Dempseys owned all o' that land. But they came to hard times after the war, and they had to sell most o' their land, and that's when the colored folks started building their houses down there on that side o' the tracks. She said that she didn't care how many of 'em bought her land or built their houses down there, she was born there, and she was gonna stay right there. Now that is enough. You carry your plate out there to the kitchen and then go on in the parlor and do the reading that your mother wants you to do before the sun sets and it's too dark. I know that you are just trying to talk and delay."

"Yes, sir," the boy responded.

As he left the room, he heard his mother behind him. "Sit on that wooden chair or the floor – I do not want my settee getting dirty.

"Yes, ma'am," the boy replied.

Cyril hated reading time. Every evening after supper, it was his mother's custom to sit and read by the parlor window as the sun was lowering in the western sky and for both she and her son to use the last full light of the day to 'illuminate the mind' as she liked to say. Today Cyril laid down on his belly to read a book that he had propped in front of him and with his body turned so that his shadow fell just to the side of his book and wasn't blocking the sunlight from the window. He heard his mother finishing up in the kitchen and then her steps on the hardwood floor as she came into the parlor. He saw her shadow sweep across him as she sat down to read. He noticed how his shadow vanished into hers like her shadow was holding its son the way his mother hugged him sometimes. He also noticed that the new shadow had blocked the light from the window, so he scooted himself to the side until his book was once again in the light, and his shadow detached itself from the larger pool of darkness and was once again laying on the floor beside him.

But Cyril hated it – just lying there holding a book and trying to concentrate. He always timed it by watching the shadow of his mother, sitting tall in her chair, as it slowly crept across the floor toward the far wall. He knew that once it reached and extended some way up the wall, his mother would declare it too dark to continue reading, and he would be released from his torture and have a little time to spend with himself before bed. But the shadow always crept so slowly across the big braided rug toward the wall. He always wished that just this once, the sun would set quickly.

Finally, the shadow slid ever so slowly up the wall, and Cyril knew that freedom was near. He began to make a show by squinting his eyes to see the still perfectly clear words. Ida smiled to herself as she noticed her son's performance. "You may go; it is getting too dark to read."

"Hold on," William said to his son. "You never finished telling us about the man that you met today."

"Oh, yessir," the boy responded. "I met him outside of the store when I went this morning. He was there during the colored hours. Did you know that Saturday mornings are for colored folks only at the store?"

"Everybody knows that Saturday morning is colored hours," said the man. "Why were you at the store during colored hours?"

Ida spoke. "It must have slipped my mind. I might have been a bit piqueish and sent him too early."

The man looked at his wife with a mischievous expression and asked. "You forgot about colored hours? I remember you bein' pretty upset about the colored hours at the store when we first moved in here with Aunt Jess."

Ida gave her husband a look that would warn a wise man to step back from the edge.

The man looked back at his son and said, "So you met a man at the store during colored hours with the same name as you. How old was he, and what did he look like? I guess he was a colored man."

"Yes, he was," answered the boy. "But not like most o' 'em. He was – he was. Like when the man at the barbershop was talking about the really pretty woman, you know, the one he said was yellow."

"Which man at the barbershop was this?" Asked Ida in a stern tone.

"I don't recall Mama," said the boy. "I think he was just in town visiting someone and needed a haircut."

Ida continued. "I will take my fabric scissors down to that barbershop and cut some hair. And I bet that it will stay cut. William, you will not take my son to that barbershop again."

The man nodded in resignation to his wife, looked at his son, and asked. "And? Anything else?

"Well, he must have some good money because he bought a wagonload of stuff to work on his new house. And he sounded like Judge Haines or the Doctor when he spoke. Real clear like – because he has been to college. I think he was about the same age as Judge Haines too."

"So an educated, light-skinned man named Cyril about sixty years old then?" Asked Ida. "Just bought a house in town?"

"Yes, ma'am," answered the boy.

The woman gave her son a stern look. "You need to have care about who you are seen speaking to and spending time with in this town. You do not want to start getting a reputation. And you start wearing a hat to keep the sun off your face."

William said, "I think that he'll be fine. I don't think that people will get too worked up about who a ten-year-old boy is talkin' to."

Ida looked at her husband and spoke to her son. "You run outside while a few minutes are left before the mosquitoes come out. Your father and I need to speak."

"Yes, ma'am, thank you, Mama," Cyril said as he hurried to get outside for the last few minutes of dimming twilight. He needed to be back outside to run off the last of his energy.

After a short time, Cyril heard his mother call his name from the back porch, and he headed to the pump to wash his face, feet and hands before going in to get ready for bed. After his wash, he went inside to change into his nightshirt. After changing, he headed into his parent's room to say good night. As always, his mother was sitting in front of her mirror, already wearing her nightgown. It was the only time Cyril ever saw his mother with her hair down from her daily bun. She was sitting there humming a hymn and brushing her hair out with a boar bristle brush and brushing oil through her hair. She always used her hair oil and skin lotion at night before bed. He could smell the hint of coconut that filled the air around her. That smell that always said 'mother' to him. Cyril also noticed that, as usual, his father was sitting in a rocking chair with a Bible open in his lap, where he had stopped reading a few passages by the lamplight. And just like every night, he sat quietly, watching his wife as she prepared herself for bed. He was holding a Bible and worshiping a woman. This also comforted Cyril – knowing how much his parents truly loved one another.

Cyril glanced down at the braided rug lying on the floor between his parents – an empty braided rug. No little sister there anymore, quietly playing with dollies and waiting to be put to bed. How could someone be so present in their absence? He felt that same lump in his throat as always and the wet sting behind his eyes. He looked up and could see his mother looking at him – noticing where he was looking. He saw that same wet sting in her eyes.

Ida turned and held her hand out to her little boy. "Come here to

Mama and give her a hug."

Cyril walked the few steps to her, felt her arms around him, and breathed deep, the smell of Mama.

Ida pushed him back to arm's length and said, "Look at you. You must stop losing those hats and running around in this Alabama sun with no hat on. It tans you so. Your face and your arms get so dark. People are going to wonder what kind of mother you have." She immediately grabbed her lotion and applied some to his face and neck.

"People are gonna say that he is a beautiful child who takes after his beautiful mother," her husband's voice filled the room.

Ida smiled, shook her head, and said, "Eleven years married, and your father still talks like he is a young man courting."

William responded, "Never hurts to be reminded how lucky you are."

Ida looked at her son and asked. "Do you wonder if he is trying to remind himself or me?" Then she tapped her cheek with a fingertip and leaned toward the boy who dutifully kissed her goodnight.

Cyril headed to his father to kiss him good night, and as always, he walked around the braided rug – the empty braided rug. Everyone walked around that rug like it was some piece of holy ground where a foot dared not tread.

As Cyril climbed into bed, he heard his mother say, "I believe that there were a few more verses to read in that chapter William."

Then as he snuggled into the pillow, he heard his father's voice. "Verily, did it come to pass…" A voice that faded into the distance as sleep settled quickly on the boy.

The next morning, Cyril was smelling the pomade in his hair as he sat in the back of the wagon on his way to church, feeling miserable. His greased hair was combed straight, and the skin on his face was burning from having been scrubbed. 'Good pants, good shirt, good shoes – good God, what a waste of time,' he thought. But he was not about to say it – nope, not about to let it show. He would keep that 'happy to be going to church' look painted on his face no matter how hot the clothes or the morning became. The paddling the wagon under his backside was giving him on that bumpy dirt road was nothing compared to the one he would get if he let his actual feelings show. 'Hot day, itchy clothes, tight shoes, and a stuffy church – Praise the Lord and sing for Jesus. And all the people said AMEN. Couldn't there come just a breath of a breeze?' The smiling little boy thought.

'Same as last Sunday,' he thought to himself. 'Wake up and have an early breakfast, then get yo' face scrubbed clean – clean off. Then your hair gets combed until it feels like Mama's trying t' pull weeds an' 'en a big glob o' grease t' make it stay put. Wear yo' good clothes an' yo' good shoes – 'at don't never fit. When ever'body is dressed, and the wagon is hitched, then Mama gonna fix her hat an' it's time t' go – well, it will be after she fixes daddy's hat even though we all know he gonna fix it back when she ain't lookin'. Then ride on the hard wagon all five thousand miles of rough road. Then daddy gonna git down off the wagon and help Mama down. Then daddy gonna set his pocket watch to the clock on the train station an' he gonna go talk t' the men about the weather while Mama gonna talk t' the ladies about they hats. Mama gonna tell me not t' run around in m' good clothes, so I gotta just stand 'round talkin' t' my friends. And all tha's just t' git ready for church!'

'And then it begins, an' the people start filin' into the church an' ever'body goes t' his same pew like last week – like last year. All the old widows sittin' together on one row an' 'at crabby old school teacher mean muggin' when y' walk by. Then we gonna sing Power in the Blood or somethin' – don't nobody need the hymnal 'cause we always sing the same few songs. A million songs in 'at hymnal, but we gonna sing the same ones. The people gonna clap an' start gittin' the Holy Ghost an' dance around a bit. Then the music gonna stop and ever'body gonna settle down. Then the preacher gonna come up t' the lectern an' he gonna open the bible an' read a piece. Then he gonna close the Bible an' hold it up in his right hand – an' 'en he'll preach. Start real quiet, like he gonna cry. But 'at won't last long 'fore he start t' gittin' louder – an' he commences to pacin' back and forth a bit and pointin' at the Bible. A little bit louder an' he gonna strut a bit like rooster an' he gonna slap the Bible a couple o' times – 'en he gonna yell an' slam the Bible down on the lectern. Pound on it like a judge with his hammer lookin' out at the accused.'

'Then somebody'll yell back an AMEN. Then the preacher gonna start thunderin' an' pointin' an' looking right at y' like he knows what y' done. Then he gonna yell some more, an' the people gonna yell back. Preacher gonna start hoppin' an' hollerin' like the flames o' Hell makin' the ground too hot t' stand still – then ever'body'll be hoppin' an' hollerin' when they feel the heat risin'. There I'll be, in all these hot clothes an' tight shoes an' I better hop an' holler too so don't nobody wonder if I don't love Jesus. 'cause they might be filled up with the Holy Ghost but they ain't so full 'at they ain't looking t' see if I ain't doin' right. Then Sister Compton gonna start prayin' with her hands in the air, and nobody gonna know what she prayin' for 'cause it ain't in English. She could be prayin' for rain or fried chicken, I 'on't know – don't nobody know. At least they don't bring snakes like them crazy people I heard about.'

'Then half the church gonna start dancing down t' the front an' 'en somebody gonna kneel. Then the next one gonna kneel with 'em and put they hand on they shoulder. An' 'en they gonna gather – some kneelin' an' some still standin', with a hand on a shoulder here an' there. Then it starts t' quiet down and Sister Compton will be the only one y' can hear since she's still whispering in gibberish. An' a few folks crying, but it won't be me – not this time. Then even Sister Compton will go quiet and just stand there rockin' from one foot t' the other real slow with her hand in the air. A quiet comes like no other quiet in the world. I think 'at moment is the only time 'at you know 'at God is here. All 'at, for only one moment with God. People say there'll be singing in Heaven, but I 'on't thank so – I thank 'at it'll be just 'at quiet – the quiet 'at comes when God is there. 'At quiet what came over my little sister. 'At quiet like 'at rug where she used t' play in the middle o' the room. People said 'at she's wi' God now, and she was so quiet. I reckon I 'on't like God much 'ese days."

Four: Automobile

Cyril Bratton stepped out of the store into the bright light of the late morning to hear the familiar voice of a little boy.

"Hey," said the boy. "I thought 'at y' might be here this mornin', it bein' Saturday an' all."

"Yes," said the man. "I needed a few things, so I stopped into the store to get them. Men are working at my house today, and it is always best if I stay out of the way and let them get on with it." He began to walk toward the train tracks, and the boy fell in beside him.

"Looks like you bought a new fishin' pole," said the boy.

The man responded. "That I did. As a boy, I loved fishing, but all those years of school and practicing law kept me pretty busy. So now I will try and find a few good spots around here and catch up on my fishing."

"I know some good ole fishin' holes," the boy said. "I know 'em all. I'll show y' one today – after y' show me 'at automobile like you said you was goin' t' do."

"Oh, did I say that?" Asked the man.

The boy looked a bit wide-eyed and said, "Well – well, y' didn't say no."

The man looked thoughtful and said. "So because I 'didn't say no,' that was the same as saying yes."

"Pretty much," said the boy.

"That will never work on a judge," said the man. "But it might convince a jury."

"What?"

The man smiled and said. "If you are going to be a lawyer, you must learn how to make a good argument."

The boy looked offended. "I know what a good argument is. You seen me have one with Mr. Dawson over 't th' store. We always argue – but he argues with a lotta folks anyways. The white Mr. Dawson, that is. Though the colored one seem a little arguey too."

"Argumentative." The man corrected.

"What?"

"Argumentative," said the man. "He is argumentative, not 'arguey'; that is not a word."

"See, you noticed it too; they both argamentive," said the boy. "Must be the last name. D'ya reckon that ev'ry Dawson in the world likes t' argue. Or just 'em two?"

"Not that kind of argument," said the man. "That manner of argumentation will get you in trouble in a courtroom."

"So they's differ'nt kinds o' argument?"

"Many varieties of argument," answered the man.

"Oh," said the boy. "I only know the one kind."

"You have a lot to learn," said the man. He stopped and turned as they reached the train tracks crossing the road. "I will tell you what. You walk home and get your fishing pole, and then you meet me at my house just beyond the livery stables on the other side of the street. You will see the men working there. I will show you the automobile, and then you can show me a fishing hole."

"Alright," responded the boy. "I ain't gonna walk though; I'm 'onna run, s' I'll be there directly – and see 'at automobile sooner." With that, the boy was off as fast as his feet would carry him.

The running boy looked down at the ground as he crossed the

train tracks while returning to the south side of the town. 'Still mornin'' thought the boy. 'Ain't much shadow to see with the sun this high, and it's behind me trying to keep up anyways.' The boy noticed that he was running passed the livery stable on his right, and he looked ahead two houses to his left. And there he saw it – a big house with a couple of ladders leaning against it and a half dozen Black men around it painting. He ran through the opening in the old picket fence where the gate was supposed to be – and barely noticed as he passed a man at some saw horses building a new gate. The excited boy was looking around for the already familiar face of his namesake. He spotted the older Cyril standing near the back of the house, just in front of the old carriage house. He was speaking to a much taller and darker man who was very muscled from years of hard work and had the look of a confident man. The boy ran up to the two men and began to try speaking while still catching his breath.

Cyril Bratton held his hand up to keep the boy from interrupting. The boy was so excited that he thought that he would burst, and he just stood there rocking side to side from one foot to the other as he listened to the men finish their conversation. After what felt like an eternity, he saw the taller man nod and turn away, raising his voice to yell instructions to the men working on the house.

Mr. Bratton turned to the boy. "Well, there you are. You must have run the whole way."

"I told y' I was gonna run it all the way – and I did just like I said. Bet 'at m' shadow don't even catch up wi' me any time soon." Responded the boy, who was peering around trying to locate the automobile. "I wanna see that automobile. Where's it at?"

"You are in luck," said the man. "I garage it right here in the old carriage house." The man turned toward a dilapidated building behind him and began to walk to the doors. "I must move her out now so these men can work on the old carriage house. They will do some repairs and widen the doors before they paint it, and then it will be a proper garage. So today, you are going to get to see her operate for a few moments." The man reached the double doors and began pulling them open.

"D'ya need some help with the doors?" The boy asked as he tried to see around the man into the carriage house.

"No, thank you," said the man. "You just stand out of the way, and I will get her started and back her out. It is a very tight fit getting through these doors."

The boy watched as the man propped both doors open wide and then disappeared into the dark room. He could see the very back of the automobile in the sunlight near the doors. He could hear the man moving inside, and then he listened to the motor jump to life as a puff of blue smoke came out of the back of the automobile and floated away as the air filled with a funny smell – the smell of an engine. There was a slight sound, and then the automobile slowly started to inch backward out of the carriage house ever so gently to make it safely through the tight doorway. The boy watched in amazement as the big metal beast appeared. The old shell carriage drive crunched under the weight of the tires. Moments later, the automobile was out and had stopped right in front of the boy.

The man leaned a little toward the boy and spoke through the open window with a smile. "Well, what do you think about her?"

"It's… I mean, she's beautiful," yelled the boy. "I ain't never been this close t' one b'fore. It's bigger 'an I thought too."

The man laughed. "Run around to the other side, and there is a handle on the door; grab it and give it a twist so you can pull the door open and climb into the seat."

"Really!" Shouted the boy. "I'm a git to ride in it?" The boy was so excited that he jumped up and down a few times before dropping his fishing pole and bucket and running around to look for the door handle. In a moment, he was in the front seat of the automobile with his head zipping around as he tried to look at everything all at once.

"Now you sit back," said the man. "I just need to back her out, and then we will take her for a short drive to let her warm up, and then we can park her in the street.

The boy watched as the man pushed down a pedal. "What's 'at do?" The asked.

"That is how I put her into her reverse gear so she goes backward." Answered the man.

The automobile began to move slowly back toward the street and eased out through the opening in the fence. The excited boy held onto the door handle tightly, not knowing what to expect as he watched everything the man did to control the machine. The boy quickly looked around and saw that the entire crew had stopped to watch the automobile. "I reckon they ain't never seen no automobile up close neither," he said as the car stopped.

"They probably have not seen one up close. These machines are still quite rare in the country, though more people have them in Memphis," The man responded as he pressed the clutch to put the machine into low gear.

"What y' doin' now?" The boy asked.

"Shifting the gears to tell her to move forward," the man responded.

The boy looked like he was studying as he said, "So they's a gear what makes her go backwards and a gear what makes her go forwards."

The man responded. "There is one gear for reverse and two forward gears. There is this first low gear so that she starts gently or to use if I want her to pull a load, then there is a high gear for when we are at speed, and I am ready for her to just walk on for a while."

"Well, let's just walk on then," said the boy.

The man smiled. "The edge of town is not that far of a drive."

After the most exciting five minutes of his short life, Cyril felt the automobile stop back in front of the house. The boy climbed out of the automobile excitedly speaking. "We shoulda drove through the whole town an' not just down t' the South End an' back. Did you see the way 'at ever'body was lookin' at us?"

The man said, "Seeing an automobile is new for many folks. And down to the edge of town and back was enough of a ride to warm her engine up – no need to go uptown and bother folks who might not like the noise."

"It don't bother 'em none when Judge Haines drives his automobile through the town," the boy said. "Or the sheriff, he got one too. Well, it b'longs t' the county, but he drives it like it's his own. And the doctor got one what he drives when someone needs him quick like."

The man nodded. "That is the judge and the sheriff, and if they make a bit of noise, people will put up with it. But I am not a judge, a sheriff, or a doctor, so I will just let that dog sleep. Now let's grab our fishing poles and buckets, and you can show me this good fishing hole. I need to speak with the builder briefly and add another job to his list."

"You already got 'em paintin' and doin' y' roof, and they gonna redo the carriage house, and they almost finished with the fence. What else you got fo' 'em t' do?"

"I would like for them to dig up this shell walkway to replace it with brick paving. I cannot abide the sound of shells crunching like they do when you drive or walk on them."

Five minutes later, both man and boy were walking north toward the train tracks that so neatly divided the town. The younger Cyril said, "we just gotta go a ways across the tracks an' 'en we'll cut through near the store an' they's a trail what will take us down t' a slow-moving creek. Somethin' 'at you carryin' shore smells good."

The man nodded and responded, "I figured that you were in too much of a hurry to stop long enough for lunch when you got home earlier, so I made us a couple of fried egg and bacon sandwiches to eat before we start fishing."

"My Mama makes those for m' daddy sometimes when he gotta do somethin' an' can't come home for lunch. I love 'em too," said the boy. "They's a place up here on the north side o' town what sells a boxed lunch with a piece o' fried chicken, an ear o' corn, an' a biscuit – ev'ry now an 'en if I got a nickel I like to go there and git me one of them boxes. But them sandwiches will be good 'cause I did forget t' get me some lunch 'cause o' me bein' in such a hurry."

A few minutes later, the boy pointed to a building with big picture windows on the front. "At's the place with them chicken boxes, an' we go right in between 'at an' the store an' out passed the lumber yard and shed, and we'll see the trail."

As the two began to aim toward the space between the buildings, they heard knocking coming from the diner. They looked to see a well-dressed white man in his sixties sitting at a table next to the window. The man was looking at the two of them and knocking on the window to get their attention. As he caught their eye, he pointed at the boy and motioned for him to come inside.

"Oh no, 'at's old Judge Haines – I 'on't wanna be in trouble wi' the judge; he can have y' hung. And iffin I git in trouble wi' th' judge, my daddy gonna be mad."

The man responded. "It will be good if you go in and see what he wants – best not keep the man waiting. And I doubt that he will hang a ten-year-old."

The boy ran over to the diner, set his fishing pole and bucket beside the door, and went inside. The older Cyril watched the judge and the boy on the other side of the window as the man spoke animatedly at the boy and pointed toward the man waiting outside. He could see the boy nodding in response. He watched as the man waved the boy away and turned his attention back to the plate on the table in front of him. He saw as the boy exited the diner and began approaching, forgetting his pole and bucket by the door. The man just pointed behind the boy, who turned and ran back for his pole and

36

bucket and then jogged over to his new fishing buddy.

"He was askin' 'bout you," said the boy. "Wanted t' know if you was 'at new colored lawyer what just come t' town. I told 'im you was. He said 'at he wanna talk t' y' later today. I said 'at we was goin' fishin' an' he said for you t' come by his house after we done. Said 'at he gonna be home all afternoon settin' on the porch in the shade."

"Is that what he said?" Asked the man as he looked hard at the judge sitting inside. Just then, the judge looked up and out through the window at the pair, gave a quick nod toward the boy and a short half smile, and then looked back down at his meal.

"Missy, she's the maid over at his house; she makes the best lemonade anybody ever had. Sometimes people in the town will send me over there for an errand t' the judge, you know, like take a package t' him or somethin' an' when I git there, Missy will always gimme a glass o' that lemonade. You should try her lemonade when you git there."

"Well, when we return from our fishing trip, you must show me where Judge Haines lives."

Twenty minutes later, the two Cyrils sat in the shade on the banks of a dark, slow-moving creek with their fishing poles beside them as they ate their sandwiches.

"Thank y', this sandwich is good," said the boy.

"Thank you for showing me this fishing spot," responded the man. "My wife used to make these for my lunch occasionally, and I always enjoyed them."

"What went with your wife anyway?" The boy asked.

The man looked out at the dark smooth water and could see the reflection of the bright sky above. "We lost her to influenza two years ago."

"I'm sorry," said the boy. "At's how we lost m' little sister. We all got sick, the whole family, but she just never could seem to git no better, an' finally, I guess it was jus' too much." The boy sat quietly for a while before he continued. "I reckon 'at she was jus' too small. It like t' kilt Mama. She just never seemed t' git over it – least not yet. We don't never talk about her; it just hurts Mama so. But sometimes I wish I could talk about her – about Celine."

The man sat quietly for a moment as he finished chewing the last bite of his sandwich. "Well, Cyril, if you ever want to talk about your little sister, you can tell me all about her."

The boy shrugged his shoulders. "You 'on't need to hear 'bout her; she wasn't nobody t' you – just a little girl you didn't know."

The man nodded as he picked up a fishing pole and began to tie a new line and hook onto it. "I would have liked to know her. And I still want to hear all about her, tell me everything you remember. It will be good for you to hear yourself remembering. It keeps her memories fresh in your mind. If you share memories of someone, then there are more people to remember that person."

"Maybe I will tell y' 'bout her sometime then," said the boy. "Still kina hard thinkin' 'bout her." The boy picked up his pole and began to unwind the line from around the pole, and soon he had a worm on the hook and was watching his cork float on the water.

The two sat there with their hooks in the water, waiting for the fish to bite. Finally, the boy spoke. "D' y' have any other family besides your wife 'at passed?"

"One daughter," answered the man.

"Does she live back in Memphis? Asked the boy.

The man shook his head. "No, she moved away almost a dozen years ago; I have not seen her since."

"Not even when her Mama passed?" asked the boy.

"She was pretty sick herself and could not travel, but I believe she would have been there if she could have been," the man said.

"A dozen years, 'at's longer 'an I been a'livin," the boy said. "D' y' ever hear from her?"

"Oh yes, I hear from her from time to time. We have continued to exchange letters over the years," answered the man.

"That's good 'at y' hear from her," said the boy. "You know, iffin y' ever wanna tell me 'bout your wife, I can help y' remember her how you talked about."

The man turned and smiled at the boy. "That would be nice; I would like very much to tell you about her and know that someone will help carry those memories and stories."

The boy smiled and said, "Who knows, maybe your daughter will come to visit you sometime, an' she can tell me memories too."

The man sat quietly for a time before he spoke. "I don't think my daughter will ever visit me here, but that is alright. I know she has the life she wanted; that is all a father could ask for his children. I wish that I had realized that a dozen years ago." The man pointed at a cork that was disappearing under the water. "Looks like you are getting a bite."

Five: Peaches and Lemonade

It was mid-afternoon when they stepped back onto the main street of town, and the boy said, "Well, you caught three, and I caught three. You keep 'em all; that'll be enough for yo' supper. Next time we should go early when they like t' bite."

"Then next time, early it is," the man responded.

The boy continued. "The judge, he lives up hye on the edge o' the north side o' town a couple o' streets up, an' then we take a right an' his house ain't far passed 'at.

They continued to walk together, and after a few minutes, the boy said, "She was five."

"Excuse me?" Responded the man. "I didn't hear you."

"Five," said the boy. "She was five years old when she passed. The last thing Mama did was to tuck Celine in with a quilt what she said was passed down t' her from her own Mama."

"I am sorry," said the man. "That must have been very hard for you and your family."

"It was 'specially hard on Mama. She was just gittin' over being sick herself. She got outta bed long enough t' dress my little sister an' t' fix her hair one last time an' go t' the funeral. And then she just took back t' her bed for weeks. Could hear her cryin' ev'ry day an' into the night. And Celine looked so much like Mama – almost more like

Mama than Mama does if y' know what I mean. Mama always fussed with her hair to make it look right, but she didn't fuss with it much 'at day – she just took her time with the hair grease an' the brush an' all the skin lotion. My daddy just sat there watching. They made me go outside, but I could see 'em through the winduh. Mama looked like she was singin' that same ole lullaby, but I couldn't hear nothin' from outside. Mama didn't let none o' the other women folk help her none with Celine. She said she was gonna take care o' her baby all by herself. Started t' rain at the funeral like the whole world was cryin'. Mama just knelt there in the rain by the grave 'til some of the church folk helped my daddy git her back up on her feet.

The stoic-faced little boy noticed a hand move beside him, and out of the corner of his eye, he saw the man take out a handkerchief and wipe his cheek.

"You ain't gotta cry over a little girl you never knew," said the boy. "I never did – I couldn't for some reason. I wanted to, but it just wouldn't come. Reckon Mama cried for us all."

They walked a few steps in silence, and then the boy took a deep breath and shook his head. "Hye's the last turn, and then we'll see the judge's house. He'll be settin' on the porch drinkin' lemonade and lookin' like he owns the world."

As they turned the corner, they looked down the short side street and saw the judge sitting in a rocking chair on the porch of a big white house. Some giant cedar trees shaded the porch. The judge had rolled up his shirt sleeves, his suspenders were off his shoulders, and he was holding a nearly empty glass in his hand. A pair of well-shined shoes were beside the chair, and the man was in his stocking feet. He smiled when he saw the pair turn the corner and come into view. He raised his empty hand and waved the two toward him like some Flavian emperor signally for the start of the races at the circus in Rome.

As the pair approached, the man said, "I was beginning to think you two had forgotten about me. How was the fishing?

The Black man answered, "Well, sir, we caught enough to stink the pan and make a good supper but not enough for a fish fry."

The white man laughed. "I remember my mother saying that when I was a boy and would bring only two or three fish home. 'That isn't enough to stink the pan,' she would tell me. You picked a strange time to go fishing anyway; most folks want to be out there before sunrise."

"It was a last-minute thing, Your Honor,' responded the older Cyril.

"We had to take a ride in his automobile first," interjected the boy.

The white man raised his eyebrows and took a long speculative look at the Black man standing in his yard. "You have an automobile? That'll be interesting to folks here about." The man turned to the boy and asked, "You're that Ledbetter boy, aren't you?"

"Yes, sir," the boy responded.

The judge nodded and said, "I'll make you a deal. Next Saturday, you get up early, before the sun, and you stop by the ice house and get a penny worth of ice in your bucket, and you go down to the river, and you catch me a good mess of fish, and you bring them around to my kitchen and dump 'em in the sink, and I'll leave a quarter out for you. Here is a penny for the ice." The man reached into his pocket, pulled out a coin, and tossed it to the boy.

The boy caught the penny and said, "Yes, sir. Thank you. I'll see you with a mess of fish on Saturday."

The judge turned to the other man and said, "You two make a strange-looking pair of fishing buddies."

The Black man glanced down at the boy. "I guess that we do. He wanted to see an automobile up close, and I wanted to know where to go fishing, so we made a trade. A ride in the automobile for the location of a fishing hole."

The white man looked thoughtful for a moment and said, "I guess that's alright – sounds like a fair trade. Anyway, I heard you just moved into town – bought the old Dempsey place."

"Yes, sir," responded the elder Cyril.

"I also heard that you had retired from law practice up in Tennessee," the judge continued.

"Yes, sir," Mr. Bratton responded as he nodded. "More than thirty years."

"I see," said the judge. "What kind of law did you practice up there?"

The Black man answered, "A fair bit of everything, but mostly wills, property, and business law."

"So you know a good amount about property and contracts then – that's good. Has Reverend Scolfield over at the Second Baptist Church spoken to you about anything yet?"

"No, sir," the Black man responded. "I have not met the reverend yet."

The judge looked surprised. "Been here two weeks, and you haven't met Reverend Scolfield yet? You'll meet him at church tomorrow; he'll probably want to talk to you a little. He has some questions that, as a judge, I can't answer. He's a good man, and he has some interesting concerns that I can't rightly speak to since these concerns just might end up before the court. And well, the county court being seated here in town and me being the judge and all, we want to keep to propriety."

The screen door from the house opened, and a lightly built medium brown-skinned lady in her mid-forties stepped out onto the porch with a pitcher. The judge held his nearly empty glass up to be filled and said, "Thank you, Missy." Then he looked back at the man standing in his yard. "Missy here makes the best lemonade in Alabama – learned it from her mother who used to keep house here for my mother."

The woman and the Black man exchanged a nod and a smile, and the man touched his hat brim. The woman turned to go back inside;

the judge leaned and looked over his shoulder and said. "I left a book sitting out on my desk Missy. Would you bring it to me? It's brown leather with Alabama and a bunch of big words on the cover."

She paused for a moment and responded, "Yes, sir. Be right back with it."

The judge turned back to the man in front of him and continued, "I know that you are retired and all that, but I am going to loan you this book on Alabama procedures for you to look through – just in case you are interested or ever want to bring a little something before the court. So that we can dot all the 'I's and cross all the 'T's.

The elder Cyril said, "Well, Your Honor, if the reverend has an issue, he should see a local attorney."

The white man gave a slightly pained look and continued. "That is the rub; we don't have a lot of lawyers out here in the country. And to tell you the truth, none of the ones we have are interested in looking into an issue that concerns a bunch of colored folks and poor white farmers down yonder in the Bottoms. Don't get me wrong. They're all good, hard-working folks down yonder, but they have small farms and not much money."

"I see," responded the Black man. "Well, sir, if the reverend brings some questions to me, I will hear him out and at least try to give him some sound legal advice."

The white man smiled and said, "That's all I ask; just give a listen and help him to consider what would be best for all those poor folks down there. I hate to see them brought into court one by one and lose their homes. I have to follow the law in each individual case." He slightly emphasized the word individual.

Just then, the Black woman returned with a brown leather-bound book. The judge nodded toward the Black man, who stepped over to the porch to take the book from the woman with a "Thank you."

"By the way, what is your name?" asked the judge almost as an afterthought.

"Bratton, Cyril Bratton," answered the Black man.

The white man slowly sat back in his rocking chair, raised his eyebrows as he looked closely at the other man, and nodded slowly. "Cyril Bratton, now that is a particular name around here. That name was passed down from father to son around here for a hundred years. That name used to have big feet in this county. Now that – that's interesting." The judge paused thoughtfully and then said, "You all go on around back to the kitchen door and get a big glass of that ice-cold lemonade – the best lemonade in Alabama." He leaned toward the Black woman with a smile and said, "Missy, you fix these boys up; it's hot out there."

Moments later, the pair were at the house's back door as instructed. The door opened, and the woman looked out at the two of them and said, "You two can come in here, out of the sun."

"Thank you," said the man.

The woman quickly took out two glasses, opened the ice box and filled both glasses with chipped ice, and then poured the lemonade. She shook her head and said, "That man drinks a bucket of this a day – but I guess it's a sight better than what some men sneak around drinkin' at that ice house in the evenings."

The boy said, "Thank you, Missy."

The man took his glass and said, "Yes, thank you, Miss –?"

"Jones, Misses Jones," answered the woman.

"Well, Mrs. Missy Jones, it is nice to meet you," said the man with a smile.

"Missy," the woman said with a smirk. "That's not my name. When I started coming here to help my mother when I was a little girl, old Mrs. Haines didn't like the name my parents gave me, so she decided to call me Missy. Now all the white folks call me Missy and always have. Guess they think that it's my name."

The man nodded and said, "I see. Well then, what is the name that your parents gave you?"

She looked at him and said, "My name is Peaches."

The boy spoke up. "Wait, your name ain't Missy? How can someone just decide to change your name?"

The woman looked down at the boy and said, "Some folks get to do pretty much whatever they want."

"But 'at ain't right," the boy said.

"It might not be right, but it is what things are like," answered the woman. Then she turned back to the man. "I have seen you at the general store, and I know you have been in town for a couple of weeks. People startin' to wonder when we are going to see you in church. A couple of the widow ladies will be stoppin' by your house later when it cools down a bit to ensure that you know you are welcome in church and when services are. They'll probably have a plate of something with them, too, since they found out that you are a single man.

"How d' they know that he ain't got no wife no more iffin he ain't been to the church to meet 'em?" Asked the boy.

The woman glanced at the boy and said, "Drink your lemonade before the ice melts, and let the adults talk. Tell you what, you run outside and finish your lemonade out there under that shade tree by the back porch."

The boy closed his mouth with an indignant expression and glanced at the man, who he saw had a slight grin in response to the woman's chastisement. He slowly walked to the door and went out onto the back porch. But that is where he stopped. Instead of going out to sit under the tree, he stayed on the back porch to hear everything through the screen.

"Anyway," the woman said as she turned back to the man. "The reverend would like to speak to you. He stopped the judge in town one day to ask about his concerns, and the judge told him that a lawyer should look into them and that he couldn't advise him. But I will tell you this, the judge there – he is not too happy with the whole thing himself. He spent the whole afternoon looking through his law books like he used to back when he was still lawyering and preparing cases. This business with this fellow from Texas has already got the judge irritated.

The man nodded. "I am afraid that with my being so new to town, I do not understand the business with the Texan of which you speak."

The woman turned and started putting clean dishes in the cabinets. "The old Bratton plantation used to go all the way down to the river. That is where they used to put the cotton bales on barges to send to market. Anyway, they used to call that the bottom land because it was real good for growing, but it does flood from time to time. Old man Bratton came to hard times after the war and started selling off small parcels down there in the bottom land. Different folks bought the parcels for their own little farms some colored families and some poor whites bought down there, and we call it the bottoms now. About two years ago, a man from Texas came to town, went down there and looked around, and started trying to buy up all that land. Now some of the colored folks did decide to sell and move north like folks have been doing here lately. But most families said no to this man from Texas – and he wasn't too happy about it either. Eventually, he set himself up like a bank and offered the same folks loans against their land. Many of them took these loans and are having trouble paying them back. If you are late on a payment, even by one day, he takes you to court. Three families have already lost their little farms. The judge is mad about it, but he just says a contract is a contract, and he can't interfere and that folks need a lawyer."

"Colored families lost their farms – and that upset the judge?" The man asked.

The woman got a sour look and continued, "Truth be told, if it was just colored families losing farms, that judge would not care at all. The first two families were colored, and he was fine ordering it. But when this Texan put a white family with five kids out of their place, let's just say that then the judge took a dislike to the Texan. Now the man is bringing more families into court; some of them are white too, and the judge is not too happy about it. Part of it is that the man is not from around here. When one of the bigger white farmers wants to put a colored family or some poor white trash off of their land, he is happy enough to sign the court orders. But this man coming in from Texas with money and trying to take over just gets all over the judge for some reason.

"I see why the judge wants them to speak to an attorney," responded the man.

There was a small knock at the screen door, and the woman turned to see the boy standing on the other side of the screen, smiling and holding up an empty glass. She shook her head, walked over to the door, opened it, and took the glass from the boy.

"I was hoping for another glass."

The woman cut him off. "Too much sugar's not good for you, so one glass is enough. Now you go on out there and wait under that tree like I told you. If you stop on that porch again, I got a broom that I clean with, and it'll clean you right off the porch."

"Why d' I gotta stand under the tree?" Whined the boy.

"You don't have to stand under the tree," said the woman. "If you are dumb enough, you can stand in the sun. Or you can go back fishing, or you can go home, or you can play with your friends, or you can soak your head in a horse trough. But you are not going to stand on my porch eavesdropping."

"It's the judge's porch anyway," said the boy, turning away in a huff.

"Off the porch," he heard the woman's voice say as he walked away. He stood in the yard under the shade tree, watching the house. He could see the woman through the kitchen window. He could see her talking, but he had no idea what she was saying.

48

The boy waited under the tree for what seemed like hours until his friend came out. "Y' ready to go back to your house now? D'ya reckon that it's time t' move that automobile back into the carriage house?"

The man nodded and said, "Yes, we can return to my house; I have some fish to clean. And I imagine it will be a couple of days before the automobile can return to that carriage house – it needs quite a lot of work. Mr. Fletcher is fast, but he and his men need a few days."

"Oh, I see,' said the boy. "So it don't need to go anywheres else today?"

The man said, "No, it does not need to go anywhere else today."

"A'ight then," said the boy. "Well, I'll git me another good look at it anyways."

The two fell into walking side by side as they headed for the south side of town. "How d' you set your clocks t' the right time?" The boy asked.

"What do you mean?" asked the man.

The boy continued. "On Sund'y. How d' you set your clocks iffin you don't go t' church? My daddy sets his watch t' train time every Sunday mornin' an' 'en when we git home, he sets all the clocks – 'ats how ever'body does around here. I just figured 'ats how ever'body in the world does it. So if you don't go t' church, yo' clocks're gonna be wrong."

The man chuckled. "I live a two-minute walk from the train station, so I can set my watch by it any time I am walking by and then adjust my clocks at home. But yes, I did set my clocks every Sunday just like that for my entire married life. That is how my father did it when I was a boy – but he was a preacher, so there was never any question about attending church. We went three times a week."

"Thought 'at you said 'at you didn't know your daddy until you was growed up an' came back here t' meet him," said the boy.

"Yes, that is true," said the man. "When the war was over, and my mother and I were free, she took me to Atlanta, Georgia, and married a preacher who raised me like his own son."

"So you was borned a slave – down on 'at old Bratton plantation??"

"Yes, my mother was enslaved when I was born, and so I was born into slavery," said the man. "Being enslaved and being a slave are two different things."

"I 'on't understand what y' mean," said the boy.

The man continued. "To be enslaved, well, that is something that other people do to you. But being a slave is what you are – who you are. My mother wasn't a slave. She was enslaved by someone else."

"I thank I understand," said the boy. After a few more steps, he spoke again. "So why'd you stop goin' t' church anyways?"

After a pause, the man answered. "After my wife passed, I just could not bear it. We had been going to that same church for over thirty years – our whole adult lives. We raised our daughter there. I could not stand to go in and sit in that pew with an empty place beside me. I had enough empty places at home."

"Is 'at how come y' t' move here?" Asked the boy. "T' git away from the empty places."

"That is certainly one of the reasons," said the man. "There are others, but that is a strong reason. I do not have to look at her empty dining chair or her empty kitchen. New house, new bed, new furniture."

"New Church?" asked the boy.

"Now you are starting to sound like Mrs. Jones back there," said the man.

"I 'on't blame y' though," said the boy. 'I 'on't wanna go t' church most o' the time neither – since my sister passed." After a few moments of silence, the boy continued. "Why they got a Second Baptist Church and a First Baptist Church anyways. Seem t' me like they ought t' just call 'em Baptist Churches – or maybe just have one Baptist Church."

"There is a bit of history behind that," answered the man. "You see, the white folks had a Baptist Church for a long time and called it the Baptist Church. But then, after the war, the Negro folks built their own Baptist Church. So the white folks added 'First' to the name, and then the Negro folks started calling their church Second Baptist. It is like that in most towns now. You have a First Baptist Church for white folks and a Second Baptist Church for Negros."

"Hmm," said the boy. "I never thought o' that, but I guess ever'body got they own church. So d' you thank y' gonna start goin' t' this new church."

The man said, "Probably should, especially if the widows are coming by to invite me. No man does well in a town if he gets the widows upset with him."

"Might be nice t' meet some new people," said the boy.

The man gave the boy a sideways glance. "Mrs. Jones told you not to be eavesdropping, and here you are sounding word for word just like her."

"She a smart lady," said the boy. After a short pause, he added, "But kinda scary too."

The man chuckled.

Six: Bull

As the Cyrils approached the house where the men were working, they noticed a second automobile stopped in front of the house with a very tall white man standing beside it, speaking to Mr. Fletcher.

As they approached, they saw Mr. Fletcher nod in their direction, and the white man turned to look at them. The boy said, "at's the sheriff."

"I see," answered the man.

The white man spoke loudly. "So you the one 'at bought this ole place."

Mr. Bratton responded, "Yessir, Sheriff. My name is Cyril Bratton; I moved to town a couple of weeks ago."

"I know when y' come t' town," the white man responded with an edge in his voice. "And y' name. Don't nuthin' happen 'round hye 'at I don't find out about. My name's Atkins, Sheriff Bill Atkins, but mostly they just call me Bull."

"Nice to meet you, Sheriff Atkins," the Black man said.

The white man glanced over his shoulder at the house and the automobile. "Come t' town, bought a house, spendin' a lot of money gettin' it fixed up – and you got an automobile. And as far as I can tell, y' ain't got no kinda job. 'At's a lot o' money fo' a boy with no job. Make it my business t' figure out where somebody gits money like 'at."

"He retired," the boy spoke up. "He was a lawyer up there in Tennessee, but he retired now an' he come to live hye."

The sheriff slowly shifted his gaze to the boy and looked at the child hard for a moment. "Oh? Is that what you heard? What you doin' down hye on the south side o' town? Does your daddy know 'at 'u down hye?"

"I come down t' see the automobile – and then we went fishin' too," answered the boy. "An' I didn't just hear it. Judge Haines, he know it too. We was just there an' the judge asked him t' look into somethin' fo' him. An' the judge, he gonna give me money t' go catch a mess o' fish fo' him next Saturday mornin'."

"Been t' see the judge?" The man queried. "Best not be lyin' t' me, boy." He turned his gaze from the child to the man. "I gotta go over t' see Judge Haines directly – I'll be sure t' ask about all 'at." The sheriff turned back to the boy and asked. "You 'at Ledbetter boy, ain't y'? I been hearin' a lot 'bout you. 'At sundown whistle gonna blow at the station hye shortly, an' when it do, you best git yo'self back up on the right side o' town. You don't wanna be down hye when it gits dark."

"Yessir, Sheriff," the boy answered. "My name is Cyril, and my daddy is."

"I know who yo' daddy is," the white man snapped. "And yo' mama. Cyril, is 'at what they named you? I been hearin' 'bout you a bit too much lately. Tell y' what, when I finish up hye in town, I'll be shore t' stop by out at your daddy's farm – make sure he knows where I fount 'u today."

The boy dropped his gaze to look down at the shadows on the ground and avoid the harsh eyes of the sheriff. The sun was behind the tall white man, so his shadow stretched across the ground toward the feet of the boy standing there in front of him. It was as if the shadow of the sheriff was hulking toward the boy – it somehow looked darker and more ominous than other shadows. 'How can a shadow look mad?' Cyril wondered in his head.

The sheriff shifted his glare back to the man. "So y' was a lawyer up in Tennessee – and y' already been by t' talk t' the judge?"

"Yes sir, Sheriff, both true." "The Black man answered.

"Defendin' crim'nals and gangsters for a livin' I reckon," said the white man.

"No, Sir, mostly probate, property and contracts," said the Black man. "Much calmer type of legal practice."

"A'ight," the sheriff said. "Make shore 'at you don't drive 'at automobile too fast around hye. And be careful where you drive it – don't want nobody bein' disturbed by the noise." The man nodded toward the automobile. "And don't be showin' it off s' much. Don't nobody like a show-off. Besides, walking places is good fo' y'."

With that, the white man turned back toward his car and took a long slow look at the carpenters and painters working on the house. Each worker was diligently doing his job, acting as if he had no idea that Sheriff Atkins was present. "A'ight Isaac, you keep them boys workin' – we don't want no idle hands bein' the Devil's playground." The sheriff glanced back at the lawyer and remarked, "I don't much trust idle hands." After a moment, the sheriff nodded to himself and climbed back into his automobile to leave.

After the sheriff drove away, the boy said, "He must be in a sour mood. I ain't never seen him talk so mean t' nobody before."

The man was standing there, still watching the car drive away. "He is just a man doing his job – a job that he seems to enjoy doing."

"Shouldn't ever'body enjoy his job?" Asked the boy.

"Not all jobs should be enjoyed," said the man. "The job might need doing, but they do not all have to be enjoyed."

The pair walked into the yard and toward the back of the house. About halfway along the house, the man stopped to look more closely at the work. And the boy spoke. "Y' know what I 'on't understand? I 'on't know why they always call 'at the sundown whistle. It blow a good hour before sundown ever' day an' a good hour an' a half 'fore it actu'lly gits dark. Seem like they'd call it somthin' else other'n the sundown whistle since it don't blow at sundown."

One of the painters, who had nearly ebony skin speckled with drops of white house paint and who appeared to be about eighteen, looked up and spoke. "O' course it blows before sundown – exactly an hour before sundown ev'ry day. How do you not know that?"

Mr. Fletcher was nearby and answered the question. "He doesn't have to know that. You have to know that. It don't mean anything to him but that he better git home or miss his supper. Just like it tells you that you better git home." The master carpenter gave the young painter a stern look and said, "Maybe if you pay more attention to your paintin', you might not wear so much of it."

"Yessir, Daddy, "the teenager responded.

"What do he mean, Isaac?" The boy asked, looking at Mr. Fletcher.

The carpenter looked down at the boy and said, "Nothin' important for you. Everybody hears what he needs to hear when that whistle blows. And for a little boy like you, it just means you better git home if you want your Mama to feed you. Matter o' fact, that whistle will blow here shortly – so you might better run along. Maybe you'll beat the sheriff to your house."

The boy looked up at Mr. Bratton for confirmation. The man said, "Mr. Fletcher is right; you probably should run along."

"I reckon so," the boy responded. "I'll maybe see y' next Saturd'y." Just as he turned to walk away, he heard the sundown whistle blow at the train station, so he broke into a jog that would get him home quicker.

It wasn't long before he could see his farmhouse in the distance as he jogged along the red clay road. He could feel the sun burning down on his left shoulder and see his shadow running along the road a little ahead of him and to his right side. Sure enough, there was an automobile sitting in front of the house. He could identify the tall man standing in the yard talking to his father, even if he had not already known. He saw the men shake hands and the tall man climb into the automobile. He heard the engine roar into life and saw the automobile back out into the road and head in his direction going back into town. A minute later, the sheriff passed by the boy, and the look the man gave the boy made his heart sink just a little as he thought about what the sheriff must have been saying to his father.

Moments later, he was heading up the carriage lane beside the house when he heard his father. "Cyril, wait up a minute." The boy stopped and turned toward the sound of the voice, and he could see his father stepping around the back of the house. "I gotta do somethin' out at the barn while you puttin' your fishin' pole away – we need to talk a little bit b'fore we go in fo' supper.

"Yes, sir," the boy answered as he fell into step beside his father.

"I understand that you saw the sheriff today. And more importantly, the sheriff saw you. He was by here just a short bit ago talkin' t' me about it. First thing I will tell you is that you will start watchin' your mouth with adults. You can't argue with the storekeeper like that. You draw the wrong kind of attention 'at way."

"Yes, sir," the boy answered. "But that storekeeper, he do like to argue with people, Daddy. It ain't all me."

"You right and you wrong," the man said to his son. "Old man Dawson, he'll argue with a clock over what time it is. But he still a grown man, and you still a little boy who is goin' t' show respect fo' his elders."

"Yes, sir," responded the boy. "He say that he gonna wear out a razor strap on me."

The man chuckled. "Let's hope that y' start holdin' yo' tongue an' he don't have to."

"Yes, sir," Cyril responded.

"The Sheriff also said that he saw y' on the wrong side o' the tracks earlier today. So, I reckon you was visitin' with that lawyer that moved into town."

"Yes, sir."

"I ain't a gonna tell y' that you can't visit with your new friend. But y'all might want t' be a little less obvious about it. Don't just walk down the middle o' the main street. It upsets some folks with old-fashioned ideas. You don't want t' start gettin' a reputation with people like the sheriff. He'll start lookin' into things and askin' questions 'bout you – and askin' questions 'bout yo family. It's just best not to have that kind of attention. D'ya understand what I'm tellin' y'?"

"Yes, sir." As they reached the barn, the boy stopped in the doorway and turned to his father. "Daddy, why do they call it the 'wrong side o' the tracks' anyways?"

"Well, now that goes back a ways," said the man. "The train station is in the middle of the town – always has been. And as the town has grown, the white folks live on the north side o' the train tracks, and the colored folks have always built their houses on the south side. Some folks are of a mind that each set o' folks ought o' keep t' their own side an' their own people."

"D' the sheriff thank like 'at?" Asked the boy.

"Oh, the sheriff, he most definitely do," answered the man.

The boy nodded. "So I gotta stay away from the sheriff 'en?"

"Not s' much stay away as try not t' git noticed by s' many folks." The man looked down at his son. "Don't argue with adults an' take the trails around behind the buildin's and houses instead o' just walking down the main street. Keep yo' head down a bit – and a lot o' politeness goes a long way. If you see dust coming, it's prob'ly the sheriff in his automobile, so you just step down a side road or into the trees an' let 'im pass."

The man pointed the boy over to the corner of the barn to put his pole and bucket. "We best git inside before the dog ends up with our supper."

"Yes, sir," said the boy as he rushed to put his pole away and join his father for the walk to the house. "Ain't never seen the sheriff talk so mean t' people b'fore, like I seen him talk today."

"Was 'at when you saw 'im on the south side o' the town?"

"Yes, sir."

"It's just gonna be 'at way sometimes with folks like the sheriff."

The pair stopped at the pump to wash their hands. As they washed, the boy spoke. "Does my Mama thank like 'at about them people on the south side o' the tracks?"

"Why'd y' ask that?"

"I remember you sayin' she was mad 'bout the store lettin' colored folks in on Saturday mornin'."

"'At ain't exactly why she was mad. See, yo' Mama grew up in a small city where the colored folks had their own stores in their neighborhoods. So, they could go shoppin' in their own store any time they wanted. She was mad t' know 'at some folks gotta wait for one day a week or go around t' the shed in back. 'At's all she was mad about."

The pair walked into the house through the back door and quickly passed through the kitchen to get to the table where their food was waiting. They sat down, acting as if they didn't notice the look they were getting. The man looked at the table and then smiled at his wife. "That looks good – I love me some peas and okra. And your cracklin' cornbread is the best in the world, especially with some molasses." He looked down and began to say grace. A few moments later, they were eating.

"So what did that sheriff want earlier?" The woman asked.

The man swallowed. "Nothin' important. He just wanted to remind me that elections are coming up and hopes he will get my vote."

The boy noticed again how his father always spoke clearer when speaking to his wife. "I saw Judge Haines today," said the boy. He told me he'd pay me for a mess of fish next Saturday. So I'm 'onna dig me some worms Friday ev'nin' and go first thing in the mornin' to catch a bunch of fish."

William looked over at his son. "I'll tell you what. I'll go with you, and you can catch a mess for the judge, and I'll catch a mess for us. Your mother is having some of the ladies over from the Church to piece together their quilting squares all day. So I'll take care of making supper and teach you how to fry fish and hush-puppies and cook some grits. I'll teach you the secret to making good grits."

"Really?" The boy asked excitedly. You almost don't never go fishin' – you always too busy with the farm an' all."

Ida looked at her son and said, "You are starting to sound like your friend Billy, that Holstead boy. You need to slow down and speak clearly."

"Yes, ma'am."

The woman continued, "You said that you saw the judge today. Where did you see him?"

"He was havin' lunch at Miss Belle's when he saw us goin' fishin', and he flagged us down to come over to his house after fishin', and that's when he told me to go catch him a mess o' fish next Saturday."

"Slow down and use the entire word," Ida said to her son. "What did the judge want with you at his house? Surely it was not just to discuss your fish."

"No, ma'am, I mean Yes, ma'am. Er er, I mean..."

The woman smiled and held her hand up to stop the boy. She reached over and placed her hand on his arm. "Slow down." She reached up, gently stroked across his hairline and onto his hair, and then let her hand rest on his shoulder for a moment.

The boy always felt calm when his mother stroked his hair. Her hands were always so cool when she touched him. He took a deep breath and started slower as his mother pulled her hand back. "Judge Haines, he wanted to talk to Cyril about something about that man from Texas and those poor folks in the Bottoms losing their farms. He couldn't explain it himself on account of him being the judge and all. So he told Cyril to talk to the colored preacher about it. Then he told me to go catch him some fish and sent us around back to get some lemonade from Missy. Did you know that her name is really Peaches and that old Mrs. Haines just started calling her Missy because she did not like her real name, and now everyone calls her Missy instead?

"I did not know that about her," the woman responded. "But I do know that she is married to Samuel Jones and that she is an adult. Do you call adults by their Christian names now?"

The boy looked confused. "No, ma'am, not generally. But she is – I mean, everybody calls her by her first name."

Ida nodded. "I am aware of that. But you are not everyone. You are a young gentleman who will address adults with respect – all adults. She is Mrs. Jones, and Mr. Bratton will be addressed as Mr. Bratton. You will address all adults either as Miss, Mister, or Misses. Unless, of course, they are members of the Church, in which case you may use Brother or Sister."

"Yes, ma'am," the boy said. After a pause, he quietly added. "I did not mean any harm or disrespect. I was just doin' - I just always seen it done that way."

"I know that," Ida said gently. "But it is the little harms and bits of disrespect that wear at a person. And the little shows of respect that are most important."

"Yes, ma'am," Cyril said. "I will be sure to remember that, Mama."

William chuckled and spoke. "So the judge wants this lawyer to look into that man from Texas? This should be good."

"Daddy, what is wrong with that man from Texas anyway?" The boy asked.

The man leaned forward with a mischievous grin. "Mostly seems to be that he is from Texass." The man stressed the last syllable of the word and dragged out the hiss at the end.

Ida cleared her throat lightly.

The man glanced toward his wife before continuing. "He uses his money to bully folks and push people around – mostly them poor people down in the Bottoms."

"Cyr.. erm, Mr. Bratton has money from his retirement, and he does not bully folks with it."

The man nodded and said, "Folks from Tennessee have more manners, I reckon."

Ida spoke. "Any man can act like a bully to get what he wants or thinks is right. Even Jesus took a stick to the moneylenders. You put that empty plate in the kitchen and go in there and start your reading.

"Yes, ma'am," said the boy, getting up quickly. As he walked into the kitchen, he heard his father behind him.

"In all fairness to Jesus, I think the moneylenders did have it comin'."

"Don't let your food get any colder, Mr. Ledbetter," said Ida.

Seven: A Busy Day

The sky was just starting to lighten, projecting a rippling silhouette over the creek punctuated by two corks plopping into the calm water. William Ledbetter said, "Perfect timin' – the sun's 'bout to come up, an' fresh worms are in the water. Wake up down there, little fishies – breakfast is ready."

Cyril added. "Come an' git it."

"Speakin' o' breakfast," said William. "Yo' Mama, fried up some salt pork and put it on some o' them biscuits from last evenin'. You know how she does 'em when she slices 'em in half an' butters the open faces an' toasts 'em up on a skillet an' 'en she puts a little honey on 'em while they still hot. Sometimes I want t' take a day off an' go fishin' just so she'll make these for me." The man took out a bundle and placed it on a nearby rock, and as he pulled back the cloth, the smell of bacon and biscuits filled the air, and the two of them began to eat.

Shortly, the fish started to bite, and the pair of them were pretty busy pulling fish out of the water and putting them in their buckets.

"Daddy, do that ice house stay open all night, or do it just open real early?" Cyril asked.

"Oh, they open up bout five o'clock every mornin' so people can get their ice for their ice boxes and fishin' and whatever else they need it for. Though on Friday and Saturday nights, they stay open pretty late."

"What d' they stay open so late for Daddy? What d' folks need with ice 'at late at night?"

"People like to go down there t' git a cold drink an' sit an' listen to some music."

"Why d' they have music at the ice house?"

"They have people t' come in and play some guitar, and the women folk will sing a bit so that folks will pay to sit and have a cold drink. Friday nights, they have the colored folks, and Saturday nights, they have the white folks. Though they have the same women from the south side o' town singin' both nights."

"D' they sing like singin' in church?"

"Well, it's a little like church singin', but mostly things y' can't sing about in church," the man said with a slight grin.

"Can we go there tonight an' have a cold drink an' listen to the singin'?"

The man paused and gave his son a stern look. "Nope. Tha's for grown people. Ain't no little boys allowed."

"Oh," came the disappointed response, "D' you ever go to the ice house at night?"

"Nooo, not in a long time. Not since I married your mother. I only go to the ice house early in the mornin', like we did today. And when you are grown, you best do the same."

"Yes, sir," said the boy. "Reckon how old you have t' be 'fore you grown enough to go to the ice house at night?"

"I'd say at least thirty-five," the man answered.

"Oh – 'ats a good long time." The boy sounded disappointed. "Daddy….."

The man cut the boy off. "Hush up now – them fish gonna stop bitin' if you ain't holdin' yo mouth right.

It was only nine in the morning when the father and son headed back into town, each with a mess of fish in his bucket. William said, "We need to stop up here by the Post Office fo' jus' a moment. Then I'll cut you lose and you can go on." They stopped in front of the Post Office. "You stay righ here and keep my pole and bucket with you, til I git back out."

"A'ight Daddy," said Cyril. The boy watched as his father went toward the door of the building. Cyril noticed that his father paused for a moment in front of the large window looking at his reflection as he straightened his hat. Cyril admired how tall and strong his father looked standing there in front of that window. Then the man continued on inside for a few minutes.

After he returned, William said,"you go on over to drop 'em fish off with the judge an' git yo' money. I'm gonna head back to the house an' clean 'ese fish. And you can come back home for lunch in a few hours."

Cyril said, "After I git my money from the judge, I thought that I'd go an' play fo' a bit, an' then when the noon train come, I'll go down there an' git me a piece of chicken an' a biscuit at the station."

The man nodded. "Well, it's yo' money, and far be it for me t' stand between a boy and some fried chicken. You be shore t' git back home in time t' learn how t' fry these fish. Now give me yo' pole, an' I'll take it with me so you don't have to drag it around all day."

The boy handed his fishing pole to the man and said, "Thank you, Daddy." With that, the boy was off like a shot running toward town.

Fifteen minutes later, Cyril had a shiny quarter in his pocket and was on a trail heading over the train tracks just outside of town to come around the back way to the south side of town. He did not much use the trails around the outside of the town since he was accustomed to just walking down the main street. As he trotted along, he saw two boys approaching who looked a bit familiar, but he did not know their names since they went to the other school on the south side of town with all of the other Black kids. One boy looked about the same age as Cyril, and the other looked a few years older and was carrying a shotgun. Cyril stopped running and smiled. "Is y'all after birds or squirrels?"

The younger boy answered. "My big brother and me goin' over to that big farm where old man Hughes got them pecan trees. He gives us a penny for every squirrel we git – and we can take the squirrels home t' eat."

"Sounds like a good deal," the white boy answered. "I just dropped off some fish for the judge m'self."

The older boy looked down at Cyril and asked. "Why you goin' 'at way? Don't you know where that end o' the trail goes?"

Cyril said, "Yeah, I know where it goes. It comes out somewheres b'hind y'alls church down there on the south side. And 'at's just down the street from where I'm a-goin' to."

The older boy gave Cyril a strange look. "Who are you goin' to see down there?"

"Just somebody," the white boy responded. "I gotta git goin' anyways. Good luck wi' y'alls squirrels." He started to walk south down the trail without waiting for an answer.

The boy exited the trail behind the Second Baptist Church and crossed the churchyard. As he passed the building, he could hear female voices through the open window. He heard a familiar voice and glanced into the building to see Mrs. Jones speaking to some other ladies. "He's over there now," she was saying.

Cyril continued on his way and soon walked through the freshly rebuilt and painted white picket fence in front of the newly painted house with a shiny, pressed tin roof. He could see Mr. Bratton sitting on the porch in a brand new white wicker chair, and another somewhat darker brown-skinned man was sitting in a similar chair. The two men were conversing, so the boy just quietly approached them and sat down on the bottom step leading to the porch to wait his turn.

Cyril Bratton glanced at the boy and continued his conversation. "Reverend, I cannot promise anything, but if you leave these copies of the contracts with me, I will read them carefully. It is hard to overturn a contract or get an injunction, but we may be able to convince the court that these contracts were not entered in good faith."

The other man said, "I understand. That is all that I can ask. But they are good people who do not deserve to be used this way just because they are poor. I spoke to the judge, and while he did not say much, his expression tells me he is not well pleased with the situation himself. It was he who recommended that I speak to you about it. There is not much in the way of money among them to cover legal fees, but I am sure they will do whatever they can."

Mr. Bratton said, "Well, Reverend, we are not sure there is a case. Aside from that, I am retired, so money is not an issue right now."

The preacher stood up, reaching out his hand; Mr. Bratton did the same. As the men shook hands, the minister said, "Thank you for your time, Mr Bratton."

Cyril Bratton smiled and said, "You are quite welcome, Reverend; time is something which I have in full measure lately."

The minister turned toward the steps and looked down at the boy who was starting to stand, and he smiled and asked. "Now, who is this young man?"

"I am Cyril Ledbetter," said the boy. "Mr. Bratton and me, we friends now 'cause we got the same first name. You 'at preacher from the colored church, ain't y'? I figured you'd be here when I heard the womenfolk talking inside y'alls church a few minutes ago. But I would o' knowed it was you anyway 'cause o' that hat – every preacher wears that same black hat when he out visitin' folks."

The man chuckled. "It seems that you do not miss much, young man. Why were you over at the church just now?"

The boy continued excitedly. "I don't miss a thang. I took the shortcut through the churchyard when I come out o' the trail behind the town to git hye. 'Cause my daddy said 'at it would be quieter an' fewer folks'll notice me if I don't walk down the middle o' town. Some folks might not like me bein' down here visitin'. Like 'at sheriff – he was by hye the other day actin' real mean like an' he told me I shouldn't be down hye on 'is side o' town." The boy turned to Mr. Bratton. "D'ya know that when I got home, 'at sheriff was at my house, just like he said, tellin' on me t' my daddy? He was tryin' to fetch me a beatin' – but my daddy, he don't thank that chil'ren need to git beat too much. Which is fine by me."

"I told my sons to take the same trail just a little while ago," the minister responded. "And yes, I am Reverend Scolfield. I am glad Mr. Bratton has such an energetic young friend."

"This mornin'? D' y' got two sons? Goin' squirrel huntin'?" The boy asked.

"Yes," said Reverend Scolfield.

"I saw 'em," said the boy. "The big one, he had him a four ten shotgun, an' we talked about squirrel huntin' and some about fishin' too."

"They must have been a bit surprised to see you," said the minister.

The boy looked up at Reverend Scolfield quizzically and said, "You bein' a preacher and all, I bet you know the Bible pretty good. I got a question 'bout somthin'. Was Jesus a bully? You know, like when he chased 'em men out o' the temple with a stick. Was he bein' a bully?"

"I have never thought of it that way," said the man. "What would put that in your head?"

The boy said, "We was talkin' at supper the other night – 'bout that man from Texas. My daddy said 'at he has money an' 'at makes him act like a bully. So I said 'at Mr. Bratton got money from being a lawyer an all an' he don't never act like no bully. My daddy said 'at folks from Tennessee got better manners than folks from Texas anyway. But my Mama, she said any man can be a bully to git what he wants or iffin he thanks that he's right about somethin' – even Jesus with 'at stick. So she reckons that even Mr. Bratton can be a bully. But she don't know 'im like I do." The boy noticed Mr. Bratton slowly sitting back in his seat, but he continued. "Anyway, my daddy said that he figured 'at 'em money lenders had it comin' anyway. And she told him not t' let his food git cold and sent me t' go read."

Reverend Scolfield took all of this in and nodded. "Well, now, I can't say either of your parents is any less right than the other. The man from Texas is surely a bully and does use his money to push people around. And your mother is right that all men can be bullies – or take to any sin, for that matter. And the money lenders certainly had it coming for engaging in commerce in the temple. As to whether or not Jesus was being a bully or bringing justice, I will have to sit and study on that for a while. So I will get back to you on that." The man raised his hand toward Mr. Bratton as he stepped onto the top step to leave. "Thank you for your help, Brother Cyril."

Mr. Bratton said, "Thank you for stopping by, Reverend. I should have more information for you after services tomorrow."

As the minister went through the gate, the boy trotted up the steps and plopped down in the chair the reverend had recently vacated. And he looked at Mr. Bratton, who appeared a bit distracted. He saw that the man was holding a few sheets of paper. "Is 'at them contrac's 'at dem people signed? What kind o' case do we got – is it a good'ne?

The man looked at the boy. "What kind of case do 'WE' have? Do 'WE' have a case?"

"Well, iffin I'm 'a be a lawyer too; I figured that I could help y' with this case an' maybe learn more about lawyerin'."

"If you want to be a lawyer, you need to start by speaking clearly and doing well in school," the man responded.

"Oh," the boy said. "I'll try. And don't you worry about what my Mama said 'bout you bein' a bully an' all. She didn't mean nothin' by it. She just been a little bit outta sorts since – well, since a while now."

The man momentarily looked off into the distance and turned back to look at the boy. "Did you get those fish to the judge? If we take a case before him, we want him to be in a good mood."

"Yessir! First thang this mornin', I caught him a big ole mess o' fish. An' I got me some shiny money for it too. And my daddy come fishin' with me, an' he took a mess o' fish home for our supper 'at he gonna cook on account of my Mama having all th' church ladies over to piece together a quilt. My Mama likes makin' quilts – she makes some nice ones too. She learned it from her Mama when she was a little girl."

"That's generally how they learn. I hope that she cherishes those memories. My wife always liked quilting and spending time with our little girl. I have several fine quilts that she made. I will have to show them to you some time."

"I'd like to see 'em," the boy said politely. "D' y' reckon 'at your daughter still makes quilts too?"

The man's expression softened, and he said, "I am sure of it."

"I heard the preacher man call you 'brother'. So I reckon 'at you started back to church. I figured 'at was gonna happen when Missy… I mean Mrs. Jones said 'at the widow ladies was gonna come see y'. I saw 'em when they was headed to your house. I figure if the widow ladies at your church is anythang like the widow ladies at my church, you probably can't say no and expect t' live a peaceful life."

"Yes, the ladies were quite convincing – and I do appreciate a peaceful life," chuckled the man. "And it is nice to hear the voices of the people around me. Mrs. Jones was correct – I did miss that part of the process. And it would seem that she was also correct that you were eavesdropping."

"Not s' much eavesdroppin' as just happened to be in earshot," the boy explained. So, what are we gonna do today? Do you have t' go anywhere in yo' automobile, maybe?"

"After lunch, I was going to walk down to the barber shop for a haircut and close shave," the man said.

"I thank 'at you ought t' drive your automobile down there. Y' know, just to keep the engine oiled an' runnin' good. And speakin' o' lunch, when the noon train come today, I'm 'a go down t' the station an' git me some fried chicken an' a biscuit. They's a colored woman what meets the noon train with a basket o' fried chicken an' some buttered biscuits an' corn on the cob. She sells it to the folks on the train while the train is fillin' up from the water tower. She walks up an' down the platform, an' people just buy it from her right there through the train winda's. They tell her how many pieces of chicken they want, an' she wraps it up in a sheet o' newspaper fo' 'em. Do the women folk sell chicken on the train platform where you from?"

The man nodded. "Pretty much every station in America has someone selling food on the platform for noon trains. But the fried chicken in the South is the best. That sounds good. Maybe I will walk to the station for a good chicken lunch myself."

"You prob'ly ought t' drive – man your age and all."

"Walking keeps you young," the man said.

"Then I reckon 'at I won't never grow up seein' as how I gotta walk ever'where," the boy said in a frustrated voice.

"Tomorrow after church and after I speak with the reverend, I will take the automobile out to start teaching Dr. Barnes how to drive."

"Is 'at doctor gittin' an automobile too?" The boy asked.

"No," answered the man. "The doctor is a very busy man. He has weekly clinic hours at several locations in the towns around here. For some towns, he can take the train, but for others, he needs his horse and buggy to visit. I offered to let him borrow the automobile on those days to make his trips faster."

"Can I come along an' learn how t' drive too?" The boy asked.

"Perhaps when you are older," the man answered.

"Alright," the boy sounded exasperated.

Just then, they heard a very distant train whistle. The man looked at the boy and said, "Sounds like lunchtime."

Ten minutes later, the two of them were back and sitting inside at the kitchen table, each with an opened newspaper bundle in front of him. Around a mouthful of biscuit, the boy spoke. "Thank y' for lunch. I could o' paid for it m'self though with the shiny money the judge gave me."

The man said, 'You are quite welcome. And if you are going to law school, you should start saving your money now."

"Oh," said the boy. "Do law school cost a lot?"

"It can be expensive – if you get in. Speaking like that will not get you in."

"Oh, I'll… I will try to remember that. S' tell me about our case."

The man shook his head. "The case – if there is a case – will rest on the issue of whether or not the contract was entered into in good faith. But I have to read the contracts very carefully. And suppose we can convince the court that the contract was not intended in good faith and that the man from Texas likely had ulterior motives. In that case, we can petition for some relief or an injunction to stop the man from seizing the farms and give the families more time to pay him back. It is not a strong argument, but I believe that the judge is inclined to entertain it."

The boy looked thoughtfully for a moment and then asked, "Do I gotta learn what all that means iffin I wanna be a lawyer?"

The elder Cyril responded, "Yes. Now eat your chicken and then we'll head over to the barber."

A half-hour later, the two Cyrils reached the barbershop. "I gotta wait out here for y'." The boy sat down just outside of the door to wait. He could hear and see everything happening inside, but he technically was not 'in' the barbershop.

Mr. Bratton walked into the barbershop, where there was a rowdy

71

conversation, occasionally punctuated by much laughter. The conversation stopped as the man entered and was greeted by the barber, who introduced him to a few local men he had not yet met. The boy looked inside and saw one barber chair with a man sitting in it and the barber behind him. There was a shoeshine chair with a teenage boy sitting in it, but he didn't even have on shoes, so he wasn't there for a shine. A bench and a couple of other chairs held three more men.

The barber spoke. "That's an interesting shadow that followed you to the door Brother Cyril." he looked down at the boy sitting just outside the door. "You here for a haircut?"

"No, sir," the boy answered. "If I come home with a haircut from a barber, my Mama will wear me out for being' in a barbershop."

"So, she doesn't like barbershops then?" the man asked.

"Not lately," said the boy. "Not since I slipped up and repeated somethin' that I heard. She said I ought t' not be in a place where men are talkin' an' there ain't no Bible."

Laughter filled the room for a moment. "She said 'at she had a mind t' take her scissors over t' the barbershop on the north side o' town an' do some hair cuttin' herself. She said that she bet it'll stay cut too."

Another round of laughter broke the air. The barber gave the boy a severe look. "Don't ever repeat anything that you hear in a barbershop or an ice house. And don't tell your Mama you were here."

"Don't nobody gotta worry about me tellin' my Mama that," said the boy. "I wanna live a good long time. B'sides, you don't cut white boy's hair, do y'?"

"I did when I was in the Army," said the man. "But not much anymore; y'all got your barbershop on that side o' town, and they got me here on this side."

The man went back to cutting hair, and the boy just watched and listened to the men inside while he waited for Mr. Bratton to have his turn for a haircut and shave. As far as he could tell, the conversation was pretty much the same as the conversations at the other barbershop always were. After a few minutes, the boy felt a sizable shadow settle on him, and he turned and looked up at a large man with very dark skin. The man looked down at the boy and said, "Excuse me."

The boy hurried out of the doorway to let the man pass. As the man entered the shop, the barber looked up and said, "Looky comin' here. I wondered if you would make it in today – after all that at the ice house last night."

The newcomer looked at the barber and said. "Brother Jones, Samuel – I don't know what you mean. And I'm afraid that you don't know either." There was another round of loud laughter, and the barber smiled. "So, why is there a little white boy sittin' in your doorway, Brother Sam?"

The barber said, "Because his Mama won't let him come in the barbershop because she heard that you were going to be here." Another round of laughter filled the air. "How is sister Helen this mornin', George?"

The newcomer answered. "She is doin' fine. Still worried about Fredrick after all that trouble in Tulsa. He says he is comin' back here shortly and bringin' that girl he met out there. They are getting married sometime soon, and her little brother is comin' back with 'em. After her parents were killed like that, she and her little brother got no close family left. He was preparing to ask her father for permission to marry anyway."

"How old is Fredrick now?" Asked another one of the men.

George said, "He's nineteen now, and the girl is sixteen, and I reckon that her little brother is only four. Same age Fredrick was when his father was killed in Atlanta."

"Oh, I remember when you went down there to Atlanta to get him and his sister,' said the barber. "You buried your brother, and then you had his two children to raise. And you with no wife. And then Sister

Helen took pity on you and agreed to marry you. And there you were, twenty years old with a four-year-old boy, a two-year-old girl, and a wife that was way too good for you. I don't care what everybody else says; you are a good man George Powell." More laughter.

Mr. Powell raised his eyebrows and looked at the barber. "I don't know about 'what everybody else says,' but I doubt you ever stop talkin' long enough for anyone else to say much of anything." More laughter filled the room.

Another voice spoke. "Reckon how many they kilt in Tulsa?"

The Barber answered. "Nobody knows. They don't ever say – they don't count everybody the same way. Could be hundreds – just like them doin's in Elaine two years ago. Or Atlanta when they killed Sam's brother or Wilmington twenty-somethin' years ago. Or whatever town they decide to burn down here in the next few years. Or in Haiti – who knows how many folks them marines have killed in Haiti in the last six years."

The barber shop was silent for a few minutes until the barber broke the stillness with a single word. "Next."

Slowly the men went back to talking about the usual things that country people talk about. Things like late trains, harvest, wives, and who has the biggest yearling or the most of any particular crop; any subject would work to keep the conversation alive.

The boy continued to sit and listen to the men and wondered about all the places the barber mentioned. 'I'll ask my daddy about 'em later,' the boy thought – ' if I remember 'at is.'

After Cyril Bratton got his haircut and shave and after the walk back to Mr. Bratton's new house, the boy watched the machine drive away, heading down to pick up the doctor for his driving lesson. He then set off on foot toward the churchyard to return to the trail he had used earlier that day. He looked down at his shadow stretching out to his left and said, "Guess it's just you 'n me. I shore wished I could o' started learnin' t' drive. Seems like all 'ese people are gettin' automobiles an' I just gotta walk ever'where. As he neared the back of the church building, he saw the two boys from earlier stepping out from the trail. They were carrying five squirrels. He waved and said, "Y'all got some. 'At'll make a good supper an' a nickel in yo' pocket."

The younger of the brothers held up the two squirrels that he was carrying and said, "My brother is a good shot, didn't miss any but one – and it was runnin' pretty fast.

As Cyril passed the two other boys, he said, "I gotta git home an' help my daddy fry some fish. Y'all tell the reverend I said t' enjoy his squirrel supper."

"We will – bye!" said the younger brother while the older boy gave Cyril a suspicious look as he wondered how this strange little white boy knew their father was the preacher.

Cyril was heading into the back door after washing his hands and face at the pump. As he entered the kitchen, he heard his father say, "There you are. I was just fixin' t' light the stove and start cookin', but the ladies are packing up to go home, so you go in there and see if you can help yo' Mama or any o' the other ladies.

"Yes, sir," the boy responded. He headed straight through the kitchen toward the front room, where he could hear female voices.

"Cyril, just in time," said Ida. 'We just finished this quilt for Sister Shields, and I want you to help her carry it out to her buggy. Then you can come back for her sewing box."

"Yes, ma'am," said the boy. He picked up the folded quilt and headed out with it. He quickly made his second trip and placed the sewing box in the buggy. He turned to see Sister Shields slowly descending the steps from the porch. She was the oldest person he knew, but she still cooked and shopped and drove her own buggy to church every Sunday.

"Is there anything else 'at I can do for you, Sister Shields?" He asked.

"No, thank you, young man," the woman said. "You are a good boy – you remind me of your father when he came here to live with his aunt."

"Yes, ma'am, you have a good evening, Sister."

"Thank you, young man. Remember always to clean your plate and say your prayers. I will see you at church in the morning."

"Yes, ma'am, bye now." He waited until she was sitting safely in her buggy. Then he headed in to put away the quilting frame since that was always his job after the ladies left. He listened to the ladies as they packed to leave while he disassembled the old wooden quilting frame. There was a chorus of 'bye Sister Ida' and 'Thank you, Sister Ida.'

"This is a very good supper, William," said Ida. "You excel at frying fish and hush-puppies."

"Thank you, my dear. You do so much in the kitchen; it's only right to spell you from time to time, especially when you have the ladies over. And Cyril here was good help – and he will be cleaning up. So, you can just go and sit with your book. It's good to have a day off from outside work for me, and good for you to have a day off from the kitchen."

"Yes, it is good, and I thank you," agreed the woman. "Though I do believe that you like the fuss that the ladies make when you bring out the tea and sandwiches for them mid-afternoon. You do it every time, and they always act surprised to see a man serving them tea. Then they compliment your auntie for raising you so well. I think that if you were to forget their tea and sandwiches one time, they would think that the world was coming to an end."

William nodded. "My aunt did love her tea, and I enjoy the ritual when I pull out that tea service. Reminds me of being a boy. But mostly, I do it so that they can tell you how lucky you are to have such a thoughtful husband. Never hurts to remember that." The man smiled and winked.

If they ever see your laundry, they might reconsider their praise." her deep brown eyes twinkled as she playfully scolded him.

The man responded. "Preacher said for better or for worse. I reckon that's the worst of it."

"So far," the woman added.

The man changed the subject. "When I was coming back from fishing this morning, I heard that one of the fellas over at the county farm was sick and might not make it. Got bit by a copperhead movin' a log on the chain gang. With Doc Harrison out of town, for a couple of days to go bury his sister, there is not a doctor available to treat the man."

Cyril looked at his father and asked. "Why don't they just send for the doctor on the other side o' town? He's right there, and even Doc Harrison sent for him one time."

William shook his head. "That won't happen. The sheriff, he'll wait for Doc Harrison to get back. He's the official county doctor for the jail. The sheriff is set in his ways about things like that."

Eight: An Afternoon With Mother

Cyril's mother had kept him home this Saturday and not let him go out to play. Colder weather was coming, and she had a list of chores that had kept him busy all morning. The first thing on the list for today was to accompany her to the general store to help carry things. The harvest was in, and his mother had been busy canning food and making jellies and jams. She had threaded a bunch of beans for string beans which Cyril had taken up and hung in the attic to dry. Potatoes, turnips, and rutabagas were all gathered into hills and covered over to protect them for the winter.

His next task was to go and hitch the mule up so that he and his mother could go into town. A short time later, he was sitting on the wagon seat beside his mother holding the reins and driving the wagon along the dusty road. He felt so grown to be sitting there driving the wagon.

Cyril spoke. "Mr. Bratton said that his wife liked to make quilts too, just like you. He said she taught their little girl how to make them as your Mama taught you. He said that she treasured those memories and hopes his daughter treasures them too."

After a pause, Ida responded. "I'm sure that she does. A daughter always treasures such things."

The boy said, "I was thinking that if you wanted to, you could teach me how to make them."

Ida smiled and said, "I doubt you have taken a sudden interest in quilting."

"I could learn to like it," the boy said. "I just think that you ought t' be able to teach somebody, is all."

Ida said, "Thank you. You truly can be a sweet boy sometimes. Perhaps someday you will have a wife who will want to learn. Then, I will teach her."

"Mama, do you reckon that the man bitten by the snake last week passed away before the doctor could get back and tend to him?"

The woman said, "That I do not know. He may have passed, or he may live. Snake bites are a strange thing. Some men can come through it fine while others die straight away."

Cyril said, "It just don't seem right that the sheriff wouldn't let the other doctor see that man just because he ain't the official doctor for the county farm."

Ida said, "No, it does not seem right, but the sheriff gets to run his jail as he sees fit. If he does not want a man to see a doctor or he does not want a particular doctor in his jailhouse, for whatever reason – that is just the way it is."

"Why do they call it the county farm anyway, Mama?" the boy asked. "There are farms all over the county."

Ida answered. "Well, it is the working farm where men are sent when they have been sentenced to hard labor by the county. It is where the men grow most of their food. If they want to eat, they have to work."

"What about the chain gang?" The boy asked. "That ain't particularly farm work."

Ida said, "The chain gangs are a different thing entirely. They clear the roads and tend to the county property, leaving the farm with guards to watch over them while they work."

"Mama? I have only seen colored folks on the chain gang. Do

they only send them to hard labor? What do they do with the white folks who break the law?"

"They go to jail, too," Ida said. "But the sheriff does not like for them to mix with the Negro prisoners, so they work in different groups. The white prisoners mostly work on the farm, though the county does hire some out to work on the farms around here during busy times. Negros get put on the chain gangs and work on the county farm too – but separated from the white prisoners."

Ida nodded. "There is the store, so just pull the wagon up front, and we can go in and give the storekeeper our list."

"Yes, ma'am."

Mr. Dawson looked up from his counter and said. "Mrs. Ledbetter. Wonderful to see you here on this fine Saturday afternoon."

"Hello, Mr. Dawson," said the woman. "Colder weather is coming, and I have quite a list here of things that I will need to be better prepared. And there are one or two things on here that Mr. Ledbetter will need from around back. And he will be stopping by sometime next week to settle up with you."

The storekeeper hurried around the counter to meet the woman and start filling her list while she shopped. "Yes, ma'am, be glad to handle all that for you." He looked down at the list. "Did you want a dozen large or small jars? And the flats and lids to go with them, I'm sure."

"Oh yes, the large jars, please," said the woman.

The man looked at Cyril. "I will start gathering things, and you can start moving them out to your wagon for your mother."

"Yes, sir," said the boy. Cyril looked around and saw several other ladies from town shopping and one little girl with whom he went to school. He nodded toward the girl and smiled. "Penny, how are you today?"

The girl smiled briefly and nodded as her mother gave the boy a disapproving look. The girl said, "I am well today, thank you."

Then, Cyril noticed that the school teacher Miss Bevis was standing over in the corner of the store. She had been looking at the sewing notions, but as soon as she noticed Cyril, she was now giving him a cold look with her piggish eyes. He had always thought that her eyes looked just like a pig. He saw the woman change her expression to a sugary smile as she turned toward his mother.

Then, the woman spoke with a sweet voice. "Sister Ledbetter, I'm so glad to see you here. I have been intending to speak to you concerning young Cyril here."

Ida looked over at the woman. "Oh, is there a problem? Has he done something or are his grades slipping?

The school teacher shook her head. "Oh no, nothing like that. If anything, he has been more studious of late."

Ida smiled. "That is wonderful to hear. His father and I are always concerned that he may not apply himself sufficiently to his studies."

Miss Bevis continued. "Nothing to worry about there. This does not concern his school work or his time at school."

Ida looked a bit confused. "I am sure I do not understand then if it does not concern his education."

Miss Bevis smiled. "It concerns his afternoons after school and what he does on some weekends. I am not sure that you are aware that he has been spending a good bit of time visiting down on the south side of the town these last few weeks. I thought your husband and you might wish to be informed about his after-school activities."

Cyril was holding his breath and even Mr. Dawson had stopped to hear the conversation. Cyril saw the smile on his mother's face change ever so slightly. It was still a very formal smile, but a wave of ice had come over her eyes.

Ida continued to smile, and after a couple of quick blinks, she said. "Thank you for your concern. Yes, his father and I are well aware of his activities. I am glad to know that he is doing well in school. You are a gifted educator, and you do so much for the children when they are at your school and in your care. But after he leaves your schoolyard, you need not concern yourself with his activities. As his mother, I will see to him, and you can give your mind a much-needed rest with you being so constantly busy – with the children." If anything, the smile on Ida's face sweetened though her eyes conveyed no warmth.

The school teacher looked a bit startled, and her pale face reddened ever so slightly. "Yes, quite right. You have a nice day Mrs. Ledbetter." The woman walked directly to the counter and placed an item beside a small pile of goods. "Mr. Dawson, please add this to my order and have your boy bring it to my house later today. Thank you."

With a growing smile, the storekeeper watched the woman turn and head directly for the door. "Yes, ma'am, Miss Bevis. You have a nice day."

"Are you finding something entertaining, Mr. Dawson?" Ida's voice broke his moment of pleasure.

The man lost his smile. "No – No, ma'am. Just recalling something I heard this week while I was getting my hair cut."

"I see. Something that you heard in a barber shop." Ida said.

"Yes, ma'am," said the storekeeper. "I will get back to your order here."

Ida smiled at the man and said, "Thank you, Mr Dawson." She looked at her son. "You should be loading things into that wagon as they are placed on the counter."

"Yes, ma'am," the boy said. That is when Cyril noticed the other women in the store had all stopped to hear the exchange between his mother and school teacher.

Ten minutes later, they were back on the wagon and pulling it around behind the store. As they pulled up, Jeremiah Dawson walked out of the storage shed behind the store and tipped his hat to the woman. "Mrs. Ledbetter."

The woman smiled and said, "Mr. Dawson." She elbowed her son.

"Set the brake, get down, and help the man with your father's things."

"Yes, ma'am," said Cyril.

Ida rode in silence on the trip back from town. Cyril was afraid that his mother was angry with him about what the teacher had told her – or maybe about how much time he spent on the other side of the tracks. Or maybe about who he was spending time with. He wasn't sure, but he knew that she was upset about something from today.

As they arrived home, the boy spoke. "Mama, I am sorry if you are upset with me behind what Miss Bevis told you today. I'm just..."

Ida cut him short. "You are fine. I am not upset with you in the least. You carry things into the house; I am going to the barn to see if I can find your father. I need to speak to him."

Cyril said, "I can go find him and tell him you want to speak to him. You don't need to…"

Ida held up a hand to stop the boy, then waved it toward the stuff in the back of the wagon.

"Yes, ma'am," the boy said. He grabbed an armful of things and headed into the house with them. Most of the stuff was headed for the kitchen, and while he was putting it in there, he saw his mother through the window as she neared the barn. He saw his father walk out of the barn and meet her just outside the building. He watched through the window, imagining what she must be telling him. He wondered how much trouble he would be in when he next spoke to his father. He could see his mother speaking animatedly to his father, shaking her head and pointing toward town. He could see his father reach out and take his wife's hand and hold it close to his chest while she spoke. The boy could see that his mother was quite upset. He imagined his father's voice as he would speak deeply and calmly like he did when someone was upset. He saw his mother lean her head on his father's chest and saw his father put his arm around her and hold on to her. After a few minutes, his mother pulled back from his father and looked up at him. The man bent and kissed his wife. Then, he said something to her and she nodded and turned to walk back to the house. The boy headed back out to finish carrying things.

After unloading the wagon, Cyril drove the wagon out to the barn to unhitch the mule and put the wagon away. As he arrived at the barn, he saw his father walking toward him. "Daddy, I'm sorry that Mama is so upset. I didn't mean to cause any trouble for anybody."

William held up his hand to stop the boy. "Boy, you didn't do anything wrong, and yo' Mama ain't upset with you. What hurts her is that someone could appear to take pleasure in hurting other folks. She doesn't understand why that school teacher likes to gossip and act like a busybody. Yo' mama just wants folks to leave us alone and not try to get into our business. Sometimes, it gets to be a little more than she can take."

"So I didn't do nuthin' wrong t' upset her?" Asked Cyril.

The man chuckled. "As hard as you may find this to believe, this ain't about you, so you forget about today and just go on inside the house and help yo' mama a bit and try to make her day a little easier."

"Ok, Daddy,' said the boy.

Cyril spent the rest of the afternoon quietly helping his mother inside the house as she got things ready before the cold weather set in. Several times during the day, he would notice his mother lost in thought while standing at the sink gazing out of the window. Very little was said between them the rest of that afternoon, just Ida occasionally directing the boy as to what she needed him to do next or a quiet 'thank you' here or there and an occasional cool hand on his shoulder or neck. Mostly Cyril just watched to see what she was doing, and he would quietly just help or move things as she appeared to need them moved. The boy enjoyed watching his mother's hands as she went through her work; her fingers were long and delicate even though they worked so hard. They were tanned from being out in the light so much, just a very light bronze color. Those hands seemed so magical, especially when she used to play her violin – something she had not done in quite some time.

After a simple supper of turnips and greens with cornbread dumplings, they sat in the parlor reading as was their custom. Cyril was not sitting in his usual spot on the floor. He sat on the floor right in front of and against his mother's chair and leaned a little to the side to rest against her leg. Occasionally he felt her gentle touch as she would absently stroke his hair while holding her book in her other hand. He noticed she sat holding the book but seemed to be looking through it into another world, and she never turned the page. The boy wondered what it was that she was studying so intently, but he did not want to ask and risk disturbing her. He watched his mother's shadow as it crept slowly across the floor toward the far wall. For once, he was not in a hurry for the shadow to reach the wall and free him. It had been a peaceful afternoon with his mother, and he did not want the quietude to end just yet.

The following morning was a peaceful Sunday as they prepared to leave for church. Cyril was dressed pretty quickly after breakfast. The boy noticed that his mother took a little more time with herself as she prepared. He watched as she pulled her hair into the tight bun she always wore when going out. She picked up her powder puff and gently patted the white powder around her face and neck. Then, she applied a rose powder to her cheeks. Cyril always found it odd that women folk would put a powder all over their faces to make them look milky and then use another powder to put the color back on their faces. She was wearing one of her nice dresses – one that she had made recently. He watched as she used the hook to fasten the high tops of her shoes that would cover her ankles – he was always amazed at how deftly she could accomplish this task. She pinned her hat in place so the wind could not take it from her head. This hat was newly decorated – she would buy a basic hat at the general store and then use her lace and ribbons to decorate it for church. Then lastly, she pulled on her white gloves, two button length, to reach up to her sleeves – it would not do for a lady to have her arms showing at church. As the last thing to signal that it was time to leave for church, she reached up and adjusted her husband's hat, picked up a small handbag, and led the way out to the wagon that was already hitched and waiting.

Nine: Preparing a Case

Later that week, Cyril felt like paying his lawyer friend another visit. He walked through the gate in the picket fence, hoping that Mr. Bratton was home and needed to go somewhere in his automobile, though he certainly never seemed to need to drive anywhere. The boy thought, 'Iffin that was my automobile, I would drive it ever'where I go' as he looked toward the carriage house door. As the boy stepped onto the porch, he could see Mr. Bratton through a window sitting at a desk in one of the front rooms with books open in front of him. The boy walked over to the window and looked in at the man, and then he said, "Hey."

The man looked up from his desk and said, "Hello, I was wondering if I would see you today."

"Yeah, well, I been stayin' close t' the house to help my Mama git everything ready fo' winter. Spent all day last Saturday with her an' been goin' back ever' afternoon after school t' git the woodshed filled up. You know, in the winter time, Mama keeps the wood stove goin' to keep the house warm – so she uses a lot o' split wood. Not like in the summer when she only lights the stove long enough to cook and not git the house so hot." The boy looked behind the man and saw a large set of bookshelves filled with books. "Is them yo' law books?"

"Excuse me?" The man arched an eyebrow toward the boy.

"I mean, to say. Are those your law books?"

"Yes, they are – among other subjects. Classics, American writers, Aurelius, Shakespeare, Mark Twain, Anna Cooper, Edgar Poe, both his literature and science, J. W. Johnson, W. E. B. Du Bois, Albery, Whitman, and many others."

"Have you read all of 'em?"

"Yes, I have – and you should read them too. Would you like to borrow one?"

"Uhhhh, not just yet, but thank you. Do you have that Song of Hiawatha up there on a shelf?"

"Longfellow? Yes, I have it."

"I 'on't much like 'at one. We been readin' it in school lately, but I just cain't understand it. S'posed t' be about some Indian, but it don't much seem real at all. Like he just made up a bunch o' stuff 'at he don't really know about Indians. But Miss Bevis, that mean ole school teacher, she shore loves it an' says that we can learn a lot about Indians, before they was tamed, from readin' it. But I don't know."

The man chuckled. "Perhaps reading that one for its structure and literary qualities is better than any cultural or historical value."

"Don't seem right to me, is all. B'sides 'at she makin' ever'body memorize a part of it an' hye shortly we gonna have t' take turns each one recitin' our part. That's just ridiculous."

"Learning to speak in public confidently and clearly will be valuable if you become a lawyer."

"I 'on't know if 'at's the best thang to practice on. Appears to me that if you gonna be speakin' in front of a judge, you prob'ly should be saying thangs what make good sense."

The man laughed out loud. "That could have come from Twain himself."

"Who's 'at?"

"Twain, Mark Twain. The writer and commentator – Tom Sawyer, Huckleberry Finn, Mysterious Stranger. Actually, his name was

Samuel Clemens though he wrote under the pen name of Mark Twain. But you could say that Mark Twain was the most important character he ever created – one which he himself played."

"Oh, him. We read that Tom Sawyer book last year. I liked that one pretty good, but it seems to me that a boy like 'at prob'ly fetched himself a lot o' beatin's. Or he would o' iffin he lived around here. What's a 'commentator' anyway?"

"A commentator is a kind of public speaker who comments on current events and news, usually in a humorous way, and folks will pay to go and hear him speak."

"Did he make good money doin' that?"

"He seemed to make a good living from his writing and speaking."

"Did you ever pay to go and hear him speak?"

"I did hear him speak once but did not pay."

"They let you hear him for free?"

"No, not exactly. I would have happily paid if I could have done so. Only white folks were allowed to be in the audience. But I found my way to an open window near the stage, and I could hear him speak if not see him."

"Was he funny?"

"Very funny – and very relevant."

"Well, I wished 'at my teacher would have us t' read more o' his books an' less o' that Long-fella' stuff. Do you know what 'at teacher did last Sat'day? She tried to tell on me to my Mama when we was over at the store. Tryin' to sound all sweet like and makin' 'at she was just wantin' to help my Mama keep track o' me an' what I been a doin'. She 'on't thank 'at I should be comin' down hye t' this side o' the tracks s' much an' 'at I should be careful who my friends are. She told me 'at in school one day too."

"And how did your mother react? Did you get your beating?"

"No, I didn't git beat at all. It was pretty funny. My Mama just smiled – but not with her eyes; they wasn't smilin' at all. Then, she talked real sweet soundin' but not really sweet. Kinda like when my Mama makes 'at cornbread where she puts in sugar to sweeten it but chops up some peppers in it too. Tastes real good, but it'll burn y' mouth if you ain't careful. Told 'at ol' biddy 'at she was just too busy all the time with takin' care of the young 'uns so well at school, and 'at she need not concern herself with what I git up t' when I ain't at school. Then, 'at ol' teacher left straight away like she was a scalded dog. I thought the storekeep was gonna bust out laughing till my Mama asked him what he found s' entertainin' at the time. Then, he said somethin' about the barbershop, and she just looked at his haircut like it was somethin' stuck t' her shoe. Then, he put his head down an' went back to keepin' the store. Guess he figured 'at hole was deep enough."

"Ah, so he stopped digging."

"He shore did."

"And how was your mother after that?"

"She was quiet the rest of the day an' I thought she was mad with me. But Daddy said it weren't about me noway. I thank she cried on my daddy's shoulder a little bit, but we was pretty busy with things what needed t' git done. But she didn't talk much an' seemed to be studyin' on somethin'."

"And she did not tell you to stay away from here?"

"No, sir, she didn't tell me anything about you. So I'll keep comin' t' visit and just try t' be quiet about it so's folks will keep out o' my bidness."

"I regret any difficulty I may have caused your mother."

"You never caused her any trouble – it's 'at ol' school teacher causin' the trouble. But I bet you gonna cause that man from Texas; a whole bunch o' trouble, ain't y'? How's our case developin' now? Is it a good 'ne?"

"I believe that I can present a good argument to the judge that the contracts were not entered into in good faith by the gentleman from

Texas and get injunctive relief to allow the people more time to repay their loans without losing their property."

"So, what does all 'at mean in English? And you prob'ly shouldn't ought t' argue with the judge."

"I have no intention of arguing with the judge. I will be presenting arguments to the judge in his role as the person of the court." He saw that the boy looked even more confused now. "I will tell you what; I will explain it all as we walk. I must return this book on Alabama court procedures to Judge Haines."

"You shore 'at you don't want to drive your automobile over there instead of walkin' – it's a pretty good piece over t' the judge's house."

"Walking will be fine."

"Ok, but we prob'ly should take the trail around the outside o' town – just t' keep folks quiet like, I seen y'alls preacher's sons usin' it b'fore. I reckon 'at a lot o' colored folks do. "

The man looked at the boy thoughtfully. "Show me this trail."

A short time later, the pair were returning from dropping off the book."Still don't know why you didn't wanna go 'round front and talk t' the judge while we was there. Tell him what we got planned for the case for gittin' that 'junctive relief." The boy spoke as they stepped back into the front yard of the man's house. "Instead o' just droppin' the book off at the back door with Misses Jones like that.

"It is easy to understand," said the man. "Neither the judge nor myself would want there to seem to be any impropriety related to this case, so I will not discuss it with him in any way; in fact, I will not speak to him at all before the case."

"Ain't the judge a lawyer too?" Asked the boy.

"He is indeed."

"Then don't he already know what you gonna tell him an' ask him to do anyway? Why don't y' just ask him right now, an' he can just order it?

"That is not the way that this works. The judge has to hear the case and the arguments presented in a formal court proceeding in his capacity as the person of the court. Until the paperwork goes before him, after having been filed with the clerk, he officially knows nothing about the case as far as the role of the court is concerned. And yes, as an attorney, Judge Haines certainly already knows the main thrust of our arguments. But everything must transpire in a certain order and process to fully inform and prepare the respondent and his attorney."

"Is the 'respondent' that man from Texas?"

"Yes, he is the one who will respond to our case – or he will more likely have an attorney act for him in the court."

"Well, why do he git to talk in the court if ever'body already knows 'at he's a liar an' a bully?"

"He has the right to defend himself, and the court has a duty to hear a defense or explanation of his actions and allow him the chance to show that he entered into these contracts in good faith and that he has continued to act in good faith."

As they approached the porch, a woman stood up from a chair, smiled, and said, "Brother Bratton." She was a very tall, thin woman with the darkest skin that the boy had ever seen, and she looked to be around the same age as his mother. And she had the finest and smoothest skin on her face – she was wearing no kind of powder, yet her skin looked as smooth as glass. The boy was stunned by her and not just the surprise of seeing a strange woman waiting at the house. The woman glanced down and recognized the expression on the boy. It was an expression that she had seen on the faces of boys and men aged eight to eighty. It is the expression that every woman of extreme beauty recognizes on men's faces.

The elder Cyril was somewhat less stunned and responded questioningly. "Yes, Sister…?"

"Powell, Helen Powell," said the woman. "You met with my husband and a few of the other men about saving our farms."

"Oh yes, Sister Powell. So nice to meet you"

"Please, just Helen," the woman said.

"Sister Helen," the man said, looking up at the woman. "Such a well-fitting name."

The woman gave a slight smile and continued. "You being a widower, the least that I can do is see to it that you have a good meal from time to time. There was no answer to my knock, so I just left a plate of macaroni pie and pork chops on your table inside."

"Thank you very much – two of my favorites. I am sure that they will be delicious." He said with a smile.

"Thank you for your help," the woman responded. "I will see you at church in the morning, I am sure."

"I will see you and Mr. Powell tomorrow." Mr. Bratton smiled and touched his hat as the woman departed.

"She just brings you plates of food?" asked the boy.

"Yes, these days I have been getting plates of food brought to me, and sometimes I just return to find them in the kitchen waiting. It is not just her – many ladies drop by with food. It is their way of trying to pay me for my legal services."

"I thank that I would like to git paid in pork chops from time to time, but mostly I would want to git paid in money. Prob'ly even in paper money. What did you mean about her name that made her smile."

"There was once an ancient queen known as the most beautiful woman in the world. One man stole her from another man, and their nations went to war for many years over this woman. Eventually, through deception, one side was victorious and destroyed the other nation, killing its men and enslaving the women."

"I see. I reckon 'at men have prob'ly fought over Mrs. Powell a time or two."

"I would imagine so."

"You said that they enslaved the women folk. Is that when they started making people slaves?"

"No, slavery is far older, perhaps as old as mankind."

"I don't know much about it. I know they used to be a lot o' slaves 'round here, 'specially down on 'at old plantation. But they don't never teach about it in school or nuthin' like 'at. But I reckon 'at you right since it does talk about in the Bible – it must be an old thang t' do t' people. Do you ever wonder iffin it was a sin in the Bible? The Bible talks about it, but it don't never call it a sin or nuthin' like 'at."

"The Bible can sometimes be confusing, but slavery was most definitely an evil practice."

"Yep, it shore confuses me to read the Bible," the boy said shaking his head.

By this time, they were standing inside the house's front room. The boy looked around and saw a quilt folded in half and draped along the top of the settee. "Is 'at one o' them quilts 'at yo' wife made?"

The man smiled, "Yes, she was particularly fond of that one. She made it with our daughter, and I keep it out to remind me of those days."

"I told my Mama about your wife always rememberin' those times together and how you hoped 'at your daughter remembers those days. Mama said she remembers her mother teaching her, so I'm shore 'at your daughter feels the same way."

"I am certain that she does," the man said with a gentle smile.

"D' y' ever hear from your daughter 'ese days? I know 'at you ain't seen her in a long while, but d' y' ever git letters or anythang like 'at?"

"Actually, yes, I do get the occasional letter from her. After she got married and settled in, she sent a letter to her mother, and they maintained regular correspondence. Eventually, I sent a letter that she answered, and we have occasionally corresponded to stay in touch."

"Oh, so she knows 'bout her Mama passin' an' all 'at then?"

"Yes, she knows. She could not attend the services since she was, herself, quite ill at the time with influenza."

"I shore hated 'at influenza."

"Yes, it has been a horrible thing to many people worldwide. Especially hard with it having come at the end of such a terrible war. So many young men struck down, if not with bullets and gas, then with a sickness."

"Was you ever in the Army?"

"No, I never went into the military."

"I reckon 'at's a good thang; y' don't want them foreign people shootin' at y' an' all." The boy got closer to the quilt on the back of the settee and gently stroked it. "It's a nice quilt. I like all the colors in it. Y' can imagine 'em both sittin' there at the quiltin' rack together. I bet they was talkin' an' laughin' an' singin' songs like the women from the church do when they come over." The boy looked over to see the man using his handkerchief to wipe his eyes. "O, I'm sorry, I didn't mean t' upset y' none."

The man smiled down at the boy. "Not at all; it is a fond memory. And the way that you describe it is as if you were there. I remember sitting in my study sometimes and listening to them in the parlor – just as you say, laughing and singing."

"I love t' hear my Mama sing."

"I'm sure your mother has a beautiful voice – lovely to hear."

The boy looked around the rest of the room. "Is all this furniture hers, or did you get it all new when you come here?"

"I kept only her favorite chair." The man said, motioning to a straight high-backed Victorian chair with ornate woodwork on the legs and purple upholstery with a fringe underneath. "She would sit in that chair each afternoon and read by the window."

"My Mama does 'at too – only she makes me sit on the floor an' read too. I kinda don't always like 'at part."

The man smiled. "But someday, many years from now, it will be one of your most treasured memories."

The boy gave the man a sideways look and rolled his eyes. "I 'on't thank so."

The man smiled at the words and the mannerism.

"I like to sit in my Mama's chair when she ain't lookin' 'cause it smells like her. It's almost like gittin' a hug from her when she's too busy doin' somethin' else. Do you ever sit in 'at chair? Does it still smell like your wife, Mrs. Bratton?"

"No, I never sit in it. But you may if you would like."

"A'ight," said the boy. He went over to the chair and slowly sat in it. The wings of the back of the chair were right at his face level, and he closed his eyes and turned his face toward one of the wings, and slowly inhaled. "It smells nice."

"I hope so – I think she would have liked you sitting there. Would you like to hear about Lucille?"

"Lucille, was that her name?"

"Yes, it was."

"I like it, 'at's a nice name. Shore, you help me remember my little sister, an' I'll help you remember your wife. How'd y'all meet, an' what was she like? Was she a good cook too?"

The man smiled. "Yes, she was an excellent cook. I was just preparing for law school, and she was just graduating from high school and preparing to attend The Atlanta Baptist Female Seminary. I was invited by my former classmate, her brother, to the celebration of her graduation. I laid eyes on her and I was enchanted straight away."

Later that evening, the boy sat at supper with his family. "I was over yonder visitin' Mr. Bratton today. Tryin' to learn about lawyerin' and help him study this case about that man from Texas – on account of me wantin' to be a lawyer someday. Don't worry, Daddy, I went around the outside o' town t' git there like you said." The boy noticed that his mother looked across the table at her husband with a fleeting strange expression. "He told me how when y' make a contract, you gotta have 'good faith' an' if y' don't have that, then you are breakin' the contract. So If we can git the judge t' side with us, he can stop 'at man from takin' other folk's property."

Ida said, "Slow down and speak properly, please. If you wish to be an attorney, you don't want to sound like you are selling soap and brushes. Salespeople speak quickly, but an attorney must speak clearly and evenly – which means speaking more slowly."

"Yes, ma'am, 'at's what – that is what Mr. Bratton told me too. He said that the judge will start hearing the case Monday week. He told me that it is not a trial because nobody is charged with breaking the law but that it is a hearing over a silver dispute – so nobody is going to jail or anything."

"Civil dispute," William corrected his son.

"I think the man from Texas ought t' go to jail for lying and trying to trick folks into signing away their property. So today is Saturday, that leaves a day and then a week from Monday. I can't wait to see this."

"You will be in school," said Ida. "And children are not allowed in the courtroom during hearings or cases unless they are the cause of the trouble."

"Oh, I didn't think about 'at." He saw his mother arch an eyebrow as his language slipped. "I shore would like to see that court case since I am helping Mr. Bratton prepare for it."

"You are helping him prepare the case? Exactly how do you help?" Asked William.

"Well, I listen to his ideas as he explains things to me, and I go git law books from the shelf when he needs a particular book, and then I put them back when he finishes with them. He said that his daughter used to help him the same way when she was little. He showed me a quilt he keeps on the back of his settee that his wife and little girl made together. He still has his wife's chair in the parlor – a pretty purple old-timey-looking chair. I guess that those things help him remember the two of them. I asked him all about his wife, and he told me how they met after she finished school. Her brother was his friend from school. He let me sit in that purple chair, and if you close your eyes and lean back, you can still smell Mrs. Bratton a little bit. I told him that I would help him to remember his wife the way he said that he would help me to remember – things."

William noticed that Ida had stopped eating and was quietly sitting and listening to her son speak. He reached over and laid his hand gently on his son's arm. "Quiet down, your supper is getting cold, and you will miss your reading time."

Ten: A Day in Court

After a week that felt like forever and a weekend that felt even longer, it was Monday again, but this wasn't just any Monday. Cyril stepped out of the bushes and back onto the road he took every weekday to get to school, but the boy had no intention of going to school today – he was going to the courthouse to see this hearing. That morning he had placed his Sunday church clothes in a paper bag and dropped them out of his window so he could run around to the side of the house on his way to school and pick up his clothes. He had ducked into the bushes up the road from home, and he was now dressed and ready for Monday morning in court.

A short time later, the boy stood outside the courthouse watching as people filed into the building. He was waiting until there was a crowd so that he had a good chance of slipping in unnoticed. Many people were there today to see the proceedings and he knew that the farms of five families were hanging in the balance. They were five Black families because none of the white farmers agreed to join the case to have their farms protected by Mr. Bratton. But Cyril noticed that there were many folks from down in the Bottoms here at the courthouse today, both Black and white folks. They may not have joined the case, but they certainly were interested in the outcome. And everybody was wearing their church clothes too. He casually walked over to the building acting like he was just looking around but did not outright join the line of people so that somebody might notice him. He stood around at the door for a few minutes as the people passed, and then he just quietly squeezed in beside a stranger who was tall and heavier than most folks, like he was just the man's shadow easing into the building with him.

Inside the foyer of the building, Cyril noticed that some folks were making their way through the big double doors into the main courtroom while others were taking some stairs up to the gallery where the Black people sit. He could hear the sheriff's voice loudly talking to someone in the courtroom. Cyril thought that if he joined the folks going up the stairs to the gallery, he might find a seat where the judge or the sheriff would not notice one little boy sitting quietly in the crowd. It wasn't long before he had managed to wedge himself into the front row of the gallery and from his perch he could see the whole courtroom open below him. He saw the people milling around in the main courtroom as they found their seats. He could see the man from Texas sitting behind a table in front of and a little to the left of the center from where the judge would sit. And he could see another man with the man from Texas. 'Must be his lawyer,' the boy thought. And sitting at another table to the other side of the courtroom and before the judge's bench was Mr. Bratton.The man normally looked pretty well put together, but today Cyril could tell he meant business. He wore a very nice, well-fitted suit and freshly shined shoes. His hair was neatly trimmed, and his face was shaved from an early morning visit to the barber. The boy watched Mr. Bratton as he unpacked and organized his papers neatly in front of himself.

Cyril watched as the opposing lawyer leaned in, conferring with his client. The two men kept looking at Mr. Bratton and whispering to one another. The other lawyer glanced up at the gallery, and Cyril shrank back to avoid being seen by the man. Cyril did not like how the other lawyer looked over at Mr. Bratton and then whispered and nodded – he didn't like it at all. He knew that Mr. Bratton must be able to feel the other men looking at him like that, and he wondered why Mr. Bratton wasn't looking up or paying them any attention. "If it was me, I'd ask 'im what he was lookin' at like that." the boy whispered to himself. "He looks like he tryin' to pick a fight."

People were settling in their seats now, and a man walked in wearing a suit and a badge, but he wasn't the sheriff. The man cleared his throat and spoke. "Good morning, the Court of Escambia County, Alabama, the Honorable Bradley Haines presiding will now be in session. All rise."

The boy watched Judge Haines walk in, wearing his judicial robes and looking very official. The judge stepped up onto a platform and sat down behind his desk. "Everyone be seated, please."

As the boy sat down, he leaned forward to get a better view, and he felt a hand close on his shoulder and pull him back from the rail of the gallery. He glanced at his shoulder and saw a white-gloved hand, and then he looked up to see the eyes of the owner, who happened to be Mrs. Helen Powell, and sitting beside her was Mrs. Peaches Jones. The two of them gave him a look that conveyed that he should sit back and keep quiet.

The judge looked around the room at a packed courtroom and glanced up to see that folks had even packed the gallery. "Bailiff, it's been a chilly morning out there, but with all these people in here, it'll be warming up right quick. Go ahead and open the windows and let some of that cool air in here." The Judge looked up at the gallery. "A couple of y'all open them windows up there too to draw the heat out." The judge looked at the court reporter and began. "The Court is ready to hear arguments in the matter of Clarence Brudeaux et al. versus Harvard King. Let the record show that Mr. King has requested that the Court allow his attorney from Texas, Mr. Fallwell, to represent him in this matter and that Mr. Fallwell, being a practicing attorney in a friendly state, we will grant that request."

The white lawyer stood up and said, "Thank you, Your Honor."

The judge turned to Mr. Bratton and continued. "The plaintiffs will be represented by counsel also, that being one Cyril Bratton lately of Tennessee. Attorney Bratton, are your clients present?"

The Black lawyer stood up. "They are, Your Honor."

Judge Haines looked up at the gallery. You all stand up so I can see you."

Five Black men sitting in the first row of the gallery rose and stood at the rail. That is when Cyril realized that he was sitting on the front row where the plaintiffs were seated – the boy tried to lean back so as not to be noticed.

Judge Haines continued. "You can all sit back down. Now will somebody tell me why that Ledbetter boy is sitting in my courtroom? And sitting right in among the plaintiffs? Stand up, boy!"

Cyril leapt to his feet. "I'm sorry, Your Honor, I didn't know this row was for them. I'll move back if – if it pleases the Court."

The judge looked at the boy. "You have been looking over somebody's shoulder at some law books – 'if it pleases the Court' - like you are some kind of lawyer. What in the name of bleeding Jesus made you think nobody would see your shiny white face up there among the colored folks?"

Cyril said, "If it pleases the Court, I could come downstairs and sit with the white folks."

"What will please the Court is for you to come downstairs and go outside. Children are not allowed in court. And white children are not allowed in the gallery."

"But Your Honor, I even wore my Sunday goin' t' church clothes. And I been helpin' prepare the case too"

There were a few anonymous snickers scattered about the crowded courtroom. The judge scowled at the room. "Somebody laugh again at that foolish boy." The room went silent. The judge looked back up at the boy. "They are about thirty seconds from being your Monday going-to-jail clothes. I can have the bailiff take you into custody and send for your daddy."

The boy hurried from the gallery and ran down the stairs, hoping he had made it outside in less than thirty seconds. "Damned ol' judge. An' after all 'at helpin' to prepare this case, an' now I cain't even be there for it." Then, he thought about the open window, and he ran around to the side of the building, found the window, and stood beside it to hear what was said inside.

"No, sir, Your Honor," came the voice of Mr. Bratton. "As far as I knew, he is supposed to be in school."

The voice of the judge came through. "Well, then we will let the school teacher tend to him not being in school, and his daddy tend to his backside for sneaking into my Court. Now you may proceed."

"Thank you, Your Honor. Today..."

Cyril heard another voice cut Mr. Bratton off just as he started to speak. "Your Honor, before we begin, I have some concerns regarding the opposing counsel."

Judge Haines spoke. "Concerns? And what, Mr. Fallwell, might those concerns be?"

The new voice continued. "Well, Your Honor, specifically, we question the legal qualifications of the opposing counsel. We are not satisfied that he is even qualified to act in this capacity and to bring this spurious complaint. We move to have this complaint dismissed unless a more qualified attorney decides to take up this case."

"More qualified attorney, is it?" Asked the judge. "He has practiced law out of state, but the same can be said for you, Attorney Fallwell. The request that the Court allow you to act as counsel said that you have been practicing law in Texas for a good fifteen years, and I respect that experience. And likewise, Attorney Bratton has practiced law for over thirty years in Tennessee. If I let a Texas lawyer of fifteen years have the courtesy of acting in this matter, it is only fair that a Tennessee lawyer of thirty years is extended the same courtesy. Besides that, attorney Bratton now lives here in Alabama and has familiarized himself with the procedures of the Courts of Alabama."

Mr. Fallwell said, "My questions concern his basic legal knowledge and ability to understand and articulate the law fully."

Cyril heard Judge Haines speak to Mr. Bratton. "Attorney Bratton, where is it that you went to law school?"

"I graduated from Howard University School of Law, Your Honor."

Judge Haines said, "Well, there you are, Mr. Fallwell. He graduated from Howard. That's up there in Washington. Pretty far north, but we won't hold that against him. From what law school did you graduate, Mr. Fallwell?"

Mr. Falwell spoke. "Your Honor, Texas is a large state with few advanced schools. And so, the state allows people to sit for the test to practice law with or without a law degree. I studied the books and curriculum and then sat for the examinations, which I passed, and then I was allowed to begin to practice law."

Judge Haines' voice took on a firm edge. "That is admirable, and I am familiar with a good number of jurisdictions that have that option. I am impressed that you educated yourself in law. But the fact remains that your opposing counsel has a formal education in law at a long-established university. But all of that aside, we have both seen his petition, and I would say that it was very clear and concise and shows both a deep knowledge of the pertinent law and a firm understanding of right and wrong. I found it to be well articulated, so this conversation is over, and your request is denied."

Cyril heard another voice break in. "This would not happen in Harris County, Texas. This isn't right."

Judge Haines said, "Perhaps not Mr. King. But we are not in Texas. We are in Alabama, and I suggest you let your hired attorney address the Court. I don't know what they let you do in Texas, but another outburst like that will get you a night in jail in Alabama.

Attorney Fallwell, you might want to speak to your client. Now, if it is fine with you, we will hear what Attorney Bratton has to say."

The proceedings went on for several hours, and Cyril stood beside that window until he got tired, and then he sat under it listening until his stomach growled and he heard Judge Haines speak. "Well, gentlemen, if neither side has anything further to add, we will adjourn for lunch. Usually, it is too hot in the afternoon to come back, but with it starting to turn cooler, I think we can all be back here in two hours. That gives me an hour for lunch and an hour to review everything. Let's see if we can get this figured out today. See you all in a couple of hours."

"All rise." Immediately, the sound of people talking and moving inside filled the air.

Cyril did not want to risk the judge or sheriff seeing him, so he slipped into the trees and onto the trail that ran outside town and headed for the south side. He hoped that Mr. Bratton would come home for lunch because he had a lot of questions for the attorney. It was only a few minutes before the boy was standing in the front yard of the restored old house. He was so fidgety that he couldn't stand still. He noticed a small ant hill, picked up a stick, and squatted down to study the ants for a bit. He had his back to the sun so his shadow fell over the ants, and he pretended he was a giant as he worried them with his stick. He was so deep in thought that he didn't hear footsteps behind him. He only noticed that Mr. Bratton was there when the man's shadow fell over him and engulfed his own shadow and the ant hill. He wondered for a moment if one shadow could get lost inside of another shadow or if the little shadow was still there somewhere. He turned and looked up at the man. "I didn't mean no harm by bein' there – I just wanted to see it all. But I did sit outside the window and listen t' ever'thang like you did that time. I reckon I'm gonna be in a lot of trouble when I git home. But it was worth it."

"Was it worth it?"

"Oh yeah. I gotta be a lawyer now. I didn't even understand half of what you was sayin', but it was amazin'. Between you and me, I ain't s' sure that other lawyer fella understood ever'thang 'at you said neither. I got a bunch o' questions."

"I thought I might find you here, so let's go inside and have lunch. I can hear your stomach from here, and the wives brought me more food than a single man can eat." He held up a basket, and the boy could smell lots of good things filling the air, and then he felt his stomach start to ache in hunger."

After lunch, Cyril sat back down under the window of the courthouse. That two-hour wait had seemed eternal, but the judge had just gavelled and started speaking. The coolness of the late autumn morning had burned away, and it was another hot Alabama afternoon, so the boy did not expect that the Judge would take too much time with his decision.

Judge Haines spoke. "After reviewing all of the evidence and arguments, I have to say that the plaintiff's arguments are quite novel and strong. Now, I cannot claim to know what was in any man's head when he signed a contract, but I can look at the contracts and the actions of the men involved. I find that there is reason to doubt the full good faith of at least one of the parties in these contracts and that these contracts seem destined to fail by execution if not by design. Now you all still owe this man his money, and I can't change that, but I can grant an injunction so that you will have more time to pay that money back and as long as you are making a reasonable effort in good faith to pay these loans back, you will not lose your farms. And the Court will have a say on whether your efforts are reasonable. The Court finds in favor of the plaintiffs and grants injunctive relief."

Cyril heard the loud voice of the man from Texas. "What? You cannot do this. These are contracts made in good faith. I will go to the Supreme Court of Alabama. We will see what they have to say about you siding with the likes of them."

Judge Haines raised his voice. "That is enough, Mr. King. If you want to take this to the Alabama Supreme Court, that is your prerogative. So, you go ahead and do that if that's what you wish. As a matter of fact, I have been having lunch with the chief justice every first Thursday of the month since we graduated law school together thirty-five years ago. That will be three days from now, so I will be sure to tell him to expect you. Now, we are done here unless you need the bailiff to help you with a room for the night."

Cyril was startled by the sudden crack of a wooden mallet, and he was sure that the judge must have broken whatever it was that he hit. The boy waited outside the courthouse to speak to Mr. Bratton – and he was in no hurry to get home anyway.

Mr. Bratton came outside the building carrying his briefcase and was surrounded by a group of Black folks. Everyone seemed happy and celebratory, and there were many more folks than the ones who would keep their farms. It looked like every Black person in the county had been there today to see this case – and they all seemed so happy. It was as if he had won a victory for the whole community, not just those few farmers. Man after man stepped up and shook hands with Mr. Bratton, who, for his part, spoke and listened to each one of them. Eventually, the people cleared, and Mr. Bratton turned to walk home with a satisfied smile. The smile grew brighter when he saw the excited boy heading toward him. Just as the boy opened his mouth to speak, he heard a female voice behind him. "Excuse me, Lawyer Bratton?"

The man turned to see a white woman wearing a clean but well-worn dress and shoes and with a bonnet on. "Yes, ma'am," the man answered. "What can I do for you?"

"It's about our farm. I was at the courthouse today and saw what you did for them, folks. We got a farm down in the Bottoms too – and we got one o' them King contracts. And he gonna take our farm away here shortly. We got five kids, and my Mama lives with us too. She stayed back takin' care of the young 'uns today so's I could come hye. We ain't got no money, but I promise I will pay you one way or t'other if you can help us."

"Might your husband be with you, Miss…?"

"Evers, I'm Polly Evers, and my husband is Isaiah Evers," answered the woman. "He ain't hye; he didn't want me t' come down hye neither. He said that there ain't nary lawyer gonna help us. He already talked to one or two, and they said they cain't help us at all – especially without we got money to pay 'em. They didn't even wanna talk to us."

"Polly!" an angry male voice cracked the air. "Whut'chu doin' still down hye? I told you not to come down hye. They finished all that court doin's, and you need to come back home with me now."

Polly said, "I ain't goin' nowhere till I talk t' this man. He just won 'at case and saved them people's farms. I heard the judge say it myself, they still gotta pay back the money, but he cain't just up an' take their farms no more. We need to talk to him an' see if he can help us."

"Polly, I cain't ask him for help. What are people gonna say? Just you bein' out hye talkn' to him is embarrassin' enough."

The woman raised her voice. "You know what they gonna say? Worse than they say now. Instead o' 'look at that poor white trash over yonder in the Bottoms'; they gonna say 'look at that poor white trash living in a tent by the river cookin' on a campfire. They lost ever'thing to a rich fella what was too smart for 'em.' That's what they gonna say."

"They might call me 'white trash,' but at least I'm white," the man yelled.

Cyril just stood and watched this exchange taking place right in front of Mr. Bratton. He saw the white preacher walking toward them with intention.

The reverend said, "Isaiah, you need to stop yellin' for once."

The woman turned and said, "Reverend, please talk t' him – make him understand that his pride gonna starve his children."

The reverend said, "Sister Polly, you go on back home, and we'll sort this all out."

The woman paused momentarily, nodded, and turned to head home.

The reverend looked at Mr. Evers. "Isaiah, you listen to me now. I already talked to Harold and James, and they are heading to the church to wait for me to return there. I'm gonna go find Parcell Sims and bring him back with me, and we all gonna sit and talk. Then, if you wanna lose your farm, that's between you and God. But here directly, you will sit and listen to what I have to say."

Mr. Evers clenched his jaw and glared at the preacher, and then he looked at Mr. Bratton with disgust, turned, and walked toward the First Baptist Church just up the street.

The preacher watched the man go and then turned to Mr. Bratton. "I'm Rev. Harrigan over at the First Baptist Church, and I wanted to congratulate you on winnin' that case today. You did a fine Christian thing for them folks down yonder in the Bottoms."

Mr. Bratton said, "Thank you, Reverend. I am just trying to do the right thing."

"And you will be rewarded in the next world for it," said the man. "Don't study on Isaiah Evers too much; sometimes he's like a dumb dog huntin' the wrong trail – no idea what he's barkin' about. But he works hard, and Polly and her mother are good Christian women, and they got a bunch o' children. I wanted to ask you if there was any way that you could do the same thing for a few more families that are about to lose their farms. Now, I can take up a collection at the church to pay for your time if you want."

"Reverend, I am doubtful that they would want my help."

"Evers is one man with a big mouth, but there are other families who are good folks and don't deserve to be tricked outta their homes," said the reverend.

"To be honest, Reverend, since the judge has already ruled on some of the same contracts, it would just be a formality with paperwork. There would be no big hearing. It would be an easy thing to manage. But the men who signed those contracts will have to want it – they will have to want me to do it for them. And I will tell you now that they refused a place in the original case, and I am not too inclined to consider it."

"I see," said the preacher. "I can't blame you; thank you for your time." The man turned and started walking away.

Mr. Bratton turned and caught sight of Cyril standing there with a confused and disturbed expression on his face. He stopped and looked at that little white boy's face – a face well-tanned from the Alabama summer that had just passed. The hard look in the eyes of the man softened a bit. He turned back, and he called out. "Reverend." The preacher stopped and turned. "Children are my only concern – they are innocent. If any of those men want my help, they can speak to me, and we will do the paperwork."

"Thank you," said the preacher, nodding his understanding.

Mr. Bratton turned and started to walk home. The boy stood there silently in the path of the man. Mr. Bratton stopped right in front of the boy. "I am very sorry that you saw that – you were not meant to ever have to see anything like that."

The boy stood there in silent confusion, just looking at the man. His eyes drifted down to the man's free hand, and he looked at it like he saw it for the first time. After a few moments, the boy wordlessly reached up and touched the back of the hand. He looked back up at the man's face.

Mr. Bratton put his hand on the boy's head for a moment and said, "You go home now, son."

Later, Cyril was lying in bed, glad he had eaten such a big lunch; otherwise, he might starve to death. He had expected this and the whoopin' he got, but his heart had still sank to his feet when he saw that sheriff's machine driving away from the farm as he slowly walked home feeling like a man walking to the gallows. He knew that his daddy didn't much like beatin' children, but this was one of those times when he thought he had to do it. He hoped his mother would at least let him eat breakfast tomorrow, even if she hadn't fed him tonight. Instead, he had spent supper time wishing he had a washtub of cold water to sit in after his daddy finally turned him loose and went inside. He already knew that the school teacher would give him a paddling tomorrow right on top of the blistering that he just got out behind the barn.

Eleven: A Day With the Boys

A few weeks had passed and Cyril's backside was finally beginning to stop aching. The early morning had been pretty chilly, but it was mid-morning now and the sun was warming things up quickly as William and Cyril walked along carrying their fishing poles and a bucket of worms. Cyril said, "I hope that the sun has warmed that water up enough so the fish'll bite 'cause they don't like to bite much when the water gits cold."

"Well, we'll see here shortly if they gonna bite or not," said the boy's father.

"I reckon I like it when the harvest is over, and there ain't quite so much to do at home. And we can git to go fishin' and huntin' together a little more. I saw some rabbits this mornin' when I went out to the barn before sunup. They lookin' pretty fat."

"That ain't fat; it's their fur getting thicker for the cold weather."

"I bet they'll taste good, though," said the boy. "It's cold weather now s' d' y' thank 'at we can go hunt some rabbits here one mornin' this comin' week – early before I gotta go to school? Cain't do it next Friday or Saturday 'cause o' the county fair bein' 'at weekend. We even gittin' the day off from school on Friday. I been savin' up my shiny money that I been gittin' from the widow ladies from doin' a few chores an' errands for 'em after school this last month. Got me more 'an a dollar saved up, an' iffin I do a few more chores this week, I'll have another half dollar at least."

"A dollar and a half for the fair – you gonna be the richest ten-year-old there, I reckon."

"Billy been doin' some chores too, so he gonna have himself some shiny money. But prob'ly not as much as me 'cause he cain't save like I can on account o' him always goin' by the general store an' spendin' a penny here an' there for candy."

"Does he share that candy with you?" The man asked.

"Yessir, he usually does."

"Then it sounds to me like you ought t' be spendin' every other penny and sharin' with Billy. I 'on't know if he ain't too smart or just that nice – but you don't want folks to start thinkin' that you're tight-fisted. It just don't look Christian."

"Yessir, Daddy."

"I reckon we can get up early Monday mornin' and get a few of them rabbits."

"Am I big enough now to take a shotgun too and maybe shoot a rabbit myself?"

"I reckon that you can carry that old four-ten o' mine. But you gonna have t' sneak up on 'em real quiet-like so they stand still while you shoot – they pretty hard to hit if they get to runnin'. I'll tell you what, if you can hit airy rabbit with it, it'll be yours from now on. But you gotta take care of it, and you are not allowed to take it out without me knowin' or bein' there."

"Yessir – yessir, Daddy. Thank you. Can I take it out today and practice on some cans when we git back home? I'll clean it up real good after I finish."

"I don't reckon it'll hurt anything for you to shoot a few cans out behind the barn while I'm burnin' some trash. But it all depends on your Mama's mood – if she don't want to hear no shootin', it ain't gonna happen."

"A'ight Daddy. Boy, I shore hope 'at she's in a better mood later this afternoon."

The man chuckled a bit. "Well, there's 'at fishin' hole – look like somebody is already there. Looks like it's your lawyer friend. We'll walk a piece up the creek and find a nice spot."

"We can sit with him and fish – he won't mind," said the boy.

"You don't know that – he might be out here to get some quiet. Might not want to hear a little boy chattering at him like a squirrel."

"I 'ont sound like no squirrel. I 'ont talk that much." He looked up at his father, who gave him a wink. "I'll go ask 'im."

Mr. Bratton heard the boy approaching him and heard the boy call out, behind him. And he turned to look over his shoulder. "Hello."

"Do you mind iffin we sit here and fish wi' you?"

Mr. Bratton glanced over and saw William Ledbetter standing behind the boy. "You don't need my permission for anything. But, if your father would like, I can leave you to it."

"My daddy said that maybe you was here for some peace and quiet and might not want comp'ny. Or might not like to hear me talking. So we can walk up the creek a ways t' fish if you want us to."

The man laughed. "I don't mind hearing you talk. And a man who lives alone goes fishing to escape the quiet. I was sitting here in the sun because it was chilly earlier when I got here, but that sun is getting warm, so I think I will move over there under that tree if you want to sit there and fish."

"That'd be right nice," said the boy, who turned to his father and continued. "He said that he don't mind us fishin' hye with him, but we should all sit under that shade tree on account o' the sun."

The three of them found places to sit on the creek's banks in the shade of a large tree that grew near the edge and had a very high canopy that shaded a large area. Cyril sat in the middle with Mr. Bratton a few feet away on one side and his father a few feet away on the other. They got their hooks in the water and started silently watching their corks bobbing on the water. Cyril said, "I hope that them fish start biting soon."

William said, "As the water warms up a bit, they should start showing an interest in worms."

"So how do you go fishing to git away from the quiet?" Asked Cyril. "It's pretty quiet here."

"When you are in a house by yourself, it gets very quiet, and all you can hear is yourself and the clocks. At least out here, there is the sound of the birds and the occasional squirrel. And now you are here, and quiet is not a thing that accompanies you."

"Oh. Are y' going to the county fair next weekend? We gonna go an' I been savin' up my shiny money just for the fair. We even git Friday off from school."

"I will have to look into that. I might go, but it is not as interesting to go by yourself."

"Maybe you can ask one of the widow ladies from y'alls church t' go wi' y'."

Mr. Bratton looked inquiringly down at the boy. "Ok, Mrs. Powell. One matchmaker in my life is quite enough."

"Mrs. Powell, she's 'at really pretty lady, ain't she? Real tall too. She is real dark-skinned; I ain't never seen any woman 'at dark-skinned before."

"Cyril," said William to his son sharply.

Mr. Bratton responded. "That is her, and yes, she is a beautiful woman. And she is quite dark; that is a simple fact. And another fact is that she has quite a list of potential ladies of interest for my consideration."

"She prob'ly just tryin' to help, so you won't be lonely in 'at big ole quiet house."

"The only help I might need comes from a doctor or God," said Mr. Bratton.

"Oh, okay," said the boy. Cyril changed the subject. "So, you came here to git away from the quiet an' we came here to git away from Mama. She woke up this mornin' an' set about cleanin'. And no matter what, we was both in her way, an' when we tried to help, it was worse. She finally told us to git out o' her house before she starts cuttin' wi' the big scissors. And don't nobody want her t' do that."

Cyril laughed. "I remember my own mother saying that, and since she was a seamstress, she had some very big scissors with which to cut."

"Your mother said that too? I wonder if all women folk say that an' where they learn it from."

"I imagine that they learn it from their mothers and grandmothers," said Mr. Bratton. "They pass it down the generations – probably the same set of scissors too."

"Do you thank 'at your daughter learned it too before she went away?"

"I am sure that she did," answered the man.

"Why did your daughter go away from y'all anyways?"

"That is enough, Cyril," said William.

Mr. Bratton sat for a while as if he had not heard the question, but eventually, he spoke. "It was my fault, really. A man has plans for his children – plans that sometimes those children do not share. After her debutante ball, she met a young man who was in Memphis working. He was very different, and I didn't want her to see him. My plan was for her to attend college in Atlanta like her mother. And then perhaps marry a doctor or a lawyer – a man I thought could provide well for her. But she loved this boy she had met, and eventually, they ran away to get married where nobody knew them or their families – but I guess she was running away from me. It was a complicated situation, and I was not doing well with it, and maybe I was a bit of a bully, as your mother once said."

"Oh," said the boy. "So they just snuck off then?"

"No, not really. He did the right thing, asked to marry her, and asked for my blessing. I refused and sent him away. And then eventually she packed her things and left."

"D' y' thank that she's happy with 'at man?'"

"I know that she is. She has written in her letters how happy she is with her husband, and he has taken good care of her – as good of care as any man could wish for his daughter. I guess I was wrong about him – about quite a number of things. I have apologized to her in our letters. But I have never been able to apologize to him as I should and would like to do. He has never struck her, and she and her children have never slept cold or hungry; I am grateful for that. And she has generally been happy, which is what I thought I had planned for her, but her plans seem to have been the right ones."

"I thank 'at you would make a real good grandfather. Do you ever thank 'at you'll meet any o' your grandchildren?

The man looked down at the boy. "Yes."

"Well, I know that they gonna like y' a whole lot. But if it is any time soon 'at you meet 'em, I hope 'at you on't forgit about me bein' yo' friend and all."

"I can't imagine anyone ever forgetting about you, Cyril," said the man.

"Was your wife mad when your daughter went away?" Asked the boy.

"Not angry so much as disappointed – but I think her disappointment was with me more than anyone else. And I have grown disappointed in myself about the whole affair."

"Maybe you will git t' tell 'at man 'at you was wrong an' 'at you're sorry for all of it someday."

"I hope so, and I hope he will understand," said the man. "But I can not blame him if he is unwilling to accept it."

"If he is as good a man t' yo' daughter as you say, then I bet he'll accept your apology. Don't you reckon so, Daddy?"

William Ledbetter sat quietly for a few moments before answering.

"I reckon that he'll be glad to hear and accept it. And he's prob'ly sorry for taking her so far away from her family anyway. There's only three women in your life that you'll love so much that it hurts and so much that you might hurt them; your mother, wife, and daughter. It's easy to lose sight of what you want for them."

"See, Mr. Bratton, even Daddy thanks 'at you would be forgiven. You should go an' visit them and talk to 'em about it all. Just don't stay away from hye too long."

"I wish it were that simple, but we live in complicated times, and this is a complicated situation. She knows that her mother and I have always loved her, and I know that she is loved where she is."

Cyril felt the tug of a fish on his line and got excited. The three started catching a few fish and chatting about the court case that Mr. Bratton had won.

Cyril said, "I was thinkin' 'bout the thangs you gotta know 'bout lawyerin' and stuff. Seems to me that a lot of it is about secrets. 'At man from Texas put secret intentions in them contracts, and you had to figure out what his secret intentions was. So, is all lawyerin' just about figuring out what secrets people got?"

"Secrets can be an important part of the work of an attorney." Said Mr. Bratton. "But not always figuring them out or exposing them. Sometimes a good attorney helps to keep secrets. Understand that in life, we are often only allowed our secrets by others – they permit us to keep them. Sometimes out of kindness and sometimes because they would rather not know them."

"I bet you are good at keepin' secrets," said Cyril.

"When I need to be – I am the best at it. Some secrets are kept for many years, some for a lifetime. And sometimes they last so long that the secrets begin to keep themselves."

"I see," said the boy.

Just after lunchtime, they decided to leave, though they had not caught many fish, and the Ledbetters were in no hurry to get home just yet, so they agreed that Mr. Bratton should take all the fish with him. William decided to treat his son to lunch in town.

After they left the diner, William looked at his son and said, "I'll tell y' what. We can go down to the ice house and get you a cold co'cola. Better yet, I'll git y' two o' 'em, and you can go find Billy an' give one t' him, and y'all play for a while, and you can come on home later this afternoon, and we'll see about that shotgun if your Mama is feelin' better about things."

"Or we could just stay around the ice house and see what the music sounds like. I ain't thirty-five yet, but I'm shore that if I'm with my daddy, they won't mind."

"Boy, if you don't stay clear of that ice house after dark, I'm gonna wear your britches out."

"A'ight, Daddy."

"I will go home and see how your mother is doin' with her cleanin', and I want to talk to her in private for a bit s' you take your time comin' home."

And just like that, William and Cyril made their way to the ice house and parted ways for the next portion of the day. Cyril spent that time sitting around with Billy, enjoying their sodapop and talking about how much they hated their teacher.

Twelve: Celebrations

Friday morning of the first day of the county fair, and Cyril was at the table eating his breakfast as fast as he could. He had wanted to get up and go, but his mother had made him sit down to a good hardy breakfast first. She knew that otherwise, he would get there and be so hungry that he would spend his money on food first thing.

"Slow down, child," said Ida.

"Yes, ma'am."

"Do not speak with your mouth full."

The boy swallowed hastily and almost choked on the bite, which had been too big anyway. "Yes, ma'am. Sorry, Mama."

Ida had loaded his plate with grits, tomato gravy, a biscuit, bacon, sausage, and a couple of dropped eggs with a big glass of fresh milk.

"Mama, I'm fuller than a tick. Can I go?"

"Clean your plate; I want your tummy full of good food before you go to that fair."

"Mama, they got all kinds of food at the fair."

"Yes, they do – popcorn balls, fried pies, peanut brittle, sweet rolls, doughnuts, and a bunch of other things- almost all of it is made of sugar. That much of it will make you sick and have you climbing a tree by ten o'clock and sleeping under it by lunchtime. This way, you won't have room for too much sugar."

"No, ma'am – uh, Yes, ma'am. I mean."

"I know what you mean. Now slow down and finish your breakfast."

"Yes, ma'am."

William Ledbetter sat there listening to the exchange with a smile. He waited until the boy finished the last bite; it was his turn. "Have you got all the money you saved up for this weekend?"

"Yessir, almost two dollars," the boy said with a satisfied smile. "I know how to save me up some money."

"That you do," said the man. "And I'm glad of it. And I am gonna help you with your money today."

"Are you gonna give me some more spendin' money, Daddy?"

"Noooo, two dollars is more than most families spend on food at the store in a couple of weeks. I will help you learn to manage your money like you are grown. Finish up that milk now, and we'll get right to it."

The boy picked up his glass of milk and downed it like a powerful thirst was on him, and then he said, "A'ight, Daddy, it's finished."

"Take your plate out to the sink and come back here and put all your money on the table so we can see it."

The boy jumped up, grabbed his plate and glass, and hurried to the kitchen.

"We never run in the house," Ida said.

"Yes, ma'am." The boy slowed down though he felt like he would bust apart at the seams any minute.

Ida and William exchanged a smile before the boy returned as fast as he could while still trying to look like he wasn't in a terrible hurry.

William pointed at the table and said, "Now you put all of your money right there, and I'm gonna step out for a bit, and we will sort it out when I get back."

"The outhouse? But Daddy, the fair gonna start at nine o'clock."

As the man stood, he said, "Sure is, and they will not move it

121

anywhere at nine-thirty. It's gonna be there all day – and tomorrow too. You need to learn a little patience. I'll be back directly."

The boy stood at the table, cleaned out his pockets, and got every last penny on the table, and was just standing there looking at it all and counting it repeatedly. As Ida cleared the rest of the breakfast dishes, she spoke. "You might as well sit down. You know that he is going to read some in the almanac before he comes back."

The frustrated boy sat down in the chair with a big sigh. And he heard his mother from the kitchen. "Are you feeling all right? I can dose you with some mullein and cod liver oil and put you back in bed until your breathing clears."

"No, thank you, Mama, I feel good – real good. Just kind o' in a hurry, is all." Cyril sat there listening to the clock ticking away. Usually, that constant ticking was just quietly in the background and easy to ignore, but right now, it was thundering in his ears – the laughter of time, stealing itself from him as the seconds ticked by. After an eternal wait, the boy heard the sound of his father's boots on the back steps, and he began to fidget in his seat like a dog under a supper table. Then, he could hear his father talking to his mother in the kitchen. 'OH MY GOD!' the boy thought, 'COME ON, DADDY.' Finally, he heard the boots coming into the dining room, and he let out a breath that he did not realize he had been holding as he jumped to his feet.

"Alrighty then, I see you got it all out on the table. So, I want you to divide it into four equal amounts."

The boy gave his father a funny look and bent over the table to comply quickly. "Okay, Daddy, four equal piles, but I got three pennies left over."

"Good, so here's what you gonna do. Take that first pile and put it in your pocket. And I'll take that second pile and give it to you later at lunchtime. Then those other two will be for tomorrow mornin' and afternoon, respectively. And those three pennies left over are gonna be so you can treat your friend Billy to something nice like a couple of candy apples on account of him always bein' so generous with you. And if his little sister is there, you gonna treat her too, even if it costs you more than those three pennies."

"But Daddy, he got his own money. An' 'at little sister of his is just a pain, an' she got freckles like a butter bean."

"Cyril William Ledbetter," called Ida from the kitchen. "She is a sweet little girl who cannot help her freckles."

"Yes, ma'am."

Ida continued. "You set one more penny aside and make sure that it gets spent on a nice treat for Norma Jean – and you know that she will tell me if you did next time we see her at church."

The boy almost stomped his foot as his body jerked in frustration. "Yes, ma'am."

He looked back up to see a sharp look in his father's eyes, and the boy immediately took a deep breath to calm himself down before getting into serious trouble.

William continued. "And Billy would have more of his money too if he weren't always thinkin' about sharin' with you, so you gonna think about sharin' with him and his sister."

"Yes, sir. But all o' that is my money. I thank 'at I should be able to take it all wi' me now."

"If you take it all with you this mornin', you will spend it all this mornin' and be dunnin' me for money for the next day and a half. So, you take what you got in yo' pocket, and you go. If you run, you'll be there right about nine o'clock."

"Yes, Daddy."

The boy turned and hurried toward the back door, but as he passed through the kitchen, it was his mother's turn to stop him. "Cyril."

The boy jerked to a stop and started rocking from one foot to the other, and he involuntarily rolled his eyes. "Yes, ma'am?"

"Is anything in your eye – do you want me to look at it?"

Cyril quickly rubbed his eye. "No, ma'am, it's out now."

"Good, now we will be getting there later today, around noon, and I will have a lunch basket packed. So you meet us out front, and we will have a nice little lunch under a tree, so don't fill up on trash. And if the Holstead kids are with you, bring them along too – there will be enough. Now, you be sure to stop at the outhouse as you leave, or you know that will be the first thing you will look for when you get there."

"Yes, ma'am."

"You run on now."

"Thank you, Mama."

As soon as the door shut behind him, Cy was off of the back porch like an arrow from a string. The boy ran as fast as he could so that he would not miss a thing - he ran, unseeing of the countryside through which he passed.

Cyril was out of breath as he hurried into the county fairgrounds. He could see the long barn that housed the animals that were here to be judged. And when the wind shifted, he could smell it too – but another shift of the wind and the smells improved as it blew across from the food stalls. Then, he could see the tents where they would judge the pies and pickles later. The music of a string band floated to him from a distance, and he could also hear the jazz band's banjos and horns starting to warm up. There would be a steady stream of music all day and into the evening, and races, contests, and games for prizes. The weekend of the fair was so much fun – it was even fun to come down here on Sunday mornin' for the church revival meeting in the tent.

But first things first, he could smell hot peanuts, and it didn't matter how big the breakfast was; there was always room for peanuts. He started following his nose until he found the source of the smell. He trotted right up and got in one of the short lines in front of the stall. The lines in front of the booth were for the white folks, and another line was on the side for the Black folks. The county fair was a big affair and one of the few events where Black and white folks could attend together. Well, not really together – everyone will keep to their own kind as much as possible, but there are still all kinds of folks at the fair. But everybody will compete with their animals and see who has the biggest turnips and things like that. And everybody competes in the pies and pickles. And there will always be an argument over whether cornbread should be sweet or not.

"Hey, Cyril!" A familiar voice yelled from behind.

Cyril turned to see the smiling face of his friend Billy Holstead. Cyril pointed at his own nose and gave Billy a warning look.

"I mean Cy," said Billy. "You wait right here after you git yo' peanuts while I git me some too."

Cyril said, "Naw Billy, you jus' wait right there, an' I'll git two bags."

Billy looked a little surprised and said, "A'ight."

A few minutes later, the boys walked around the fair, eating peanuts and dropping the shells on the ground. Billy said, "Thank y' fo' the peanuts, Cy."

"You welcome, Billy. You always share yo' penny candy wi' me so I can git you some peanuts here or there."

"Wanna go see 'at five-legged cow, an' 'at two-headed baby pig what they got over yonder in 'at tent?" Billy asked.

"Shore do," said Cyril. "That baby pig gonna be the same one they had pickled in a jar last year, but a five-legged cow is somethin' I ain't seen b'fore. An' they got a sheep with four horns too."

"Let's run over and play some o' them games first," said Cyril. "I wanna try and win somethin' while I'm a-thinkin' 'bout it. I like that game where y' th'ow 'em rings on the milk bottles – pretty good at it, too."

"I ain't good at it at all," said Billy. "What you trynna win anyway?"

"One o' them little dolls."

"Y' 'on't play wi' dolls," said Billy.

"No, but yo' sister Jenny does an' you cain't win her one – so reckon I'm 'a have t' win her one."

"Why you being' nice to my sister? She jus' gonna follo' us around the rest o' the day after she gits hye later with m' granny an' m' daddy. You know granny is cookin' hard for all o' the competitions."

"I'm always nice to yo' sister," said Cyril.

"Not hardly."

The two boys spent the morning wasting money on games and sweets and seeing strange things in the side shows. As noon approached, Billy knew to make his way to the food tents where the afternoon competitions would take place to help his granny unload the baskets from the wagon. "Billy," called an older female voice, and the boys headed in that direction. They saw Granny Holstead pulling baskets out of the back of the wagon. "Hello, Cyril," said the old woman.

"Hello, Sister Holstead," the boy answered.

She continued as if she hadn't noticed and looked at Billy. "Yo' daddy already took two baskets an' your sister got one, so you and Cyril take aholt of a basket in each hand and I'll git this last one and y'all help me git 'em over t' the tents. I got a lot of food to unpack."

After the boys dropped off the baskets, they headed out to meet Ida and William for lunch, and they had little Jenny in tow, happy with her new doll. And after lunch, Cyril had more money in his pocket, and they headed back into the fair, just two little boys and one little girl following along almost like a shadow, but not as quiet as one.

Cyril spotted Mr. Bratton in the fairgrounds and headed right toward the man. "Hey," said the boy.

Mr. Bratton looked at him, smiled, and started to answer when another man approached him, shook his hand, and engaged him in a brief conversation. "Cyril waited for the other man to depart. "Hello, Mr. Bratton, This is my friend Billy and his little sister Jenny. Are you having a good time at the fair? I don't see anyone wi' y'."

I came alone. I saw you walking earlier, but you had your hands full carrying baskets and following a lady of a certain age," said the man.

"That was Billy's granny, Sister Holstead. She made somethin' for every competition 'at they have, s' she brought eight baskets o' food. Every kind o' pie an' cake an' all the pickles an' jellies an' preserves. She enters every contest every year."

The man laughed. "I hope that she wins at least a few of them."

Billy said, "Oh, she do win some of 'em an' gits real mad at the judges behind the ones what she don't win. She tells 'em 'If I wasn't a Christian woman, I would tell y' somethin' – and then she tells 'em anyways."

The man smiled. "Holstead, I think I met your father earlier this week."

The boy nodded and looked down. "Yeah, he said 'at he asked you for help wi' that paper from 'at Texas fella' on account o' us not havin' much money. I shore hope 'at you can help us like you helped them other peoples. I 'on't know where we'd go iffin we lost our farm."

"Look up here, and you always keep looking up" said the man to Billy. "Billy, is it? You never be ashamed if you are not as rich as another man may be. There is no shame in working hard, as your father does. He is a good man, and you are not losing your home."

The boy looked up, smiled, and nodded.

Just then, another man approached Mr. Bratton to shake his hand and introduce himself to the lawyer. The two men chatted briefly, and the other man left.

Cyril said, "Seem like ever'body wanna shake your hand an' git to know y' after what y' did in the court fo' them people."

Mr. Bratton nodded. "Poor folks do not generally expect to win when up against money. Luckily, we had a judge open to considering all arguments."

"So, if Brother Holstead met you at the church, did the other men come for your help too?" Asked Cyril.

"A couple of them did," answered the man.

"Not Mr. Evers, though?" Asked the boy.

"I cannot discuss clients by name," said the man.

"I knew 'at he wouldn't meet y' at the church. He don't never come t' church noways. His wife an' her mother do, but we don't never see him there. His family is nice people, but I don't care for him much."

"Understandable," said the man. "You children run on and enjoy the fair; I will head home soon. I have had about as much fun as I can. And I have shaken enough hands for the day."

"Are you comin' back tomorrow?" Asked Cyril.

"Oh, I doubt very seriously that I will be back tomorrow," said the man.

"Well, I'm 'a be back – and Billy too."

"Then you enjoy the rest of your day and enjoy tomorrow. It was nice to meet you, Billy, and young Jenny."

"It was nice t' meet you too," the Holsteads responded in unison.

The man turned and walked away, and the children watched him go and saw someone else stop him for a handshake and brief chat.

Billy had a strange look on his face. "He don't sound like other colored folks – really, he don't much sound like anybody from around here. He must o' come from somewheres far away."

"He's from right here in Bratton," said Cyril. "He was borned on the old plantation back when they was still slaves down there. Then, he and his mama moved away after they was freed. He sound like 'at 'cause he went t' college an' studied law. An' he been a lawyer for a long time."

The two boys and Jenny spent the rest of the afternoon enjoying the fair and eating too much food from the stalls. They played until they heard the sundown whistle in the distance. Cyril knew that he had to go and meet his parents to head home – his mother had already warned him about not being at the fairgrounds after dark. Billy and Jenny had the same warning, so they went to find their father and granny.

Cyril found his parents already waiting for him, and he climbed up into the back of the wagon. The wheel brake was released, and the wagon lurched forward. He was sitting there just watching the fairgrounds as the mule plodded away. He noticed the sheriff standing outside the exit, leaning on his automobile, watching all the folks leave. It seemed like many folks were leaving the fair already, but the sun wouldn't be down for another hour, and then it would not be dark for a half hour after that. 'I would stay as long as I could – if I could.' the boy thought. Then, he noticed that most of the folks who were leaving were Black. It looked like all of the Black folks were leaving. 'I reckon that the sundown whistle even counts on fair days for the colored folks,' he thought. Then he looked at the way that the sheriff was just standing there.

Later that night, Cyril dropped from his open window onto the ground outside. He could feel the air starting to get a bit of a chill from the night. He had known that his parents would go to bed very early after the long day at the fair. He had waited until he could hear his daddy softly snoring. He had one more thing that he wanted to do to make it a perfect day. He started trotting up the road toward town, and he knew that at this pace, he would be in the trees just outside of the ice house in twenty minutes. Then, he could watch for a few minutes to see what they do at the ice house after dark and hear some of the music. After he sees what goes on, he can just run back home and git right to bed.

Soon, Cyril was squatting on the ground just behind some trees near the ice house, where he was well-hidden but close enough to see and hear what was happening. He could see a crowd of maybe a dozen or so Black men sitting and standing on the open-air dock where people loaded ice into wagons in the daytime. They had set up some tables and had lanterns hanging overhead, giving light. They were drinking from glasses and a few soda bottles. Some men were sitting around one table playing cards, and some were playing dominoes at several other tables. Now and again, there would be a loud crack as a man would slam a particularly good domino down onto the table. There was one white man, and Cyril knew that he was the ice man who owned the place, and he saw that people would go up and pay him for a soda or to fill their glass from a barrel.

Cyril heard the roar of an automobile, and he saw one pull up the road right in front of the ice house just a few feet from where he was hiding. He realized it was the sheriff, and he was sitting in his automobile waiting for something. The ice man hurried to the automobile, and the sheriff climbed out of the driver's seat to stand over the man. "Hello, Sheriff," said the man. "I got your money fo' y' – and a couple of bottles of that soda pop that y' like."

The sheriff cleared his throat and ensured everyone noticed he was present. "A'ight Cyrus, thank you. Now, you know I only let you open the ice house after dark if you keep things quiet, so I don't want any trouble down here from anybody."

The ice man shook his head. "No, sir, Sheriff, no trouble at all down here. We keep everything very quiet. It's mighty white o' y' to check on us like this and make sure that everything is peaceful.

The sheriff spoke in a voice that was louder than it needed to be for a man standing right next to him. "Y'all close up at midnight and keep things quiet. Cyrus, I'll see you again tomorrow night."

"Yessir, Sheriff – thank you, Sheriff."

The sheriff got back in his machine, started the engine, and slowly pulled away up the road, leaving dust-filled air behind him. The ice man stood and watched him go, and then Cyril overheard the man speaking to himself in an angry voice. "Always gotta come and git his share."

As the man started back toward the ice house, Cyril heard a small cheer from the men at the tables. He noticed a woman standing at one end of the dock, and a man was starting to play guitar beside her. And she sang a line, and some of the men laughed and called back; that was how she sang her song. She would sing a line, then wait, and some men would answer her, laugh or yell out. It sounded kind of like when the preacher would preach on Sunday morning, and he would yell out something and folks would answer back with an 'Amen.' She sounded like she was preaching, and the folks listening sounded like they were in church. Except what she was singing about wasn't anything he had ever heard in a sermon, and he did not expect to hear it in church. But the form of it felt familiar with that same call and response, even down to how some folks were tapping their feet in time with the music and the good feeling of folks just enjoying fellowship with one another.

Thirteen: An Accident

The day had been cold in the morning, but it had warmed up nicely by the afternoon even though it was late winter – Southern Alabama is still Alabama. Cyril and Billy walked along the overgrown road to the old Bratton Plantation. Cyril could hear the sound of the old shells crunching under his boots. Today was the Saturday that they had decided to go exploring and see the old house and outbuildings. They had been planning this for a while and were excited.

"I hear 'at the old family graveyard is up on a little hill across from the house," said Billy. "I wanna go look at it on account o' Granny saying 'at they buried some mean people 'ere. Granny says 'at it got stone posts around it wi' iron rings and an old iron chain around it. She told me 'at when you see an iron chain or an iron fence all the way around a graveyard, it's because 'ey buried some evil people in there an' the chain gonna make 'em stay inside on account o' they cain't pass the iron if they get up an' walk at night."

"What kind o' dead folks git up an' walk around at night?" Cyril asked.

"I 'on't know, vampires and such, I reckon," answered Billy. "She said 'ey cain't pass the iron 'causin' 'ey hate iron, but 'ey also gotta count every link in the chain. So, if the chain is made right, they just keep walkin' 'round an 'round 'cause they don't know where the chain ends or begins."

"So your granny says vampires gotta count the links in the chain?"

"Yep, they gotta count the chain or the bars on the fence iffin it's an iron fence around it. She say 'at them New Orleans witches keep beaded curtains on 'ey doorways 'cause 'em vampires gotta count every bead 'fore 'ey can come through the door."

"Do you reckon 'ey got a lot o' vampires in New Orleans?" Cyril asked.

"I reckon 'at they must have a good bit if 'ey all puttin' beaded curtains in 'ey doors," said Billy.

"I 'on't know if all 'at's true," said Cyril.

They came through the old stone gateposts, and Billy pointed to a small hill. "Look, 'ere it is. Let's go look at it."

The boys trudged up the hill through the weeds until they were standing in front of the graveyard. Billy said, "Look at it. Shore enough is a big ole rusty iron chain."

Cyril said, "Yeah, but I 'on't know 'at it's 'ere t' keep in any vampires."

"Well, then step over it an' walk right into the graveyard," said Billy.

"I didn't say I would walk into the graveyard," said Cyril. "Just 'at I 'on't thank 'at it's for keepin' in vampires. It just ain't a Christian thang t' do t' go walking in an' disturbing the dead. Just tryin' to be respec'ful is all."

"Unh hunh," Billy said with a nod. "Welp, let's go look in the old house."

"Nah, we'll save that fo' last. I wanna go down yonder an' look at the old quarters where the slaves used t' live." He started walking down the hill toward the ruins of some old shanties that he could see a hundred yards away.

"Why you wanna go down 'ere?" Asked Billy.

"I wanna see the quarters where Mr. Bratton was borned."

"You mean 'at colored lawyer fella 'at you friends wi'?"

"Yep, he was borned right here on the plantation back when his mother was a slave."

"Reckon 'at his father was a slave too?" Asked Billy.

"I reckon 'at he'd have t' been one too," answered Cyril.

"Yeah, I reckon so," agreed Billy.

Soon, they were standing among the remains of a dozen or so small wooden cabins. They looked around at everything.

Billy said, "Most of 'em is fallin' in an' 'ey 'on't look too safe."

Cyril said, "Most of 'em 'cept 'at one over there. Look like they built 'at one solid an' them cedar shingles will last forever. Let's go look in it. That one must o' been for someone that the master thought was special - it bein built better 'an the rest of 'em."

As they approached, Cyril heard a crunching sound and looked down. "He could see his shadow there on the ground beneath him, resting on the remnants of what used to be an oyster shell walkway. "The old oyster shells is still here where they used t' have they walkway."

He got to the cabin door and saw that it had once been pretty solid. It stood, still wedged into the doorway, but the old leather hinges had long since rotted away. He slipped his fingers around the edge of the door through a small space and started to scoot the door inward, and he slowly pushed it around until it was open and the door was leaning against the inside wall of the cabin. He turned and stood just inside the room as Billy walked in.

There was a wobbly table in the room with what was left of an old low stool lying on the hard clay floor beside it. It was dark inside the cabin, with just the light coming in through the door and one small window opening in the wall. There was some kind of long four-legged wooden frame with a few pieces of mostly rotted rope hanging from the boards next to one wall. Billy walked over to it. "What you reckon this was?"

"It was they bed, I reckon. Them ropes used to wind back an' forth across it, an' they slept on it with they blankets and all," answered Cyril. "Wonder who lived in this cabin 'cause this one is more solid built 'an the others. Wonder if anyone was borned in here – or died here."

"I 'on't know," said Billy. "Let's go look at the big house."

Cyril stood alone in the one-room cabin for a few more seconds after Billy left; he was wondering about the folks who had lived here – wondering if Mr. Bratton had ever been in this cabin when he was a little boy.

"C'mon, Cy," yelled Billy from outside. "What you doin' in 'ere now?"

Cyril yelled, "A'ight, I'm a comin' now." He turned and stepped back outside, and he and Billy headed up toward the old big-house.

They approached the house from the rear, where the old summer kitchen space used to be. As they neared the house, they passed what was left of the stone wall that used to surround the well. They could see various pits and piles of stones piled up and the remnants of old outdoor hearths. Billy said, "This was they outdoor kitchen, on account o' it being s' hot in the summer time they'd do a lot they cookin' out hye. My granny told me that her daddy worked hye when she was a little girl 'til the war come. She was ten years old when the war started. S' she was always hye when she was a little girl. Talks about what it was like comin' out hye t' the big house. She say that old lady Bratton never had no kids of her own, so she used to like for the people what worked hye t' bring they kids around, and she'd act like they was hers. The old lady used t' give 'er dresses an' whatnot to look pretty. And my granny liked it 'cause they was poor, an' her Mama couldn't make her many dresses. Her daddy was an overseer, an' they lived in a little house what was on the plantation. Then, when the war was over, her daddy saved up an' bought the little house an' the land around it – an' 'at's our house an' farm now. It was the first piece o' land 'at old man Bratton sold off down inna Bottoms."

"An overseer?" Cyril asked. "What d' an overseer do?"

"She said 'at the slaves, they had they own straw bosses for each gang of 'em doin' diff'ernt thangs. An' the overseer, he was a white man what told the bosses what t' have they gangs do ever' day an' keep an eye on 'em an' make shore ever'thang gits done. An' old man Bratton, he'd just ride around once e'ry day an' check ever'thang over an' tell th' overseers what he wanted done. So, the rich folks didn't much talk t' the field slaves; the overseers did all 'at. She say 'at old man Bratton would walk down most nights t' check the quarters an' make shore ever'thang was quiet too."

"You shore know a lot about it," said Cyril.

"Yeah, I like t' ask my granny t' tell me about it. Must o' been nice livin' hye with folks t' do all o' the hard work fo' y' – 'specially if y' was livin' in the big house. Wisht I was a livin' back 'en."

Cyril thought about it. "I 'on't know – seem t' me like it weren't right, 'em bein' slaves and all."

"Granny say they was all happy and smilin' all a time. They knew where they 'as gonna sleep an' what they 'as gonna eat. Didn't have a care in the world as long as they got they work done like they was s'posed t' do. Folks in the big house took good care of 'em – like when he used t' check on 'em ever' night t' make shore they was all safe an' quiet. Granny say 'at if they was unhappy, they wouldn't a been signin' all a time like they was. She say they was always singin', and they had a song fer e'ry job 'at they did, washin' an' cleanin' an' workin' in the fields an' cookin' an' ever'thang. They was all happy – right up 'till the Yankees started the war and messed ever'thang up. An' now 'ese days, the people what was rich is poor, an' the people what was poor are even mo' poorer an' folks what was slaves, 'ey the poorest of 'em all."

Cyril said, "Mr. Bratton, he was a slave, an' he ain't poor."

"I 'on't know, he diff'ernt – not like most o' 'em. He real light-skinned – act like he almost tryin' be white. 'Least 'at's what Granny thanks - she say 'at he kina uppity."

Cyril shook his head a little. "He is diff'ernt, but I 'on't know about all 'at 'tryin' t' be white' stuff. I'll tell y' one thang though; he shore helped y'all to save y'all's farm."

Billy nodded. "Yeah – at's what my daddy said t' Granny the other night. 'En she said it was a shame, an' 'en he told her 'at sometime she talk too much. An' 'en ever'body just finished they supper real quiet like."

Cyril grinned. "I bet 'ey did. Don't nobody never wanna see yo' daddy or yo' granny mad, 'specially iffin 'ey mad at each other."

As the reached the house, Billy spoke up. "Hey Cy, I 'on't wanna go in th'ough the back door like the poor folks always did. Let's go around front an' walk in the front door like the rich folks used t' do."

"A'ight," responded Cyril.

The two boys began walking around the big house toward the front entryway. The old plantation house was very run down after many years of being ignored, but one could see that it had once been a grand home with a large front porch, columns, and an impressive double door. In keeping with the previous century's architecture, there were large, closed shutters hiding what had once been a great many windows. In the hot Alabama climate, allowing constant airflow throughout the building had been important. But the once grand home was in dire need of attention and paint. The boys walked carefully across the porch due to some of the boards being rotten.

"I bet the door's locked," said Billy.

"Nah, not hardly – people's been comin' out here fo' years." Cyril reached the doors, and he turned the latch, and pushed. With a creaking sound, the doors swung slowly inward on rusted hinges.

Before them lay a once grand hall, and scattered shafts of light sneaking in through the old shutters broke the darkness here and there. It was just enough light to place the room in an eerie state of dusk.

"Look at all 'at old-timey stuff," said Billy. "Lot o' the old furniture been broke up b' peoples comin' in hye."

"I reckon so," agreed Cyril.

The boys started walking around in the large room. "Bet y' 'is is where 'ey used t' have some big parties," said Billy. "Wish I was there. Granny said 'at they used t' push all the furniture back fer space t' do the Virginia Reel right hye in the middle o' the main room."

Cyril nodded. "It shore is big enough to hold a lot o' folks." He stopped before a large fireplace and looked at a painting over the mantel. It was of an older-looking white man glaring down at the boy. The face seemed oddly familiar, and the glare made him feel like he did when his mother was angry at him – like those eyes could see all his secrets.

Billy came walking over and was also looking at the painting and whispered. "Wow, 'em eyes foller y', don't they? An' 'ey real mean lookin' too."

"He been dead a long time, but it feels like I know 'im from som'wheres," Cyril whispered. "Like I seen his face before."

Billy took a long slow breath. "He look kinda like you when you git mad. But 'at must be old man Bratton. Shore glad 'at they put 'em ir'n chains 'round 'at graveyard out yonder where he buried. Not a word of a lie. If they's anybody out there gonna git up and walk around, it's him."

After a few moments of silence, the boys quietly walked away to explore more of the house.

Cyril said, "Looks like the roof been leakin' a bit here an' 'ere. Them floorboards look like 'ey startin' t' rot in a few places."

"Smell like it, too," added Billy.

"Let's go up the staircase and see what's on the next floor," said Cyril.

Billy looked troubled. "I 'on't know 'bout 'em stairs. Some o' 'em look like 'ey been gittin' wet an' look kinda rickety."

Cyril said, "I tell y' what, I'll go first, an' you can foller me up.

We'll go slow an' test the treads as we go."

"A'ight, but you gotta go slow – an' iffin anythang starts crakin' we gonna come right back down."

"Deal," said Cyril.

So, they ascended the stairs slowly, with Cyril in the lead and Billy behind him. The treads of the stairs creaked and squeaked as they ascended. Cyril carefully tested each tread as he went, slowly shifting his weight onto each new tread.

"I can still feel 'is eyes in 'at paintin' on m' back follerin' us up the stairs," whispered Billy. "Feels like pure hate burnin' my back like the sun."

"Well, soon 's we git up 'ese stairs, he cain't see us anyways."

As they neared the top of the stairs, Cyril stepped onto a tread, which started to creak as he slowly shifted his weight onto it.

"Stop, 'at one 'on't sound right," said Billy.

"It's a'ight; I'll hold on and go slow," said Cyril. The boy took a firm grip on the railing and slowly shifted his weight onto the tread of the next stair. After a few moments, he was standing on the creaky tread. "See, it's fine – holdin' me just fine."

'Crack!' Cyril felt the stair tread give way beneath him, so he gripped the railing hard – the rotten railing. He felt the railing break under his weight and then emptiness as he fell.

Billy grabbed at his friend as everything happened so quickly, but he couldn't get a good grip and felt the denim overalls sliding through his hands. He expected to hear a scream from his friend – but Cy never screamed; he just vanished downward in silence until Billy heard a thud – and nothing.

"Cy! Cyril!" Billy yelled. He dared not lean over the edge of the stairs where the railing had vanished. He turned and saw the painting across the hall with its eyes focused on him. The boy started down the stairs as fast as he dared – all the while, he could feel those haunted eyes. He tried not to look at the painting, but that made it worse.

'Forever' seemed to crawl through the few moments the boy took to reach the bottom of the stairs. And he turned and saw Cyril still on the floor under the stairs with bits of rotten wood scattered around him. "Cyril?" He called quietly. He wanted to run to his friend – he feared what he would find when he got there. He wanted to run from the room – from the painted eyes that pierced his soul from behind. Instead, he walked slowly toward where his friend lay.

Finally, he was close enough to see that Cyril was breathing – but his eyes were closed. As he neared, he thought, 'His leg don't look right, it look all twisted 'round down b'low the knee.' He knelt beside his friend and touched him. "Cy," he whispered. "Can you hyear me?" Silence was the only answer. He noticed a trickle of blood coming from Cyril's head. "I'm 'a git help, Cy. I'm 'a git help right now."

He turned, ran across the room, and headed out the door onto the porch. He knew it would be a long run into town, but he had no choice. As he ran around the house toward the trail behind it, he saw someone down by the old quarters. "Hey!" he yelled, waving his arms. "Help – we need help." He saw two brown faces look in his direction and then start running. As they approached, he saw that one was a boy about his age and another boy that looked a few years older. They looked familiar from town, but he didn't know their names.

"What's wrong?" The older boy asked as they neared.

"It's m' friend; he fell off the stairs, an' it look like his leg broke, an' he ain't wakin' up. I was goin' t' run into town an' git the doctor. But wi' three of us, we can pick 'im up and carry 'im."

"Show me," said the older boy.

Billy turned and ran back into the house, followed by the two other boys. "He over hye by the stairs. Let's get a holt of him an' git him outta hye."

"Stop," said the older boy. "Don't touch him. If his leg is broke and he ain't wakin' up, we could hurt him worse by tryin' to move him."

The younger Black boy said. "Jimmy, that's that white boy that

140

comes down to our side of town and says he knows our father."

Jimmy said, "Yeah, it is." He pointed at Billy and said, "You know where he lives and what his name is, so come with me, and we'll run for help." Then, he looked at his little brother and said, "Charlie, you gotta stay here with him and make sure that nothing bothers him. And you must keep talkin' to him to try and wake him up. But don't shake or move him – and if he wakes up any, you got to get him to lay still even if you have to hold him down."

The younger brother nodded, "Okay, Jimmy, but y'all be fast – I don't want to be out here when it gets dark."

"We'll be back with help before then," the older boy answered as he pulled off his jacket and laid it over the injured boy. He looked at Billy and said, "C'mon." Then, he turned and ran with the younger white boy following behind him.

Twenty minutes later, the two boys were running up the main street through the south side of town. Billy knew it would take another half hour to make it through town and out to the Ledbetter farm – if he could keep running for that long. Then, he saw the Black lawyer sitting on his porch and changed plans. He yelled to the older boy who was still ahead of him. "Hey, hold on." He saw the older boy stop and turn, and Billy pointed to the man.

The teenager nodded and ran into the yard of the man who was standing up to see what the matter was. "Brother Bratton," the older boy called. "There's a badly hurt boy at the old plantation; I think you know him."

"What boy?" The man asked, concern showing on his face.

Billy finally caught up and said, "It's Cy, um, Cyril. I know you his friend, an' he told me 'at you got an automobile. He fell off the stairs an' he look like he got a broke leg an' ain't wakin' up. We got t' git the doctor out yonder to 'im right now."

Mr. Bratton looked at the older boy. "Is anyone currently with him, James?

"Yes, sir," the boy answered. "We left my little brother there with him so nothing can bother him."

The man pointed at Billy. "You run out to tell his parents what happened and that we are on our way out there with the doctor." Then, he turned to the older boy. "You run over to Dr. Barnes's house, tell him what happened, and let him know that I will be around there to pick him up in a few minutes in the automobile. Tell him to get his bag and be ready." He turned back to Billy, who was still panting from his run. "Go! Now!" The boy turned and ran as fast as he could toward the north side of town.

Fourteen: Another Ride

Cyril Bratton had never driven with as much haste as he did in those moments he went to pick up the doctor and then to the old house at the abandoned plantation. The automobile darted through the streets on its way to aid Mr. Bratton's young friend with little care for safety as all of the focus was on making their way to that run down house as quickly as possible.

"Brother Cyril, it will do the child no good if you damage this machine before we can get to him."

"You're right, Doctor," the man said as he slowed the automobile down ever so slightly. The machine still plowed down the overgrown old plantation road a bit too fast for the physician's comfort, and he clutched his doctor's bag mainly to keep it from flying around the vehicle but also to provide some semblance of comfort.

Mr. Bratton was impatient to get to the injured child. It felt like it took so long to drive around on the roads instead of the foot trails that cut directly from the town to the old place.

"It's just ahead around this bend," said Jimmy from behind the men.

Mr. Bratton said, "James, you jump out and open the gates when I stop."

"There aren't gates there anymore," answered the young man.

"All the better; I hated those gates," said the man.

Jimmy said, "If you have been out here, it must have been a long time ago."

"A lifetime ago," said Mr. Bratton. "When people still lived here."

Jimmy said, "I hear that the man who owned this place was bitter and mean."

Mr. Bratton focused on the old road ahead and quietly answered, "He was."

"They say that his ghost haunts it," added the young man.

Mr. Bratton said, "Ghosts do not haunt places – memories haunt people."

Moments later, the machine rounded the bend, and the old plantation house appeared. The automobile sped between the old brick columns that had once held the gates of many decades before and still were hanging in the memory of Cyril Bratton. The man recognized the view as if he had seen it yesterday. As they sped up, what had once been a grand carriage drive, the man looked down toward where one lone familiar cabin still stood. He could hear the tires crunching the old shells that had once glowed in the moonlight to show the carriageway – he still hated the sound of shells crunching. He shook his head to help ignore his memories and focused on the main house. He could hear the engine roaring, but the automobile seemed to be moving so slowly.

"Brother Cyril!" The voice of the doctor cut through. And the automobile slid to a stop, almost touching the bottom step leading to the porch.

The three jumped out, and Jimmy ran up the steps. "This way," he called back to the men.

As they entered the old plantation hall, the younger boy called to his brother. "He's awake, Jimmy; I have been keepin' him still and talkin' like you said. He's sayin' a little bit but not makin' much sense. He's been tryin' to talk to that old man in that painting up there."

144

The doctor knelt beside the injured boy and patted Charlie on the shoulder. "You did well, Charles; now you back up and let me see. James, go over and knock out the slats on those shutters; we need more light.

The teenager picked up a chair leg and used it to quickly hammer away the old wooden louvers of the shutters in a nearby window and let the afternoon sun flood the room for the first time in many years.

Cyril Bratton knelt beside the injured boy across from the doctor and watched silently as the skilled dark hands of the physician started to check the boy over.

Dr. Barnes began speaking to the injured child. "Son, can you tell me your name? I will check you over, but you need to lay very still."

"Cy – ever'body calls me Cy," the boy mumbled. "My leg hurts – an' m' head too," he mumbled slowly.

"Your leg is broken," answered the doctor. "But it's not anything that we cannot fix. But I am worried about your head. Can you see? How do you feel?"

"I can see that old man's eyes," the boy said with a slight slur to his words.

The doctor's face stayed calm and belied his deep concern hearing the garbled words as he felt around on the head of the boy – he felt the crack in the bone. "I have to straighten and set your leg before we can move you. I am sorry, but it will hurt a lot, but you will have to take it. I can't give you anything for the pain because you bumped your head, and I don't want you to fall asleep."

"A'ight," said the boy. "I'm ready."

"It will be a minute or two," said the doctor. "I have to get these gentlemen ready to help me. James, we need you to put your hands on his shoulders and press them down into the floor when I start counting to keep him still."

The older boy nodded, knelt down, and rested his hands on the shoulders of the boy, waiting for the doctor.

"Brother Cyril, I need you to put your hands on either side of his head so he doesn't move it. And Charlie, you come here and lay across his body to keep his hips down."

Everyone got into position and prepared to help the doctor.

"How's he doin' now?" Billy yelled as he ran in through the door.

Mr. Bratton looked up. "I told you to go tell his parents that he is hurt. What are you doing here?"

"I ran into a couple of the other fellas from school an' they was fresh t' run, s' I sent them out t' tell his daddy an' I come back hye."

"Later," snapped the doctor. "Now listen to me, Cy, I'm going to count to five, and then it will hurt as I set the bone, so you be ready for it. But first, I want you to relax, so you take a deep breath. Can you do that for me?"

Cyril mumbled something that sounded like agreement, and the doctor could feel the boy relax under his hands. The doctor looked at the others and said, "Hold him very still."

The doctor could hear the boy taking a deep breath as he counted "One" out loud. With that, the doctor quickly pulled and set the shinbone back together while the boy was still relaxed.

A scream echoed in the hall, and the boy tried to break free of the hands that held him down. Then he went silent and limp as tears rolled out of his eyes, down his temples, and into his hair. The boy slurred out a whispered, "You said on five."

"I lied," answered the doctor. "You can let him go. Now I will wrap this leg up to one of these boards to keep it straight, so we can move you. But it won't hurt like that did, so you lay as still as possible."

The boy tried to nod, and the pain in his head made him wince and take a sharp breath.

The doctor continued talking to the boy as he gently worked, explaining everything that he was doing. His intention being to keep the child awake and distracted.

They heard Billy yell, and everyone except Cyril and Dr. Barnes turned toward the sound. The boy was standing in front of the painting. "It's you, you the causin' of it! You and them evil eyes! You hurt m' friend – even from the grave, you hurt folks! I ain't never comin' back hye. I hope it rots t' the ground, an' your evil-eyed picture with it!" He picked up a piece of broken furniture and threw it at the painting as he shouted, "Damn your eyes!" The table leg glanced off of the old wooden frame. The canvas of the painting shook from the blow, but the painted eyes still glared down at them all.

Cyril Bratton looked up at the eyes that glared at him from the painting – glared at him from the past.

The doctor said, "Okay, we can move him out to the automobile if we all work together."

Mr. Bratton didn't wait; he just scooped the boy up and started to carry him to the door.

As the man placed the boy gently into the back of the automobile, the doctor climbed into the machine from the other side to continue caring for the boy. "Jimmy, you take these two back to town. You young men all did very well."

"I'll be there as quick as I can," Billy said.

The boys stood and watched as the automobile drove back out the way it came – slowly and gently, with shells crunching under the tires.

Ida Ledbetter could hear a raised voice inside the doctor's office before her husband opened the door for her. As she stepped in, she saw the sheriff towering over Mr. Bratton and Dr. Barnes, with Billy Holstead standing in a corner looking shocked. The large white man was yelling at the two Black men. She could see a door open behind the doctor, and through that door, she could see her son lying in the treatment room beyond.

The sheriff yelled. "You had no call to bring that boy here, and I'm going to take him over to see the appropriate doctor. You should have taken him to see Dr. Harris immediately instead of bringing him here."

Mr. Bratton stood before the larger white man speaking calmly. "Sheriff, Dr. Barnes has already begun treating the child, and he should not be moved again until we are certain that his head injury is properly treated."

"That is why I am taking him," yelled the sheriff. "I'm gonna take him to the proper doctor for treatment. I'm not going to have his parents upset that he is here. He will be seen by a doctor who I know is properly educated. Y'all might be fine to come hye to this boy for medicine, but this child is white and will be seen by a white doctor."

"Sheriff, what is going on here?" Ida asked.

The white man turned toward the woman. "There you are, Mrs. Ledbetter, these boys brought your son hye, but I'm going to move him over to be seen by Dr. Harris right away."

"My son is injured in his head, and there is a doctor right here to see to him. I will not have any further risk to my child by moving him until the doctor says he can be moved. He is under a doctor's care, and that is sufficient."

"Ma'am, he needs to be seen by a proper doctor," said the large man.

"There is a well educated physician right here, and rather than tending to my son, he is out here dealing with you," The woman responded.

"I will not allow it," yelled the man. "This is not how things are done 'round hye."

William Ledbetter stepped in front of his wife. "You will not raise your voice to my wife. I do not care if you are the sheriff."

Ida Ledbetter spoke barely above a whisper which still managed to fill the room as she stepped gently around her husband and walked up to the large white man. "You will not allow it? You will not allow it? I have buried one of my children, and I will not bury another one because you 'will not allow' something."

William said, "Sheriff, I think you should leave now."

The big man stood there, the fury visible on his face. After a moment, he started for the door, stopped, turned back toward the doctor, and pointed. "If 'at boy comes t' any harm, you are goin' t' hang for it." He stood for a moment, and as he turned back to the door, he heard Billy whisper.

"The judge ain't gonna hang no doctor."

The sheriff pulled the door open and turned, looking back as he spoke. "Didn't say anything about the 'judge' hanging anyone."

Ida Ledbetter stepped toward the man pulling back her hand. William moved up behind his wife and gently touched her drawn-back arm, and she stopped. She gave the sheriff one last look and turned to walk into the other room with her son. As she passed the other men, she stopped and placed a hand on the shoulder of Mr. Bratton, and she looked at him and whispered, "Thank you."

The sheriff gave a look of hatred and then turned and left. They heard the engine of his automobile come to life, and the man sped away.

Cyril was awake enough to hear all of this in the next room, and then he felt his mother's cool hand touch his cheek as she sat down in a chair beside the bed.

He heard Mr. Bratton say, "I will be heading home now."

And his father answered. "I'll walk out with you."

Cyril looked out the window, where he could see the automobile parked and waiting. He watched as his father and Mr. Bratton walked out to the car. He could see the men talking to one another and wished he could hear what they were saying. After several minutes, he saw the men shake hands, and his father nodded. He watched Mr. Bratton climb into his machine and drive away. Cyril's head hurt so bad, but the doctor told him he had to stay awake for a bit longer.

Fifteen: A Day on the Farm

A few weeks later, Cyril was sitting at the breakfast table, and it was a Monday morning, and the first day of spring break from school. It was time to plant, so the school would always take a break for a week so the children could help their families get the main body of the crops planted. "I can do some of the work, Mama. The doctor said that this cast will come off soon anyway, so my leg is mostly healed up."

"You are not going to try and walk behind a plow with your leg like that," said Ida.

"But Mama, I've got to do it – we have to get at least some seeds in the ground. And with Daddy being so sick, he can't do it. We're already so far behind. Most people been plowing and getting their fields ready for weeks."

"Your father is getting a little bit stronger every day, and he will be back out there in no time. Until then, I can walk behind a plow, so we won't get too far behind. I know how to hitch a mule."

"Mama, you can't do that. There's three forty-acre fields out there, and Daddy wanted to plant that other back forty this year too. You gotta let me do some of it."

"No, if you hurt your leg again before it heals and is out of that cast, you may never be able to walk right. I will not have you take that risk. Dr. Harris said that your father should be able to start getting up and around as soon as they remove those stitches."

"What caused his appendix to get sick anyway, Mama?"

"The doctors do not know. Dr. Harris said that it just happens sometimes without warning. Luckily, he knew to get Dr. Barnes to help him operate. He said he went to medical school thirty-five years ago, but Dr. Barnes went just a few years ago. Dr. Harris said they didn't know much about how to clean up that kind of infection when he went to school. Even today, most people don't live through it. You just be glad that we have good doctors and you have a strong father."

"Well, I'm strong too, just like my daddy. And that's why I'm gonna hitch up that mule and do some plowing – even if I'm in a cast."

"Your father said the same thing to me first thing this morning. And see where that got him, so do not test me, boy."

"Mama!"

"I told you no."

"No, Mama. Look out the windo'. They's somebody at the barn."

"English," the woman said as she looked out the window.

"Yes, ma'am. It's Mr. Bratton. I think that he must o' heard that daddy took sick, and he is here to hitch the mule himself."

"That man is a lawyer, not a farmer."

"He said that he was on a farm when he was a boy, so he must know a little about it. I'll go talk to him." There was a thud as the plaster of the cast met the floor.

Ida turned to her son. "Sit down; I will go out there and send him home right this instant." The woman left the room.

Cyril was shocked when he heard the screen door on the back porch slam shut behind his mother. He watched through the window as his mother marched down to the barn. He saw Mr. Bratton turn to face her. He could see that she was upset and felt sorry for the man. He wished he could hear as he watched the two adults arguing in the barn doorway – the argument seemed to go on for several minutes longer than the boy had expected it to last. He finally saw Mr. Bratton point back toward the house as he said something to the woman. And then he saw the man turn and walk into the darkness of the barn. He watched as his mother stood looking into the barn for a few more moments, and then he saw her turn and start marching back up to the house.

He heard the screen door slam again, then his mother in the kitchen. He wanted to ask her about the conversation at the barn, but he knew better, so he just sat there quietly. Well, he sat until he saw them coming. Seven wagons were coming, each with a man and a woman sitting in front and most of them with some kids in the back. All of the wagons had a plow sitting in the back and mules or horses tied to the backs of some of the wagons. Four Black families and three white families. "Mama! Look here coming. It's a bunch of people. It's them people from the bottoms, them people that he helped. They are all here to help him. They know how to plow and plant even if he doesn't remember much about it."

Ida hurried over to the window. Tears started forming in her eyes. "He saved their farms, and now they will help him save ours." She watched as the wagons all pulled up to the barn, and the men all started helping one another to unload plows and tools. The kids started helping, and she saw the women gather around together.

She saw Mr. and Mrs. Holstead walking up toward the house, and she met them at the door and asked them in.

Mr. Holstead asked to speak to Brother William to find out what he wanted to be done and where and what to put in each field.

He heard Mrs. Holstead. "Sister Ida, where can we build a fire out hye to cook? Them men are going to be hungry later."

Ida said, "A fire? Sister Susan, I've got a stove right here and a pump inside the kitchen. You tell the ladies to come inside, and we'll cook in here."

Sister Holstead said, "We don't want to put anybody out; we

brought plenty of food. We just need a fire."

Ida said, "Susan, you bring them all in here, and we will cook together and set everything up under a shade tree just like dinner on the grounds at church. And send Billy and Norma Jean in here, please. I need them to get some things for me."

"Okay, Ida, if you are sure. Do you want all of the women in here?"

"Every one of them, Susan – every one of them."

Cyril saw Sister Holstead walk back down, speak to the other women, and watched as they all headed toward the house. He saw Mr. Bratton walk out of the barn to be greeted by many handshakes. He heard Billy in the kitchen. "Mama said we was t' come speak t' you, Sister Ledbetter.

"There you are," Ida said. "Now Billy, go down to the smokehouse, get that biggest ham, and bring it up here. And then you go back and get a side of salt pork too. Then I will need you to get some string beans hanging in the attic. Norma Jean, you take this basket and go down to that hen house and get all the eggs; what I have here is not enough."

"Yes, ma'am, Sister Ledbetter," Billy and Norma Jean said in the familiar harmony of siblings. The sound of it gave Cyril a moment of heartache.

Then, the kitchen suddenly filled with women's voices. Some were familiar; he knew their owners from church, and other voices were new to him. But they were laughing and joking, so Cyril knew they were friendly. Then, he heard them all go silent and listened to his mother. "Thank you all for coming here and doing this for us. It is as if God sent an army of angels to help us." He could hear her voice choking up with emotion.

"We know our husbands a little too well to go callin' any of 'em angels," announced an unfamiliar voice. The room filled with feminine laughter.

Cyril sat and watched through the window as the men and

children got to work outside, and he listened to the women as they cooked together. He welcomed the sound of their laughter. He could not remember the last time that he heard his mother laugh like this.

He saw another wagon approach and recognized the driver as Reverend Scolfield from the Second Baptist Church and his two sons riding in the back. He figured that the woman was Mrs. Scolfield. Reverend Scolfield helped his wife down from the wagon, and then he and his older son headed out to help the other men while Mrs. Scolfield headed toward the house with her younger son in tow.

He heard the women greet 'Sister Scolfield' and his mother say, "He is right in there."

He saw the younger Scolfield boy walk into the room. "Hey. How's your leg?"

"Still hurts some, but it's almost all healed up. The headaches can get pretty bad, but they been gitin' some better too. My name is Cy. I wanna thank you for what you an' your brother done for me 'at day when I got hurt. I still don't remember it all, but I remember you stayin' there with me the whole time and tellin' me them stories to keep me awake."

"You welcome. My name is Charlie. I'm just glad that you are getting better now. But I'll tell you one thing. It was scary wondering if you were going to be okay. And that old man in that painting, just staring at us the whole time."

"Yeah, he's pretty scary."

"More scary than pretty," Charlie answered, and his face lit up with the joke, and both boys laughed. "I better get outside and start helping before my daddy comes looking for me. I'll see you at lunchtime."

"A'ight, see y' then."

The women took turns checking that Cyril was doing alright for the rest of the morning. He had never been so spoiled in his life. He was shocked that every one of the ladies had heard about his accident and the scene at the doctor's office. He knew they were also checking on his father and spoiling him. He thought that was funny because he knew that his father would hate it, but he would never let on to any of the ladies that he didn't like the fuss.

He could smell the food cooking. And he sat in the parlor listening as the women talked or sang songs while they cooked. Sometimes one woman would sing, and sometimes they would sing together. He recognized some of the songs from church. But sometimes, the women would sing other songs that sounded like church songs but ones that he was unfamiliar with, and he figured that they must be songs from the other church. He could hear his mother's voice on nearly every song, even the unfamiliar ones. He had missed hearing her sing like she used to.

About noon, the women started to spread quilts on the ground outside under the cedar trees where the shade was cool, and they began to carry the food out too. Cyril wandered slowly outside as the menfolk and the children gathered for lunch. Reverend Scolfield stood up and said grace, and everyone made their plates and sat around laughing and eating. Cyril sat with Billy, Charlie, and a couple of other boys around his age from down in the Bottoms.

He saw the dust of an automobile in the distance. He knew that it would be the sheriff. He watched as Brother Holstead went out, leaned on the side of the automobile, and spoke to the sheriff, who looked disapprovingly at the folks sitting together under the trees. After a short conversation, the sheriff left.

After a while, when everyone had finished eating and were sitting to let their food digest a bit before going back to work, Rev. Scolfield stood up with his Bible and read a passage about Jesus driving the moneylenders out of the temple; then, he began a short lesson. "I was asked a good question by a young man some time back. He wanted to know if Jesus was a bully when he drove those people out of the temple."

Cyril felt his face redden and was sure his mother was looking at him, but he knew better than to check. He just listened as Reverend Scolfield continued. "Yes, yes, he was a bully – a righteous bully. He was God who came to walk as a man. And as he walked as a man, he felt and experienced all of the same pains and temptations as other men. He was a righteous bully but not a self-righteous bully. And that is a hard line not to cross. It can be hard to know if we are being a righteous bully or a self-righteous bully. But he was God walking as a man, so he knew where the line was. We might not be able to tell, so we should not be any kind of bully so that we don't cross that line as some people do. Now get back out there and bully some mules."

After some laughter, the men got up and headed back out to the plows and fields, and the women started cleaning up. Cyril went back inside and decided to sit with his father so that the women would have an easier time fussing over them if they were in the same place.

He spent the afternoon listening as the women cleaned up and immediately began preparing the supper they would all share at the end of the day. The afternoon passed very quickly, and by the end of the work day, everything had been plowed and planted, and the farm was ready for the new growing season. And none of the other farms were more than a day of work behind. Everyone gathered for another meal together. Everyone was laughing and enjoying themselves, but they were all very tired. Then, Reverend Scolfield stood up and spoke. He thanked everyone for coming out to help this family and to repay Brother Cyril for what he had done to help them earlier. "Glad that you all came. Brother Cyril, you worked hard, but you are a much better lawyer than a plowman." There was laughter. "In fact, I would say that your plowing made that mule about as mad as your lawyering did that man from Texas." More laughter.

Mr. Bratton said, "From where I was walking behind that plow, I thought it was the man from Texas." There was an explosion of laughter.

When the laughter died down, Reverand Scolfield looked at Ida. "Sister Ledbetter, until Mr. Ledbetter is back on his feet, each of these men will spend half a day here each week to help you keep everything in order. My son Jimmy is fifteen, and he and a couple of the other young men will also spend half a day each week. That will allow everyone to keep up with their own work and keep your farm going until your husband is back on his feet.

Ida sat there and said nothing as her eyes filled with tears. The other women gathered around her for a few minutes. But they had to get things cleaned up, so before long, Cyril noticed his mother sitting alone with Mrs. Scolfield having a quiet conversation.

The women made very short work of cleaning up after that supper, and the men soon had their wagons loaded. Several of the ladies hugged one another as they parted. He saw his mother get a few hugs from some of the ladies who were leaving. Soon, everyone was back in the wagons and heading home by the time the sundown whistle blew. The sheriff drove back by in his automobile and slowed down to check that everyone was loaded and leaving. Cyril couldn't help but think about the 'self-righteous bully' the preacher had spoken of.

Mr. Bratton was soon the only one who remained. Cyril had been sitting on the porch, and he got up and limped over to the man. "Thank you for havin' all them people come down here to help us."

"I didn't have anyone do anything; I came to help. They came on their own because that is the kind of people they are."

"Yeah, but they came here for you. And I'm thankful all the same."

The man nodded, "Go back up on the porch and sit down. I have to head home."

"Bye," the boy said as he turned and limped away. He returned to the porch, entered the house, sat down, and watched through the window as Mr. Bratton walked back toward his automobile. He saw his mother approach Mr. Bratton, and he saw them have a peaceful conversation. As usual, the boy wished he could hear what was said.

He saw the man nod and smile before turning toward his automobile, then Cyril looked on as his mother stood and watched the man drive away.

Part Two

Sixteen: Big Changes

William Ledbetter was sitting at the supper table, just starting to cut into his pork chop. "Cyril, we will be making some changes here around the farm. Nineteen and twenty-six is going to be a big year for the Ledbetters."

"Yessir. What kinds o' changes, Daddy?"

"Now that you have turned fifteen, you are going to have a lot more to do. And we are going to start farming on the Moore farm next door. Since Brother Moore passed two years ago, Sister Moore hasn't had it tended to at all. I spoke to her today, and we made a deal that I am going to start taking care of it so that the fields stay in good shape and it stays as a working farm."

Ida said, "That farm is a good sixty acres larger than this one, so I don't see how you can work both farms."

William said, "I've worked everything out and have a plan. The Moores only have one daughter, and she lives in Baltimore now and has no interest in a farm in Alabama. So, we are going to start buying the farm from Sister Moore, and she is going to keep living there. But we are going to work the farm, and the money from that land is going to pay for itself, and in the end, we will have a much larger farm."

"Well, if you think that Cyril is going to quit school to do farm work all day every day, you are mistaken," responded Ida. Cyril felt a wave of relief that his mother was stepping in.

"I have no intention of Cyril leaving school. He is going to graduate and go on to college. But he is going to spend afternoons and Saturdays working hard around here."

Cyril asked. "When do I study and do my homework?"

"In the evening after supper, you can do it then," the man answered.

"I'll be too tired," the teenager said.

"Well, you are going to have to do it so that we can pay for you to go to college when you have finished high school."

"I don't know that this is a good idea, William," Ida said.

"Well, why don't y'all let me finish explaining the plan to you before you start on me about it?" The man sounded a bit frustrated. "So, Ford started making a new Model T for working on farms and the like. A lot like those delivery vehicles that they had been building for a while. But it is open in back so that you can haul things like you can with a wagon."

"What?" asked Cyril excitedly."You buying an automobile? I saw one of them new Fords; they call it a truck. We could get a lot of work done with that."

William looked silently at his son and arched an eyebrow.

"Yessir, sorry Daddy.

"There is still a good plow in the barn over on the Moore farm," continued William. And she still has a mule that Brother Harold bought not long before he passed. It's a young mule, and I've been going over there to take care of it these two years myself. And I'm going to hire a man to help with the work. Jimmy Scolfield is his name. His father is the preacher over at Second Baptist Church. You will remember him, Cyril; he was the one that helped you when you was hurt."

"I know him," the boy said, nodding. "Him and his brother – he's got a brother my age, and he is the one that sat with me while the older one took Billy for help. I know his father too. And Mama has met his wife."

"Alright," the man said, waving his son into silence. "So, he will start right away with the planting and work with me every day, Monday to Friday. He has friends who he can bring to do day work here and there when we need extra hands. And you can help afternoons. We can run two farms with three of us, two good mules, two good plows, and one of them new automobiles – a 'truck' I guess you called it – we can run two farms. That farm will pay his salary and pay for itself. Then, we will have a bigger farm, and when I get too old, and you finish college, who knows, maybe we will sell that farm to Jimmy Scolfield. That way, you won't have become a farmer yourself."

"That is a lot of money, William," said Ida.

"Been saving up for years. That truck is going to be worth it, and the farm is going to pay for itself." The man reiterated. "This is a fantastic opportunity. Sister Moore don't want to sell the farm, but she can't take care of it anymore. She told me that she only wants to be in her own bed when the Lord sees fit to close her eyes, and know that her farm is in good hands, so she is giving me a real good price on the condition that she can live there from now on. Jimmy Scolfield married a girl recently, and she will be coming out to help Sister Moore a few days a week. They have a new baby coming, but Sister Moore would love for the baby to be around anyway. And if we don't buy it this way, Sister Moore's daughter is going to have to sell the farm to a stranger and take her mother to Baltimore to take care of her."

"I guess you have it well figured out, Mr. Ledbetter," said Ida. "A young husband and father will have a good job, you will have a bigger farm, and Cyril will finally learn to drive an automobile. And you are doing the Christian thing by the Moores. I guess that I can't argue too much with that plan – but I would have appreciated being part of the planning." There was a long silence.

"You are right as always, Mrs. Ledbetter." William looked a bit embarrassed. "And I apologize for not speaking to you about it. Sister Betsy asked me if I wanted to buy the place on these conditions, and I guess I just ran with the hook in my mouth. If you don't like it, I will tell her that we just can't right now."

"I did not say that it was a bad plan. I just wish it had been our plan instead of yours alone." With that, the woman stood up, picked up her plate with one hand and William's mostly unfinished plate with the other, and headed to the kitchen to clean up from supper. "Finish up, Cyril; I want to get done in this kitchen early."

"Yes, ma'am, almost finished." He sat there stunned and looked at his father, who gave him a warning look to say nothing else. The idea that his mother had just decided that his father was going to bed without most of his supper made Cyril carefully reevaluate the family dynamics.

A short time later, the family read in the parlor as the sun sank. William was quietly holding an almanac but had not actually turned a page. Cyril was sitting on the settee holding a book but was not reading. He was thinking about his own disrupted plans while he stared at the page in front of him. The room was quiet since it was still cool enough in the evenings for the windows to be closed. There was only the sound of a ticking clock and his mother's chair rocking ever so slightly as she sat with her book.

Ida noticed Cyril was more restless than usual. "What is the matter with you, Cyril? You seem to be bothered by something. Is the sun not sinking fast enough to suit you?"

"No, ma'am, um, I mean… Yes, ma'am – it's not that Mama, not that at all. I was just thinking about something else is all."

"What has your mind so occupied?" The woman asked.

"It's nothing – nothing important anyway. Not as important as a new farm and a hired hand."

"Ah, I see. It must be that new automobile that your father is getting. You are excited about that."

"No, ma'am. I mean, that is exciting, but that isn't what I am thinking about."

"If it is a girl, you best put that out of your mind right now. There is a long way to go before you finish college and can think about such things."

"No, ma'am, I am not thinking about a girl."

"Talk. What are you thinking about that has you so restless?"

Cyril sat for a moment but could feel her eyes on him expectantly, so he began. "Well, Mama, you see, I was going to ask about some afternoon tutoring to help me get ready for college. We are not really covering a lot of the kind of material in our high school classes that we are going to need for college. I tried to talk to Mr. Linkway about it, but he said that he is educating people to be store clerks, bankers, and farmers and doesn't expect to see any of his students become doctors, lawyers, or anything like that. He said that I am set to inherit a good farm someday, so I would be better off paying attention to that."

Ida raised her eyebrows. "Is that what the new high school teacher thinks? Should you not bother with trying to go to college? Well, you can ignore that man and continue to work on getting into a good college. Now what is this about tutoring?"

"Well, the teacher over at the colored school on the other side of town is planning on some of her students going on to college. And she and Mr. Bratton have worked out a deal where he is going to tutor some of her best students three afternoons a week at his house to help prepare them for their entrance examinations. Since they only got one teacher there for all of the students, she can't focus as much on getting them ready. So anyway, I was going to ask if it was alright with you and Daddy for me to start going to those afternoon college preparation sessions with him. Even though we have a second teacher for our high school students, he doesn't expect us to go on to college and is not trying to help us prepare for the entrance examinations. But if we are going to be buying that other farm, I will be too busy here to go to those sessions, so I will just forget about it."

"I see," said Ida. "And have you spoken with Mr. Bratton about joining his tutoring class?"

"No, ma'am. I wanted to talk to you and Daddy about it first since I know that there might be some folks who might not approve too much. The sheriff will probably have a problem with it, and I am sure that the new high school teacher will have something to say about it. But I really did want to try and get ready for college. I guess I can get some books and study here alone in the evenings."

"Preparing for your college examinations would be a good idea, but I don't know if spending more time on that side of town is the answer. People already talk about how much time you spend down there; I am not sure that more questions are in order. Your father will need a lot of help running two farms, so it must be up to him. William, do you hear what your son is saying? Seems like he has been making plans too."

William took a deep breath. "I hear. I could use the help around here, but I also know that you always have had your heart set on college and don't want to run this farm in the future. I will have a strong young hired hand to help me, and you will have to work extra hard on the other days, and you can plan on being busy all day on Saturday, but if you want to ask Mr. Bratton to join his study group, you go ahead and ask him. And you let me deal with any folks who have a problem with it. If the new high school teacher don't think that it is his job to prepare you for college, then we will have to let your friend there help you get ready."

"So when is all of this supposed to begin?" Ida asked in a seemingly disinterested voice without looking up from her book.

"Seeing as you both have figured out so many things and have given me nary clue about any plans anyone has been making. So, I will just ensure you have clean clothes, a clean house, and hot food."

For a few moments, an uncomfortable silence hung in the room until the unmistakable sound of a stomach growl from William broke it. The sun was quickly sinking, so the room was darkening, as was the mood. Ida slowly looked at William as she leaned a little bit forward. "Did you say something, dear?"

William cleared his throat uncomfortably. "Well, Cyril has spring break all next week, and tomorrow is Saturday. I have Jimmy starting tomorrow, and he is going to bring his little brother, who is also on break, and one friend for tomorrow, all next week, and next Saturday. So, that gives us seven days with five sets of hands. The last month has been mild, so I have everything on this farm plowed and ready for seed. So, by the end of tomorrow week, we will have everything plowed and planted before Cyril has to be back in school. Then, I will have Jimmy for five days a week with plenty to keep us busy. I figure that the Saturday after that, I can take the morning train into Birmingham to buy that new automobile. I will pick up a few things that I can't get here in town that we need and drive back here before night." The man paused for a moment and continued. "Of course, if there are things that you need in Birmingham, I would love for you to accompany me, and we can drive back together and see the countryside."

"A train ride to Birmingham?" The woman asked. "Maybe so – if I don't have other plans. If I do have other plans, I will send Cyril along with a list – unless he already has other plans."

'Tick, tick, tick,' the clock seemed to thunder into the steadily darkening room. Finally, Cyril spoke. "I was going to ask if I could start the tutoring on Monday week when the break is over and we go back to school."

"Well now," said Ida, "that sounds like a good plan." She stood. "All of these good plans. I guess I need to plan a week of lunches for five grown men." The woman smiled and turned to glide from the room. William watched her go, and his eyes followed as she went through the dining room, into the kitchen, and turned from sight. They heard her close her bedroom door behind her. Not slammed but closed firmly enough to be heard from the front of the house. Another growl of his stomach followed William's sigh.

"Want me t' go out in the kitchen and get you a leftover biscuit with some butter and molasses?" Cyril asked.

"Nah, she knows how many biscuits she expects to find there in the morning. I'm good."

Cyril stood up and said. "I'll get that extra pillo' from the top o' m' closet. Prob'ly should go to bed early too."

William nodded in the darkness. "Prob'ly should."

Saturday morning came early. The sun was just lightening the sky as Ida placed the breakfast on the table. Cyril noticed that his father was moving his neck around as if it was bothering him. "Is your neck a'ight, Daddy?" Cyril asked.

"English," said Ida.

"Yes, ma'am," Cyril answered. "Is your neck alright, Daddy?"

"A little stiff, but it'll be fine."

Ida sat down at her place. "You must have slept on it wrong."

"Must've," the man agreed. "I'm sure that I will sleep better tonight."

"Maybe so," Ida responded.

Cyril studied his plate very closely as he quietly ate, admiring the light brown traces of the hairline cracks in the white porcelain.

"Let's hurry up and eat, Cyril. Those young men will be here directly, and I don't want to miss a bit of daylight," said William.

"Yessir."

A short time later, Cyril sat beside his father as they tied on their work boots when they heard a knock at the back door. William called through the door, "Be right there."

"Yes, sir," came a response from outside.

After Cyril and his father walked off the back porch, they heard Ida call from the back door. "I will see you all back here for lunch."

A chorus of "Yes, ma'am" answered her.

It was a busy morning. William had set Cyril and two of the others to seeding three different fields on their farm while he and Jimmy Scolfield were on the Moore farm walking behind the plows. But the morning passed very quickly, and by lunchtime, five big appetites were heading to the house. After a short stop at the pump to clean up their hands and faces, the men were all on the back porch. William opened the door, and he and Cyril walked in while the three Black men waited at the door. After a moment, Ida appeared on the other side of the screen door. "Are you gentlemen ready to eat?"

"Yes, ma'am," said James. "We figured we would sit out there under the cedar trees if that'd be all right."

"Cedar trees?" Asked the woman. "I know your mother. I will not feed any woman's son outside. That's where the dog eats. There are three more places set at the table. You stomp those boots off and come inside."

James Scolfield said, "Yes, ma'am," exchanging confused looks with his brother and friend as they gave their boots an extra stomp. He had worked on several local white-owned farms for the past few years, and while the women generally fed him well, no white woman had ever asked him to eat at her table. He was unsure if he was comfortable with this, but the smell of food coming through the screen door put him at ease.

Seventeen: An Important Lesson

Cyril was just crossing the train tracks on Main Street. He had decided to stay on the road instead of his usual route on the trail behind the buildings since pretty much everyone was still at one of the two Baptist churches in town. That was one thing you could depend on with Sunday morning; everyone was going to be at church – well, everyone except the man at the station who had to make sure that someone was attending the telegraph at all times. All the white folks would be at the First Baptist Church of Bratton, and all the Black folks would be at the Second Baptist Church of Bratton. Both churches were near the station in the center of town, one just a few doors north and the other just a few doors south of the station. In fact, on a hot day with the windows open, and if the wind was right, you could hear the music from one church while standing at the door of the other. The young man thought, 'Nobody's gonna notice me but maybe a dog or two,' looking at the train rails as he stepped over them, taking care not to scuff his good shoes.

The young man had told his parents that he had something to do right after church and would sit with his friends in the back this Sunday. He had waited for everyone to stand for the singing, slipped out early, and headed south. He could hear the shift from the singing behind him as it was fading and the singing ahead of him steadily growing louder. At one point, he stopped briefly and turned his head to the right. He could hear the singing from one church in his left ear and the other in his right ear. The sound balanced between them, and each was just far enough away that he could not quite make out the words, and all that he could really hear was the rich harmonies of the voices. He closed his eyes and listened to what seemed to be a single choir surrounding him in the distance. After a few moments, he opened his eyes and looked down at the ground. He saw his shadow pointing off a little to the west and leaning back toward the way he had come and away from where he was going. 'Funny,' he thought, 'shadows always seem to be leaning like some kind of wind is blowing on them. A wind that we can't feel, but it pushes the shadows just like a breeze pushes tall grass. Sometimes it wants t' push your shadow ahead of you like it is trying to beat you to git somew'eres, and other times like it is trying to slow you down and hold back from somethin'. This morning, it looks like it wants to push me back – good luck with that.' He began to walk again, but he could feel his shadow behind him, almost like it had weight and was trying to slow him down.

As he walked, he could hear the church ahead of him steadily getting louder until he could make out what song they were singing, though he didn't seem to recognize this one like some others. 'Reckon they got some o' they own songs,' he thought. By the time he opened the gate in the white picket fence, the singing had stopped, and he could hear the voice of Reverend Scolfield starting to preach, and he could hear the voices of the congregation as they answered. He stepped onto the porch, knocked on the door, and waited for an answer. When no answer came, he stepped over to the study window and looked at the empty desk. 'Reckon 'at he went t' church.' Cyril walked over and plopped down into a chair on the porch to wait. He leaned back, closed his eyes, and could hear the sermon getting louder, as did the responses. 'Bet he gonna be thunderin' over there soon. I thought I wasn't gonna hear a sermon today, but I guess I can't git away from it. Least I can sit through it and not have t' do anythang.'

Cyril heard the nearby service as it wrapped up and saw well-dressed people start walking by. The ladies all had hats, white gloves, and little handbags, and the men wore well-brushed suits and shined shoes. After a few minutes, he saw Mr. Bratton walking toward him. He smiled when he saw the man notice him sitting on the porch. He saw Mr. Bratton give him a questioning look and a smile. Mr. Bratton spoke as he entered the gate and started up the brick walkway. "Do not generally see you on Sundays; your mother likes to have the whole family home and together. I hope that you are not out without her permission."

"Oh no, sir. She knows 'at I have some thangs t' do. We was workin' all day yesterd'y on the farm, and we gonna be doin' the same ever' day 'is week while we on spring break. My daddy is buyin' the farm next to us, and he hired some fellas t' help us, and we got til next Sund'y to get both farms plowed and planted. Then, he is gonna keep one fella on t' work 'round the farm full time. So, I only got Sund'y afternoon to git thangs done this week and next. S' I wanted to ask y' a couple o' thangs real quick."

The man nodded. "I do not imagine you have had lunch yet, so let's go inside and make a couple of ham sandwiches for ourselves, and you can ask your questions over lunch." The man opened the door and led the way inside. Just inside the door, he took off his hat, placed it on a hat tree, and removed his jacket, which he carefully folded over the arm of a chair. He motioned for Cyril to do the same. Then, headed into the kitchen as he rolled up his shirt sleeves. The young man laid his jacket across the other arm of the chair, and he followed, also rolling up his sleeves, joining the man to wash their hands with water from the small hand pump poised over the soapstone sink. The man dried his hands, passed the towel to Cyril then motioned toward the ice box. "I'll get the bread out of the bread box and start slicing off some, and you can grab the leftover ham in the icebox."

The two of them worked together and soon sat at the kitchen table with ham sandwiches on well-buttered bread, sharing a pitcher of lemonade. "So, young man, what are your pressing questions?"

Cyril said, "Well, the first thing is about tutorin'. I remember you tellin' me 'at you was gonna start doin' tutoring here at your house in the afternoons for some of the fellas from the colored school because they only got one teacher for all the grades. I know 'at you talked to the colored teacher over there about which o' her fellas could go on t' college and how you can help 'em with afternoon tutorin'. I know 'at we got a new teacher at our school just for the high school students, but he said 'at he is there t' educate farmers an' store clerks, an' he don't expect any of us t' be able t' go on t' college. Told me 'at he knows 'at I'm set to inherit a farm, so I should stick to learnin' how t' be a good farmer. But I 'on't wanna be a farmer, you know that already about me. But if he ain't gonna prepare me for a college entrance examination, I got no idea how I can get into a college or law school. So, I was wonderin' if it would be a'ight for me t' come to those afternoon tutorin' sessions."

"Have you asked your parents about this? Some people will not approve."

"Yessir, I did. I talked to 'em both on Frid'y night after supper an' Mama wern't too happy, but she said t' let m' daddy decide, an' he said 'at it was fine with him an' anybody what's got a problem with it can talk t' him about it. An' 'en Mama made him sleep on the couch."

"She made him sleep on the couch for saying that you could attend tutoring sessions?"

"No, sir. She made him sleep on the couch behind some thangs what he done himself. He bought the farm next door, an' he decided to buy one o' them new Fords. And 'en he hired Jimmy Scolfield t' work for us – decided it all himself without talkin' t' her about any of it first.

He told her 'at he was sorry an' 'at he just ran with the hook without thinkin' 'bout it."

"So he slept on the couch for his own foolishness and not yours?"

"Yessir, I guess so."

"I see. Well, there are four young gentlemen who will be coming here in the afternoons for college preparatory tutoring sessions three days a week. We will cover material from various subjects and examine and discuss current events as reported in several periodicals. I am not sure you would be entirely comfortable in the group or with all the discussions."

"Not comfortable? Why not? Is it 'cause they's colored? That ain't gonna bother me none. Just yesterd'y Jimmy Scolfield brought his little brother Charlie an' one of 'is friends t' work with m' daddy an' me on the farm, an' at lunch time, Mama set 'em at the table with us and fed 'em. They was set to eat they lunch outside under a shade tree, but Mama told 'em they ain't gonna eat outside and they better sit down at the table. Nobody looked too comfortable with it at first, but after Daddy said grace and we started eatin', ever'body was just fine."

"That your father was fine with it is no surprise; he is a good man. But I am a bit surprised that your mother invited them inside, given the appearance. I would have thought that her concern would have been for what other people would think."

"Ah, you don't really know m' Mama, real good."

"No," the man said, and after a brief pause, he added, "I guess that I do not know her very well." Mr. Bratton then continued, "The nature of the conversations about current events often include subjects gleaned from Negro newspapers and periodicals. Things that might be new or feel uncomfortable to you."

"Iffin, it's somethin' I don't know anything about; I'll just sit and listen. But I need t' learn them other thangs though, t' git into college."

"I see. I cannot say yes just yet. The other gentlemen might not be comfortable with you being there. I will discuss it with them and see what they say. So, there are no promises; it will have to be up to those gentlemen to decide."

"Why would they feel uncomfortable with me bein' there?"

"We will have to see. But should they acquiesce, I will have one condition. The same condition that I insist on for everyone."

"Ok, anythang."

"English."

"Do what?"

The man spoke sternly. "You will speak English at all times. You are quite capable of managing your words, and you are careful how you speak around your mother. You will drop the constant use of local country dialect and vernacular, which you only do when she is absent. If you want people to see you as college material, if you want your teachers to see you as worthy of educating, stop trying to sound like you just fell off of the back of a hay wagon. I know that your mother has you reading books and that you know how to speak proper English. So, no more of this 'ain't a gonna' or this 'iffin' when you speak."

"Oh. I did not know that it bothered you. I'll try my best."

"Yes, it bothers me," the man scolded with a severe expression. "Some people only know their local vernacular. And some people have to intentionally speak in a way that makes them sound dumber than they are so that they can live in peace. But for you, it is a game – a game in which you mock no one but yourself. If you want to become educated and if you want to become an attorney, you need to sound educated and to sound like an attorney. When I was a boy, I had to watch my stepfather change how he spoke in different settings as if he were changing clothes. You have no need to wear other clothes, especially the suit of a circus clown. I went to college and became educated so that I would never have to switch how I speak, and my daughter would never have to do it, nor would her children. And here you are playing at it – and that playing disrespects those who cannot help but speak that way."

"I see," the young man said, looking down at the floor, not wholly understanding the anger in the voice of the man. "I am sorry."

The man looked at the chastened young man for a moment and then continued with a more gentle tone. "You are fine. I should not have scolded so harshly. Let's just say that it is a pet peeve of mine."

"Of my mother also."

"Yes, I am sure that it is. I will speak to the other young gentlemen and see if they are willing to accept your presence among them. One of them is Charles Scolfield, whom you know, so if you have a chance, you may wish to see if you can get him in your corner since, as the pastor's son, he carries some weight with the other young men."

"Charlie Scolfield? That is good. He will work with his brother at our place this whole spring break week. I will speak to him."

Mr. Bratton changed the subject. "I believe you said you had other questions for me."

"Well, really, only one, and it is about automobiles. Ford came out with a new kind o' Model T built like a wagon to work on farms last year."

The man nodded. "I have seen it advertised in the catalogs."

"So has my father. And since we have two farms to work now, he's going to get one to make the work easier. I was wondering if, since you have a Model T and all – well, maybe you might teach me how to drive it and look after it an' all of that sort of thing since my father has never driven one or even seen one up real close. That way, one of us would know how to drive it and take care of it properly. I know you regularly check the oil and the tires, and I was wondering if you could teach me those things."

"And when were you thinking about learning all of this?"

"Well, I hoped we could start this afternoon and maybe some next Sunday. My father wants to take a train into Birmingham Saturday week, buy that new automobile, and then drive it back."

"Back here from Birmingham – and he does not know how to drive?"

"Yessir, all the back here."

"What are you now, fifteen?"

"Yessir."

"You have been trying to convince me to teach you to drive since you were ten years old, and I guess that you have finally found a good reason."

Cyril smiled. "So, can we start today?"

The man gave the teenager a suspicious look. "I do not know about today. Today I planned to put in my kitchen garden behind the house."

Cyril got a look of grave concern on his face. "On no, that wouldn't do. Aren't you afraid that with you living so close to the church and all, the preacher might see you working in the garden – on a Sunday? I mean, you could end up being the subject of a Sunday sermon. Nobody wants to be the subject of a sermon – everybody in the church looking at you because they know it's you that he's talking about. No, that wouldn't do at all." He leaned back and shook his head. "Not at all."

"You should try that act while holding a skull," the man said.

"Pardon me?"

"Nevermind. So, to best avoid eternal damnation, I should work on the garden tomorrow and teach you to drive today?"

"I don't know about damnation, but I know that it can be damned embarrassing if the preacher starts talking about you in church." He paused for effect. "I know," the boy added with conviction and an eye roll.

"Well, if law school doesn't work, there is always the stage."

"Pardon me?"

The man shook his head. "Take off that white shirt. I'll not have you return to your mother with grease and oil on a white shirt. I will change clothes, and you can get these dishes cleaned up."

"Yessir," Cyril said as he shrugged the suspenders off his shoulders and reached for his top button, already heading toward the sink.

By mid-afternoon, Cyril had learned to check and fill the fuel and check the engine and tires. He had learned how to prime and start the engine, always with the left hand, and how to turn the key from the battery to magneto after starting. And he learned how to advance the spark with the lever on the left of the steering wheel and adjust the hand throttle on the right of the steering wheel, and how to adjust the choke to manage fuel usage. He was sitting behind the steering wheel with the engine idling and Mr. Bratton beside him.

"Just relax," said the man. "Push the brake pedal on the right so that it will not roll on you. Now pull the hand throttle down just a bit. And ease the handbrake forward until it is straight up. Now let the brake pedal off, press the middle pedal for reverse, to back up, and be ready to pull the throttle if the engine starts to sputter."

The automobile began to slowly inch backward, and Cyril got excited. "It's doin' it, it's doin' it."

"Ok, that is very good. And you didn't even stall the engine this time. So, let off the reverse pedal and press the brake pedal to stop moving." The automobile came to an abrupt stop. "Be careful with the brake. If you press it too fast, one side will start to catch before the other, pulling hard to that side."

"Sorry, I'll try to remember that."

"Now let's go forward. Ease off the brake again and press the clutch pedal on the left, and it will start forward in low gear. Remember that you can't turn the steering much if the machine is not moving. Now that it is moving, you can ease the throttle and pick up some speed."

"I'm doin' it. I'm drivin' it."

Another automobile was coming down the street, and as it neared, they saw that it was the sheriff. The auto passed them, slowing down, and they could see in their mirrors that the sheriff was turning around and heading back. Mr. Bratton spoke. "Ease over to the side of the road a bit and let off of the clutch and press the brake to come to a stop."

The automobile stopped on the side of the road as the sheriff pulled up and stopped behind them. Mr. Bratton said, "Pull the handbrake back and then turn the key to the off position straight up and down." The engine went still.

The sheriff got out of his automobile and saw the two looking at him in their mirrors. He motioned for the driver to get out and come over to him, and he yelled. "Ledbetter, git out and come hye."

Cyril climbed out, carefully maneuvering around the handbrake. He walked quickly back to where the sheriff was waiting. "Yessir, Sheriff?"

"Boy, what in the hell are you doin' out hye?"

"I'm learning to drive, Sheriff. My father is buying a new Model T, and I thought I would learn to drive one."

"And you just thought you would learn to drive that one?"

"Well, I don't know anyone else who will teach me."

"Five people have bought Model Ts in this town in the last two years, and all of them go to your church, so you could've asked one o' them t' learn y' how to drive. Hell, the man that sells them will teach you how to operate it before he turns you loose on the road with it. You ought' not be just ridin' around with that boy. What will folks think about you and your parents with you mixin' like this?"

"I don't know, Sheriff."

"You don't know? You have never seemed to know what is good for y' or how things is supposed t' be done. I don't have to explain 'is t' anybody but you, so I don't know if you are stupid or stubborn. You just never ever appeared to know who you are or how you are supposed to act. You go on ahead and learn how to drive that machine, but you better know that I am gonna be watchin' you. Gonna be watchin' you close. All this mixin' is gonna stop."

"Yessir."

"You can go for now, but I'm gonna be stoppin' by t' talk to your daddy about you."

"Yessir."

"I need to talk to him anyway about them new hands 'at he hired and make shore 'at 'ey know t' quit work early enough t' git back to where they supposed t' be before the sun is down. You may not know your place, but I'll damned shore make certain that they know theirs. Now you go on an' expect yo' daddy t' take this up wi' you later."

"Yessir." The young man turned and walked back to the automobile where Mr. Bratton was waiting. He climbed in and saw the Black man looking at him expectantly. "You and my mother are right; I never want to sound like that man again."

Eighteen: New Lessons to Learn

The Ledbetter family sat at the table having their Sunday supper. It had been a tough week, even with three extra workers around to help get the combined farms planted. Cyril got to know Charlie Scolfield much better and spoke to him about joining the three-time-a-week tutoring group. "So today, after church, I stopped by to speak with Mr. Bratton. He spoke to the other folks who attend his afternoon tutoring sessions, and they decided it would be alright for me to join them. So, we meet tomorrow after school, and then again on Wednesday and Friday. Are you sure things will be fine without me on those days, Daddy?"

William glanced at his son and nodded. "Yes, now that all the seed is in, Jimmy and I can take care of everything that needs doin' on those days, and you can pitch in on the other three workin' days each week. You go on and study hard with your group."

Ida asked. "Are you sure the other young men will be alright with you participating? The other boys are, after all, Negro and may be uncomfortable with you being there."

"Mama, I don't mind that they are colored. I just want to get prepared for college."

"I did not ask if you mind. I asked if perhaps the other young men may find your presence difficult. Have you considered that while Mr.

Bratton may feel one way about things, the others may feel differently?"

"Mr. Bratton told me that he would speak to them all, and he did. He told me that he let them discuss it on their own, and they took a vote, and three of them voted to let me join them."

The woman nodded and contemplated her plate for a moment. "So that means that one of them does not want you there, so that is something of which you must remain cognizant. I am still not convinced that this is the best idea."

"Mama, I don't understand how you think that. You have had three colored men sitting at this table every day this past week. I can't see how; if that did not bother you, my going to a class with some of them does bother you. I understand when the sheriff tells me he will not cotton any mixing because that is just the how man is. But I have seen you in the kitchen with colored women when Daddy was sick, and you were laughing and singing with them just like you do when the ladies from the church come over to quilt. I just do not understand you. Do you have a problem with colored folks or not? Or is it like Mr. Dawson, who only appears to have a problem with them when they are not around?"

He regretted the last sentence as it left his mouth. The look of shock on the silent face before him stunned him as much as his words had startled her. He felt a firm hand on his shoulder, followed by a painful squeeze. He watched his mother as she slowly stood, turned away from the table, and began walking out of the room.

"Boy, you have said enough," said William to his son. "Your mother does not have a problem with anyone. But there are folks in 'is town who do have a problem, and she is concerned about those people."

"I don't care what those people say," responded Cyril.

"It is not what people say that is a problem – it is what they sometimes do. Your mother just doesn't want folks tryin' to get into our business. You go on and put your plate in the kitchen and head to your room for the night. I will go and talk to your Mama."

Cyril picked up his plate and headed for the kitchen. "I gotta do something first." He put his plate in the sink and turned to see that the door to his parent's room was still open; he walked softly over and saw his mother standing turned away from the door and looking out of the window at the slowly fading day. "Mama, I am very sorry. I don't know what I was thinking." He stood there for a moment looking through the door, but she didn't turn. Ida took a slow deep breath after he finished, but that was the only sign that she had heard her son speak. "Good – goodnight Mama."

Later that week, Cyril stepped out of the forest trail behind the Second Baptist Church and quickly made his way to the Bratton house, heading to his first after-school study session. He knew that the other students were most likely already there since the Black school was on this side of town, and he had taken the longer route along the forest trails. He soon stood before the door, awaiting a response to his knock.

The door opened, and Mr. Bratton smiled, gave Cyril a quick up-and-down look, and nodded. "Last to arrive, but you have come the greatest distance. Come inside; you will find the other gentlemen in the kitchen. We start our sessions with a cup of tea and a chat to wake ourselves up before jumping into our afternoon work." Though Cyril knew the way well, the man led the way to the kitchen. "Gentleman, this is Mr. Ledbetter, Cyril Ledbetter, the young man we recently discussed joining our sessions."

Cyril stepped into the kitchen to see four young brown faces looking at him. One face he knew was that of Charlie Scolfield, and the other three faces seemed vaguely familiar but without names attached to them. All four of the young men at the table stood as he entered. Cyril was immediately uncomfortable as he realized he was the only one wearing overalls and boots. He was dressed like a farmer, while the other gentlemen had dressed like college students. He suddenly felt very out of place as he noticed one of the other young men smirk in his direction. "Mr. Bratton has a garden out back if you are here for work," the smirking young man said. Cyril heard Charlie clear his throat as a warning to the speaker.

"I apologize," said Cyril. "I just wore my usual clothes for school – I didn't realize."

"Yes," Mr. Bratton said. "My fault entirely. I should have told you that it is our custom to dress as if we are attending a college class for these sessions. No harm, and next time you will know." The man motioned toward Charlie Scolfield. "I believe you know Charles Scolfield, and these other gentlemen are Emery Dawson, Isaac Jones, and Peter Styles. I do believe that you know several of their parents.

"Hello, it is nice to meet you all," Cyril said uncomfortably as he reached to shake hands with each of the other young men.

Mr. Bratton picked up a cup from the table and replaced it with a clean cup into which he began to pour tea. "Mr. Ledbetter, take this empty chair at the table here, and you gentlemen, sit and get to know one another while I prepare a few things in the next room."

Cyril sat quietly and listened to the other young men as they chatted. After a few minutes, Charlie included Cyril in the conversation, to his relief. "Mr. Ledbetter lives with his parents on a farm north of town. How is Mrs. Ledbetter doing?"

After a few minutes of small talk, Cyril noticed the other young men glancing expectantly at him. He was unsure what was happening until Charlie caught his eye and nodded slightly down at his cup. Cyril then noticed that his was the only cup still containing any tea and realized that the other young men were waiting for him to finish. Cyril picked up his cup and quickly drained it, and as he sat it back down, the other young men stood and headed for the next room. Cyril followed as they walked into the study where Mr. Bratton was waiting, with four empty chairs crowding the room.

"Very good. Everyone have a seat. In our last meeting before the break, we decided to read some Edgar Allen Poe – or, more precisely, his science writing. Mr. Poe is widely known as a poet, and poetry certainly was an avocation of his, but his primary vocation was as a scientist and science writer. He produced a well-known textbook about seashells and wrote a highly regarded and quite comprehensive cosmology. So what are your impressions of his writing?"

After a half hour or so of this conversation in which Cyril could not participate, Mr. Bratton decided it was time to move on to the next topic of discussion. "Mr. Jones, I believe you were going to find a law you wanted to discuss."

"Thank you, sir," said Isaac Jones. "Today, I would like to discuss poll taxes." Isaac proceeded to explain the poll taxes in American history, emphasizing the more recently instituted poll taxes in several southern states, after his brief outline of the more general history.

"Wonderful, thank you, Mr. Jones, that was very informative," said Mr. Bratton. "Does anyone have any other thoughts or discussion on the subject?"

"Well, it is clear that most of these laws were instituted to take away the right of Negros to participate in elections," said Peter Styles.

Finally, Cyril thought this was a discussion in which he could participate. "I do not understand how you can say that. If it is a tax, it applies to everyone, so it does not target any particular race. If anything, it will stop poor people from voting."

"Not so," said Emery Dawson. "The poll tax in Alabama has only been in place for twenty-five years. These laws have grandfather clauses meaning that if your ancestor could vote before the Civil War, you do not have to pay the tax."

Peter Styles said, "So realistically, when you go to vote for the first time, they will take one look at you, and because you look like your grandfather could vote, they hand you a ballot, but when I go, they will hand me a bill."

184

"Oh, I did not know that," Cyril said.

"You don't have to know that," said Peter Styles.

"Alright, gentlemen," said Mr. Bratton. "Shall we move on? Mr. Styles, I believe it was your turn to find a current events topic for discussion."

Peter Styles nodded and said, "Thank you, Mr. Bratton. I have found an interesting article written by Marcus Garvey."

Most of the afternoon passed in this way, with Cyril constantly feeling like he was on the hot seat. They finished the session in the kitchen, working together for the last hour on their homework. And while the conversation at the table during this time had no tension, Cyril noticed that the homework the other young men had from their teacher was more detailed and challenging than the work he had been given. He ended up learning some things about more advanced mathematics.

Mr. Bratton said, "That will be enough for today, gentlemen. So, our next meeting will be on Wednesday, a philosophy and history day, so Mr. Jones, I hope you have an Aurelius passage. Mr. Scolfield, you were supposed to report to us about the Spanish Colonial history of some US states. And for our next Monday session, Mr. Jones, please have something from the law books ready for discussion. And Mr. Ledbetter, would you please find a current events article to discuss?

Cyril watched as the others shook hands with Mr. Bratton and departed, leaving Charlie and Cyril alone with Mr. Bratton. Charlie looked at Cyril and said, "They are going to have to get used to having you here, so they are going to do that for a while."

Cyril nodded and said, "Thank you."

Charlie nodded toward Cyril. "And maybe don't wear overalls and boots Wednesday."

Cyril started to turn red. "Oh, I'm not. I will be here, dressed for church."

"Good," Charlie said. "Bye until Wednesday." With that, the young man reached out his hand. Cyril shook it and watched as the young man turned and thanked Mr. Bratton and shook his hand and left.

After the door closed, Cyril looked at Mr. Bratton and asked, "Are you sure that they voted to let me join?"

"Let us just say that Charles Scolfield can be very convincing when he wants to be, and when that fails, he may twist an arm or two."

"All of the things that we talked about today – well, that they talked about today." Cyril shook his head. "I just don't know what I am supposed to think or what maybe they want me to think."

"The goal in this group, similar to college, is not about what one thinks. It is about how one thinks. Today introduced you to a radically different perspective on some issues. It will take some time for your mind to acclimate to a setting where so many things you think or assume are being challenged by how you are learning to think and rethink things."

Later, Cyril sat at the table quietly, eating his supper and thinking about the day's events.

"How was your first day with the tutoring group, Cyril?" Asked William.

"Kind of confusing, if I am honest. And I wish that I had known not to show up wearing overalls."

"What is wrong with your overalls?"

"Nothing is wrong with them. Just since it is for college preparation, the others dressed as if it were a college class – or church."

Ida said, "Well then, you can wear your church clothes on Wednesday."

"I don't know about Wednesday," Cyril remarked.

"What do you mean, son?" Asked William.

"That is the confusing part. They voted to have me join them, but I am not sure that everyone wants me as part of the study group. Maybe Mama is right, and they are uncomfortable with me being there. I know I was not as comfortable as I thought I would be. And their teacher gives them some pretty hard work to do. It was embarrassing for them to see what our teacher assigned us. And when we talked about current events, it was about stuff I had never heard of and came from an article in a Negro newspaper. And we talked about poll taxes. I did not even know that we had a poll tax or that it really only applies to colored folks. I don't know. Maybe I should not go back. I don't think that they all want me there. Maybe I should just leave them to it. I don't know what to think about it all – I am not even sure I know how to think about it all."

William nodded his understanding. "It does sound to be confusing. When I would get like this around your age, Auntie Jess would tell me to go out to the front room and just sit with it for a while and study on it. Seems to me that you should avoid making any decisions while you are confused."

"Yessir."

"So, the sheriff tells me you have been learning to drive from Mr. Bratton. How is that going?" Asked William.

Ida looked sharply at Cyril but didn't say anything.

"Now that, I understand," Cyril said. "He has taught me about taking care of it and maintaining the motor and mechanical details. I can crank it and drive it in reverse and both gears going forward. I stalled the engine several times last Sunday, but yesterday afternoon we drove around for a good while with no problems."

William said, "So many folks have bought themselves new automobiles lately that Brother Gerald Dawson down at the store has started carrying spare parts and such for 'em. And he says he is putting in a fuel pump so folks can fuel up at the store. I reckon that you knowing how to drive might come in handy with us getting a new Ford."

Ida finally spoke. "And when did you see the sheriff?"

William answered, "He came by during the week to speak to me over at the Moore place. Wanted to ask me about who I had hired and let me know that he has seen Cyril driving with Mr. Bratton."

"I am sure he had an opinion about it," said Ida.

William nodded. "He always does. And he always tells me his opinion, and I always thank him for his concern and tell him that I will take care of it."

"So it is settled then," said Ida. "This Saturday, the two of you can go to Birmingham to get your new automobile. And while you are there, you can pick up a few things for me – I will send a list. And you should pick up some new clothes for your college preparation afternoons. I have let your church pants down as far as they will go."

"Do you not want to help me pick out the new automobile, my dear?" Asked William.

"And then spend the better part of the day rattling down these Alabama red clay roads to get home covered in dust? No, thank you. A father and son outing will be just what you two need. And the quiet will be just the thing that I need. And besides, Cyril can help you to drive this machine back home."

Cyril was sitting in the parlor holding his book long after darkness came and long after his parents retired. It was a moonless night that was falling, and so the darkness was profound. He was thinking about the events of the day at the tutoring session and debating with himself over whether or not he should continue. It was still spring, so the nights were chilly enough that the windows were closed, and the room was silent.

He came quietly awake, still sitting in the corner of the settee propped against one of the wings and the arm. The darkness was heavy on him, as if he floated in ink. The only sound he could hear was the clock ticking on the mantel. He blinked to feel if his eyes were actually open. He glanced down to where he thought that his hand was resting on the arm of the settee – but it was so dark he could not see his own body. He had been sitting there without moving for so long that he couldn't feel exactly where his arms and legs were. He considered wiggling his fingers and toes and moving around to assure himself that he was still in a body and not just floating somewhere in a starless night, but something about the floating sensation appealed to him, so he just sat there relaxed. He thought to himself, 'This must be how a shadow feels in the night, no edges between itself and the darkness. It just wonders; who am I – what am I – where am I – where is here? Maybe it's not so bad to be a shadow after all.'

Cyril woke to the sound of his mother moving around in the kitchen. The darkness had lightened to become a grayness all around him. He could see his body again. And he could hear his mother humming and noticed the smells floating out of the kitchen, and then he was sure that he knew where he was and that he was back to being somebody again.

Nineteen: Training Day

It was a very early Saturday morning – the Saturday when the Ledbetters would become the proud owners of an automobile. Cyril stood with his father, waiting on the station's platform as the train was taking on water for the steam engine's boiler.

"Looks like she is just about topped off and ready to roll," said William. "She will make a short whistle-stop in every town between here and Birmingham, but she will only need to top off two times before we get there. Those are the only towns where she will sit still long enough to get off the train for a bit to walk around the platform. Not that we need to get off for anything."

"All aboard for Birmingham and all points north," came the conductor's voice.

The Ledbetter men moved toward the train but held back not to crowd other folks. "You sure know a lot about trains Daddy."

"I worked for a railroad company for a short bit when I was a young man – before I met y' Mama."

Most other folks had brought bags, the porters had already loaded these, and William and Cyril made their way to a short line of people getting onto one of the forward cars. The smiling dark brown face of a porter in a sharp railway uniform appeared next to the line of people.

He addressed William. "Good day to y', sir. Is there anything with which I can help you, sir? Any bags?"

"No, thank you. We're traveling light today as we'll be coming back this evenin'."

"This evenin', sir? Well, the last train out of Birmingham comin' this way will steam out right at four-thirty. You don't wanna miss 'at one, or you will have to wait for the red eye tomorrow mornin', and we don't run too many trains on Sunday."

"That's fine; we're going in to buy a new automobile and driving it back here, so we won't be takin' a train back."

"New automobile? Yes, sir. That will be nice."

"You can tell me one thing, though."

"Yes, sir. What do y' wanna know?"

"Well, I told my wife not to pack us a lunch because my favorite part of train travel is buying lunch at the stations. Where is the best lunch on this line lately?"

"Well, sir, at our ten o'clock stop, Miss Emily is going to be on the platform with her pies. I recommend the pecan pie there. But then, you hold on to that if you can resist until our eleven-o-five stop, our last top-off before Birmingham, so you'll have plenty of time. Now that is where you will want t' get your lunch. The ladies will have everything a man could want for lunch right on the platform. O' course, a man is going to want the fried chicken. And since we will be there for a little while, there might be a boy tippin' a pail in the area – but with prohibition and all, he ain't always there."

"Thank you," William said, handing the man a coin. "Ten o'clock, I will definitely ask Miss Emily for a couple of pieces of pie and lunch at eleven, and I'll pass on the pail; that's a bit early in the day for me."

"Thank you, sir; y'all have a good day." The man turned and headed toward the rear of the train.

William spoke to his son as they climbed on the train and looked for a good seat. "Always ask the porters about anything that you want to know. They know the best food and, evidently, where the best homemade beer is."

"Yessir." Cyril looked around at all of the people in the car as the train lurched into motion. "There sure are a lot of folks on the train early this morning."

"Yes, there are. This train starts down in Mobile very early in the mornin', so most of these folks started their trip there or in Pensacola."

A smallish, wiry white man in a uniform who looked to be about fifty years old entered the front of the train car and started to slowly work his way down the aisle, greeting everyone with a smile and nod or with a tip of the hat to the ladies and an occasional word. William leaned over to Cyril and whispered, "That there is the conductor; he is like a ship captain, but for a train. That conductor is named Samuel Olmstead. Sit quiet and see if he remembers me."

The conductor soon reached the row of seats where Cyril and his father sat. "William? William Ledbetter?" The man stuck out his hand.

"Good to see y', Sam," said William taking the offered hand.

"When you was leavin', you did say that you were to come down this a way t' take care of the family farm. How is that goin' for y' anyway?"

"The farm's doin' real good, Sam. Looks like you made it all the way up to conductor now.

"Yeah, I been condcutin' full time now for about ten years, but most o' that was on the Atlanta line. Now, who is this good-lookin' young man here?"

"This is my son Cyril."

"Cyril, is it? Well, Cyril, it's nice to meet you." The man stuck out his hand again.

"Thank you, sir; it is nice to meet you too," Cyril said as they shook hands.

"Your father worked wi' me on the railroad fo' a few years when he was not much older 'an you. Boy, he was a handful sometimes, too, not a word of a lie. Always sneakin' off to places 'at he shouldn't o' been, and with folks he should o' known better than t' be around. He was one fo' the ladies too – and not always the right ladies neither. And now, mind y' that was back before prohibition. The stories 'at I could tell you."

"Or you could maybe not," said William. "Half of 'em 'ill be made up, and the other half embellished too much."

"Hahaha," the conductor laughed. "There was that one girl in Memphis that you always said you was gonna marry." He looked at Cyril. "He never would bring her by t' meet any of us at the train yard. We always figured that she was either too pretty or too plain for him t' want us t' see her." He turned back to William. "Did you end up marryin' that one like you said?"

"I did," answered William. "And she was too pretty for y'all. Didn't want y'all to look at yo' own girls an' have t' cry."

The man laughed again. "There is a lot to be said for a plain woman; I been married to one for twenty-five years and never had cause t' complain even once."

"But has she had cause to complain?" Asked William.

"Eh-ve-ry day," said the man with a smile. "A'ight William, it was good t' see y' and nice to meet yo' son, but I got a train t' run." The man continued down the aisle.

William called back over his shoulder. "And Samuel, try not to get the train lost this time."

There was another explosion of laughter from the man.

Cyril looked at his father. "How can a train get lost?"

"You'd wonder, but Samuel is special like that."

The rest of the trip on the train was uneventful – and the pie and chicken for lunch were delicious. Shortly after noon, the train rolled to a stop at the station in Birmingham, and people started filing off.

"Let's tend to that list that your Mama gave y' first. There is a Woolworth Five and Dime not too far from here, and we can get most everything on it there, I imagine. And you can get yourself some new clothes for your study sessions. How has that been going anyway? I know that Monday was a rough start." The man began to walk, and Cyril hurried to catch up.

"Well, Wednesday was some better when I showed up wearing decent clothes and didn't look like the hired help any more. And Friday was pretty good. I still don't think one of them is too happy to have me there, but I think he is getting used to it anyway. I'm glad I didn't quit after Monday like I was thinking about doing – we are learning some interesting stuff. And a whole lot of new stuff about math – stuff that I have never seen."

"That's good. This tutoring is going to be a good thing for you." The man looked around and then continued. "Well, you have never been anywhere as big as Birmingham, so what do you think?

Cyril stopped and looked around and was stunned by the size and scope of the buildings and the sheer number of folks going about their business. And he couldn't believe the number of automobiles zooming by, and even a few trucks and some delivery vans – the overwhelming number of the machines were Model Ts. Cyril gave a long whistle. "This is amazing, so many folks, stores, and machines. I could live here and be happy. They have got everything in these shop windows."

"That's true. There isn't anything that you could want that you can't get in Birmingham. And up there is the Woolworth's. Git out yo' Mama's list." The man stepped up his speed, and Cyril followed.

In less than an hour, they stepped back onto the sidewalk carrying the parcels of new clothes and everything on the list. And one bolt of cloth tucked under William's arm. "This cloth here ain't available in Brother Dawson's store, and I think yo' Mama will like it as a surprise. And I remember a candy store that makes these nice chocolates. We

194

can also stop by there and pick up a box for her; they are the best chocolates in Birmingham. But it does mean that we gotta go down one o' these side streets where all o' the colored shops are – a woman from Tennessee owns the store. But it's the best chocolate in Alabama. It reminds her of the ones she liked when she was a girl"

Cyril spied a newsstand. "Daddy, Mr. Bratton said that they have a lot of newspapers here at the stands that you can't get back home – from places like New York, Boston, and Chicago. Can we stop and get some city papers to use in the afternoons for current events?"

"Lead the way."

Cyril stepped out into the street to cross it and almost had his leg torn off by a passing truck as he felt the wind off of it.

"Careful, boy! You don't want t' git hit by one of those. You better look."

"Yessir." Cyril led the way across a bit more carefully. He stopped before a newsstand and was shocked at all the papers. There were papers from all over, just as he was told there would be.

"We got it all," said the Black man working at the newsstand. He was a thin light-skinned older man who sat on a bar stool, and as he stood, Cyril noticed that he leaned heavily on a cane.

"I need to get some papers for my class back home to use for current events. We live down in Bratton, and all we get is the local paper and the Birmingham paper on the train. I was thinking about some city papers. Maybe Boston, New York, and Chicago."

"Well, now. Let me see. I got the Boston Globe, Chicago Tribune, and The New York Times last Sunday and yesterday. I got the London Times from last week. I got one from Paris from last week, but it's in French. And you might wanna git an Atlanta Constitution which just come in on th' train."

William said, "We'll take the Sunday and yesterday editions from Chicago, Boston, New York, and Sunday and today from Atlanta. And the London Times too. "That should give ' em plenty to study. Can you tie all of them into one bundle for us?"

"Yes, sir." the newsman said.

Cyril looked puzzled. "There are two others I wanted to pick up copies of for some of the other fellas and the teacher – but I don't see them. The Chicago Defender and Negro World, the Marcus Garvey paper – do you have them? My teacher likes the Defender, and my friend likes reading the other one."

The man stopped and gave Cyril a speculative look. "Those are colored papers."

"So are the gentlemen that I am getting them for."

"Well, the man that owns this stand, he don't carry any colored papers, not much call for 'em in this neighborhood. My grandson Harold is tendin' the stand that I own, and we got those papers there. But you will have to go a little way down that street over there to get to where that stand is."

"Would that be down near The Barret Chocolatier," asked William. "Best chocolate in Alabama."

The man looked a bit confused. "Yes, sir, the same street, just one block further down. And how do you know about Barrets' chocolate?"

William handed the man some money. "Excellent, I wanted to get some chocolate for my wife. I used to get Barrets' chocolate from the original shop in Memphis. One of the family moved here and opened this shop, and her sister opened one in Atlanta. And my wife grew up with Barrets' chocolate, an' she hasn't had it in a while. I figure Birmingham is closer than Memphis or Atlanta. Besides that, it makes a good peace offering."

The man handed some change back to William, laughing. "That it does; I have used it to establish a treaty more than once myself. Y'all have a good day, sir."

"I have another question for you, sir," said Cyril looking at the man as he sat back down.

The man gave Cyril a quizzical look. "What would that be?"

"Why do you work a stand here if you own a stand of your own."

"Well, sir, years ago, I got hurt, and the man that owns this stand gave me a job. Now this is a prime location, and this stand makes good money, so he pays me well. Eventually, I was able to open my own stand. It is some smaller, but it makes pretty good too. But by keepin' this job here and havin' my grandson tend the other stand, we can do pretty well."

"I see; thank you for the papers. You have a good day too, sir." Cyril turned and headed toward the street the man had pointed out.

William fell in beside his son. "Parcels and papers and one more shop and another news-stand to get to, we gonna be loaded down like a pair o' mules before we even get to the Ford place. We better step it up if we want to get back to Bratton before sundown."

"They put lights on the front of those automobiles to light up the road at night."

"Oh, well, I guess that's good. But I still don't wanna be gettin' home too awfully late anyways."

Forty-five minutes later, after having picked up two more papers and a box of chocolates, the Ledbetters stepped onto a lot full of new automobiles and could see a smiling man heading their way. The man looked a little too slick and polished and walked just a little too fast. "They are beautiful machines, aren't they?" The man said in a loud voice, just a little too quickly. "How're y'all doing today?"

"We doin' pretty good," said William. "Name's William Ledbetter and this is my son Cyril, and we here to see about one of them new Fords y'all got for farmers. We got a large farm down Bratton way, and I think we outgrowin' that old wagon."

"Well, Mr. Ledbetter, y'all come to the right place – we got 'em. Name's Toby Smith; nice to meet you. Let's go over here to the office so you can put your parcels down, and I can shake yo' hand an' show you some machines."

Two minutes later, the three stood in front of four trucks. The man was still speaking, just a bit too loud and fast. "These three here, they just come in, so they brand new – and that'n on the end there is from last year. A farmer bought it, and then he was kilt by a snappin' fence wire, so his wife sold the farm and had me come t' git this one back from her since she don't need it. Now, we got four colors, all of 'em black. Ha ha ha." The man laughed a bit too hard. "Now, we gonna throw in a spare tire and a fuel can. Have y' ever driven an automobile before? If not, I will walk you through everything on crankin' it, drivin' it, and ckeckin' the oil and the fuel – everything you gonna need to know."

Cyril said, "My friend has a Model T that I have been driving around town, and he showed me all that stuff."

The man appraised Cyril. "That's good. Prob'ly a couple o' years old, though, so I'll show y' where everything is on this one since they move things around a little bit from year to year. But if you already know how to drive, this won't take long at all. And then, y'all can go down the street here and register it with the state – and then, y'all be good to head out to wherever y'all want t' go."

An hour later, Cyril was driving the machine through Birmingham. They had already finished the process of buying and registering the automobile. Cyril was very tense since he had only driven on those country roads and was suddenly surrounded by moving vehicles, wagons, and carriages; there were pedestrians and workers with wheelbarrows and pushcarts all using the same roads. There were police officers directing everything at some of the larger intersections, but at others, it was a game of catch as catch can. Cyril could feel the tension from his father sitting in the seat right beside him. The automobile was in low gear the whole time. About twenty minutes later, they had left the outskirts of Birmingham and were on a more open road heading south as Cyril was finally able to push the handbrake forward, ease off of the clutch, and let her slide into high gear. He could feel his father relaxing beside him since there was less traffic, and he was getting used to the moving machine. "It's all right, Daddy; everyone stalls the engine the first few times they try to drive."

"Was still embarrassin'. I was plannin' on drivin' out of there in my brand new Ford. I guess that it is good that Mr. Bratton taught you to drive."

"I will tell you what, Daddy, after we get a little bit further out of town, I will pull over to the side, and we can switch, and you can take a couple more tries until you got it."

"That'd be good. I would like to be able to drive it myself before Jimmy gets t' the farm Monday mornin' and you are in school, so we won't have t' just look at the machine and hitch a damn mule to that old wagon anyway."

"You will be an expert at it by Monday, Daddy. I bet that you will be able to drive us to church in it tomorrow."

"That'd be nice. You sure have been careful with your words this past week or so. You sound like your mother is sitting right next to you. She has a good education, growing up where she did in the city. And I try not to sound like a bumpkin myself when she is around, but you are pretty much watchin' yourself the whole time now."

"It was like with the overalls."

"Do what?"

"When I showed up for that first afternoon session after school, looking like I was there to do the gardening, I felt out of place with the other gentlemen being all so well dressed. I have to make sure that I look and sound like college material and like a lawyer."

As he drove along, Cyril noticed that the sun had moved off to the west, and the shadow of the truck was running along on the red clay road on his left side, undulating back and forth as it passed across different bushes and fences. Eventually, he pulled off to the side, and William only needed a couple more tries before he had the truck cruising along, heading south.

Twenty: Memory Lane

On Monday, Cyril had tutoring at Mr. Bratton's house again, and he was excited to tell them all about his trip to Birmingham and the new automobile. Cyril shared the newspapers he had picked up with his classmates and Mr. Bratton, and they spent a good portion of the tutoring session that day combing through the articles within the papers. But soon enough, it was getting closer to the last train whistle of the day, and the boys had to head home for supper.

"I will see you later, Cyril. Have a good evening Mr. Bratton," said Charlie Scolfield as he pulled the door closed behind him.

"Bye, Charlie," answered Cyril.

"We will see you Wednesday, Charles," added Mr. Bratton.

Once again, Cyril was the last to leave after the study session. So, he and Mr. Bratton were alone in the house as the evening approached. "It was nice of your father and you to pick up all those papers while you were in Birmingham," said Mr. Bratton.

"Had to go to two different newsstands to get all of them. But I thought that Peter Styles would appreciate that Garvey paper."

"Young Mr. Styles is a good man. I think that you and he may become friends still yet."

"I do not know that I can agree with you on that one, Mr. Bratton. He was happy enough that I brought that paper to him, and he thanked me politely enough, but the way he asked me if I had bothered to read any of it was a bit sharp."

"Let me ask you this, then. Did you consider reading anything from any of the Negro papers?"

"No, sir, I did not. I assumed they were not written for me, so I did not consider it."

"So then, does that mean that the other papers are for white folks only? Do you think that Negros read them?"

"Those papers are for everyone; they are just the news. Not for just white folks," answered Cyril.

"Are they really for everyone? To be sure, they differ from the Negro papers in as much as Negro papers do discuss issues of race and issues of particular interest to Negros. And therein lies the question. Those other papers are just tacitly for everyone. Still, if you look at them, the things considered news generally do not include subject matter particular to Negros or Indians. Newspapers are just as segregated as are schools and churches. And that segregation is not loud; it does not announce itself so much as it is just the current that flows under what seems to be still waters. Certainly, there are a few loud voices here and there and a few explosions of anger occasionally. But really, it is just day in and day out the way that we live. Who gets off of the sidewalk for whom. Who is allowed to look a peace officer in the eye. Who has to order their boxed lunch from the kitchen door around the back, and who can go inside and sit down to be served. A thousand unspoken rules that we just know and which are never posted as signs or written into the laws."

Cyril stood and listened and nodded. "I do not know what to say to that. I guess that I have just not seen it."

Mr. Bratton smiled. "There is not anything for you to say to it. And that is fine. Perhaps just be open to hearing what others say about it, because it is all around you – it is all around us. We swim in it like fish, most of us just moving with the current rather than fighting it."

"I feel like a fish that did not know that he was wet – that did not know that there is water all around."

"Most fish do not notice the water since it is their whole world. But there are fish like young Peter there who do notice – he notices every drop of the water and might feel like he is drowning in it, and so he leaps into the air occasionally."

"I am going to have to think about this for a bit. I do know one thing; that new high school teacher did not appreciate me having those papers with me this morning."

"Oh?"

"Well, I come here immediately after school, so I brought the papers with me to school, and he asked about them. He told me they were a waste of paper and that he had half a mind to take them from me for even bringing them into the schoolhouse. Then, he asked me about my new clothes and coming to school dressed for Sunday when I am just a farmer. I told him that I was attending after-school college preparatory tutoring sessions. He wanted to know why he had not heard about these sessions and told him it was organized by the teacher at the colored school, and he just laughed. Then, he told me that there are more than enough smart boys in the city to fill the colleges, so they do not need hayseeds."

"I see," said Mr Bratton. "That must have stung a bit."

"He does not know me. He refuses to teach me anything to prepare for college and then picks at me for not knowing what I would need for college. He took one look at me on the first day and decided who I am and what I can do, and now, that is all that he knows or cares to know about me. Well, I am done with it. I don't want to talk about it anymore. We should discuss something more pleasant – maybe tell me more about your wife."

The man seemed a bit surprised by the sudden change in subject. "Alright, we can talk about her for a bit, but it is getting late in the day, so you might want to start heading home before too much longer."

"Ok, just for a little bit. I just need to hear something nice for a while, and I like the way you speak about her."

The man went over to the shelf, took down a leather-bound volume, and headed over to sit on a settee. "I have an album here with photos we had made over the years." Cyril sat beside the man, sharing the album on their laps. "Here she is around the time when I met her. Her family owned a candy store in Memphis – that specialized in chocolate. You can see it there behind her. Her father had a photographer come out to take a photo of the whole family in front of the shop – her and her parents and her brother and three sisters. I paid the man to take an exposure of just her. I ate cornbread and molasses for nearly a week to pay for that photo, and it was worth every penny and stomach growl."

"Looks like it was right after noontime."

"Yes, it was just after lunch, actually. How did you know?"

"Only a little bit of a shadow behind her. He waited for the sun to light her face and the sign on the shop."

"He said that he was waiting for the light to be right," said Mr. Bratton. "You do notice many details."

"There is a shop just like it in Birmingham. My father and I stopped there on Saturday to get some chocolates for my mother – kind of a peace offering. He said that it was her favorite. And it must be because she just looked at the box for a long time and shook her head at him – I think it worked for him, though. I did try one piece of the chocolate while we were there. It was so good."

"So his plan worked then; that's good," the man said with a slight chuckle. "That chocolate has saved a lot of men from wrathful women. I remember when our daughter was a little girl, and she loved visiting that shop to see her grandparents – and test the chocolate. If you went to the shop in Birmingham, that one was owned by one of her sisters who went into the family business."

"My father said he used to go to the shop in Memphis. I wonder if he ever saw your wife there. Or maybe even your daughter."

The man looked at Cyril and smiled. "He probably did." The man pointed to another photograph. "And here she is on our wedding day. She was so beautiful that it hurt to breathe when I looked down that aisle at the church. I had trouble hearing the minister because my heart was pounding in my ears."

"She was beautiful. You have told me so much about her that when I look at these pictures, she just looks like I know her from somewhere – like she is somehow familiar."

"She was like that; everyone just seemed to take to her right away. When I met her, I tried to pretend I was unimpressed. So a few days later, I dropped into the candy store when I knew she would be there, and I asked her for help picking out some chocolates for another girl, which I can assure you is not the best way to start trying to get to know a woman. Spent too much on that box of chocolates for a young fool just out of college."

"Did the other girl like the chocolates at least?"

"There was not another girl. But at least that week, I had chocolate for dessert after my cornbread and molasses."

"You ate a lot of cornbread and molasses trying to get to know her, didn't you?"

"That I did, but I did have buttermilk with the cornbread occasionally," he said with another chuckle. "I would have starved to death except that every family in the church with a daughter around my age invited me home for Sunday dinner – every family but hers. Her mother did not think too highly of me having so many Sunday dinners with different families. She thought that I was a bit too free with the hearts of the young ladies – and really, I was just tired of cornbread and hungry."

"Why so much cornbread?"

"It did not cost much, and I could buy a whole cornbread and get eight meals out of it. See, I only had my first job clerking for a bank, and I had rented a room with no cooking stove and was trying to save for law school. Here is a photograph of her just before our little girl was born."

"How did you get to know her if her mother didn't like you?"

"I went to law school. And we started writing letters to one another. And her mother thought that with me being so far away and unable to see her in person, it would be fine. That way, she had a pretense to keep the other local boys away from her house and her daughter. She was not a trusting woman where her daughters were concerned. And then, they sent her to Atlanta for school, so she was very far away from me, so letters were all we had." The man turned the page. "Here are some pictures of my daughter when she was small. She was about ten years old here."

"She sure favors her mother a lot."

"Yes, she does take after her mother – always did."

"And all of that just from writing letters?"

"Yes, we even kept writing letters our entire time together. Some days I would have a few minutes to spare in the office and would write a short letter and post it to her. We lived three city blocks from my office, and it would take two days to get there. And sometimes, the postman would leave a letter from her sitting on my desk. I had just seen her when I went home for lunch, but I was still excited to cut into the envelope to see what she had written. And if I went away for a conference or something, she would write a letter a few days before I even left and then mail it to the hotel so that it would be waiting for me when I arrived. The last one like that was at a conference in Chicago. I had a long train trip, which was not pleasant. I got to the hotel where I was staying, and a letter was sitting in my room. I closed my eyes and pretended she was standing close. I could smell her perfume on the paper. Then, I answered with my own letter and dropped it off at the front desk to post for me the next day. A couple of days later, I got off the train in Memphis and got home to find out she had taken sick. And she passed the next day in my arms. That letter from Chicago arrived for her a couple of days later."

The man paused for a few moments before he quietly continued. "She wrote letters to everyone. Stayed in touch with all of her friends from school that way. For months, letters would come for her from people who had not been informed. I had to answer every one of those letters with the sad news. Maybe one or two letters each week. That was when I stopped going to church. Instead I went down to sit beside her stone and read the letters to her. After the letters stopped, I would sit and read a few chapters from one of her favorite books."

They sat in silence for a few minutes until Cyril pointed at the album and quietly spoke. What about the next page?" He was trying to move his friend back to more pleasant memories.

"Oh, those are just photographs of my daughter as a teenager."

"I want to see those," Cyril said.

The man looked at Cyril briefly and slowly closed the album. "It is getting late. It will be dark soon, so you best head home."

Cyril decided that his usual trails would take too long, so he would just cross the tracks on the main street, just this one time. As he neared the station, he saw an automobile parked about ten yards on the other side of the tracks, and he saw the familiar hulking figure of the sheriff standing in front of it, leaning back against the machine. Cyril thought about possibly ducking around the station and going behind everything to avoid the sheriff, but he saw the sheriff look in his direction and shake his head in disgust, so he knew it was too late to avoid the man. Cyril noticed a tall, dark-skinned figure coming from the opposite direction. It was about forty-five minutes since the sundown whistle had sounded, so the approaching figure was hurrying along. The figure drew closer, and Cyril recognized him as Jimmy Scolfield.

The sheriff raised his hand and waved Jimmy over, and shouted. "Com'ere boy, we need t' talk."

Cyril heard the man yell and saw Jimmy drop his head and walk toward the sheriff. Cyril intended to walk by the pair but heard the sheriff shout again. "Ledbetter, get over hye; you next on my list."

The sheriff turned back to Jimmy. "Boy, I know you been workin' out past the north side o' town on the Ledbetter farm. And I know it's a good walk for you t' git home ever' evenin'. But you gonna have t' tell that man that you gotta go on time. That whistle at the station blew nearly an hour ago, an' hye you are, still on the north side o' them tracks."

"I'm sorry, Sheriff, I was walking this way and left in plenty of time. But the widow Moore called for help as I was passing by. She had fallen and was having trouble getting back up, so I carried her in and got her settled in her bed, and then I stopped to tell Dr. Harrison that she needs to see him right away because she was some skinned up."

"Widow Moore, is it? A'ight this time, but you better start makin' shore 'at you git back across them tracks in plenty o' time. You go on home now."

"Yes, sir," Jimmy said as he turned and quickly resumed walking.

"And I'm gonna check with the Doctor and wido' Moore too, and you best not be lyin' to me, boy."

"No, sir. Never would lie to you, sir," Jimmy answered.

The sheriff looked at Cyril. "Git over hye, Ledbetter. Boy, you just don't ever seem to learn. Ain't you ever listened to anythang that I have told you? And hye you are again on the wrong side o' the tracks. I suppose 'at you been visitin' that lawyer down 'ere. That or maybe you got a girl on that side." The man sneered. "You wouldn't be the first, an' you won't be the last – but people ain't supposed to see you. It bothers folks. You don't wanna bother nobody, do y'?"

"No, sir, I don't have a girl down there. I was just studying with Mr. Bratton to prepare for college."

"Listen t' you, 'Mr. Bratton' and tryin' to sound smart. Who do you think you are? You cain't call them Mister and Misses. You gotta use their first name, or they start to git uppity. See, people like you is what is wrong lately. Y'all start gittin' out o' place an' 'en they git confused an' don't remember their place no more an' pretty soon we got problems like they had down 'ere in Arkansas a few years ago where some white folks ended up getting killed there in Elaine. White folks – dead! Hell, they damned near burned down half o' Tulsa when they rioted there. Three years ago, down in Florida, they rioted an' burned down the whole town o' Rosewood. The whole town is just gone. They just got confused and rioted and started killin' one another like animals. I ain't havin' that hye in Bratton. I'm gonna keep folks in their place – I'm gonna make sure they know where they belong and are not allowed. And that is the gospel. I am tryin' to protect ever'body and keep order for ever'body. I'm protectin' them too; from themselves, you see." The man looked at Cyril in disgust. "An' then there's you. Don't keep t' yo' own, always mixin' – gittin' folks confused about where the lines are. hye y' are just walkin' around bein' special – no rules for you. I tried to talk to yo' daddy about you, but he just don't seem t' listen to good sense about this. If you was one o' my sons, I'd beat you like I owned y' – until y' got some sense, just like the Bible says. What do y' think about that?"

"I guess that my father does not believe in beating his children."

The man looked down at Cyril and huffed. "An' look at what he ends up with for a son – you may be the dumbest white boy there is. I should knock you flat on your back right now, but yo' Mama is a good Christian woman, so I won't out o' respect fo' her. You prob'ly breakin' her heart, always down 'ere on 'at side o' town." The man stood for a moment and then said, "Git out o' my sight. And when you git home, you find a mirror an' take a good long look at yo' face – at yo' white face. And just maybe y' might remember who the hell you s'posed to be."

As Cyril neared the farm, the night was settling in, but a full moon was rising so that he could see his moon shadow walking along in front of him. He watched it glide up the walkway and then up the steps just to vanish into the darkness under the porch as he walked onto the boards. He walked through the front door and into the parlor. His mother was sitting in her usual chair, and she looked up from her book as his father looked up from the almanac he was reading. "You are awfully late," William said.

"I am very sorry. I got caught up talking with the sheriff – or listening to him rather. He had some things that he wanted to tell me after he finished yelling at Jimmy."

"Did he tell you anything important that I should know?" Asked William.

"No, sir, not a single thing that he said was important – but he took a while to say it anyway."

"Is Jimmy alright?"

"Yessir, he is fine. He went home after the sheriff finished."

"Good to know."

Cyril looked at Ida and said, "Mother, I hope I have never embarrassed you. Please tell me if I ever do."

Ida looked at her son and said, "Your supper is on the table, and wash up your plate when you finish with it."

"Yes, ma'am," he said as he started to walk toward the dining room. "Thank you." As he passed in front of his mother, he felt her lean forward and grab his hand, and he stopped as she held it for a few seconds and gave it a firm squeeze. After she dropped it, he started walking again.

"Cyril," William said. "You have never embarrassed us."

Cyril stopped but didn't turn; he just nodded in acknowledgment.

William continued, "Except that time that you peed in the corner of the church – but you were three years old, so I'm not sure that it counts."

"William Ledbetter!" Ida said. "It was your fault anyway."

Cyril smiled as he sat down; something about when his parents played at arguing gave him comfort – he just wished that it was not about the time the preacher caught him peeing in church. They always seemed to do it when he was feeling his worst.

Twenty-One: A Journey on the Other Side

A couple of days later, the smell of bacon and coffee woke Cyril, and he sat up in his bed. He caught sight of himself in the mirror across his room. 'An' take a good long look at yo' face – at yo' white face. And just maybe y' might remember who the hell you s'posed to be…'

Later that afternoon, Cyril walked into the Bratton kitchen and saw that the other gentlemen were already there, as usual. Everyone was sitting with a cup of tea, and he saw a cup waiting for him before the only empty seat at the table. Everyone looked up at him, and he exchanged nods with them. Sitting down, he said, "Thank you to whoever poured my cup."

"You are welcome," said Peter. "Mr. Bratton stepped out for a bit and said that we were to reverse our usual order of things and begin doing our homework together at the table. So as soon as we finish our tea, we can get started."

"Stepped out?" Asked Cyril.

"Yes, he stepped out," answered Emery. "I think that he is planning a surprise for us."

Within minutes the young men had their books in front of them on the table. The four Black young men were always working on the same assignment, and Cyril was always interested in helping them, and they would help Cyril with his. This way, they all saw what the other high school class in town was learning. It was often similar, but there would be subtle differences, with the teacher for the Black school often giving the more demanding assignments. Mr. Bratton had even noted that Ms. Holyfield at the Negro school was exceptionally stringent with high expectations. Mr. Bratton had also explained to them that exposure to the assignments and materials from two different schools would give them a broader knowledge of high school material.

After a short time, Mr. Bratton returned and walked into the room. "Gentlemen, I have quite a surprise for you. When you have finished up here, please join me in the parlor, where we will spend the remainder of the day." He exited the room before any of them could answer.

The young men looked at one another. Spending the rest of the day in the parlor sounded strange to them. There was a specific order of business at these sessions. A short time sharing tea in the kitchen to start, then a time in the study where they would discuss academic issues of law, logic, philosophy, or history, followed by a session sitting together in the parlor where they would discuss literature or current events and news followed by a return to the kitchen where they would use the table as a shared desk to complete their assigned homework and study. Changing the order of the day was unprecedented. The young men hurried through their homework assignments.

Mr. Bratton looked up as the young men entered his study. "Gentlemen, please come in and find a seat." He had a large leather-bound volume in his hands and an excited smile on his face. "You will each find a small book on your seats; those are for you. I was hoping they would arrive today, and I met them at the train platform for the three o'clock train. They are a gift – one for each of you."

Each man picked up a booklet and looked at the cover. "Hamlet," Mr. Bratton said. "It is one of the masterworks of William

Shakespeare, a classic English playwright of some centuries ago. We will read it together over the next couple of weeks and discuss it."

"A play?" asked Charlie Scolfield.

"Yes Charles, a play." The man smiled broadly. "A Negro theater company will be performing this play in several weeks in Birmingham, and I would like to go and see the performance. It is a classic play, told completely out of chronological order, demanding a great deal from the audience. And I would like you to all accompany me on the trip to Birmingham. We will leave on the early train on the third Saturday from now, which will put us arriving with plenty of time to check into our hotel, see a bit of the city, get a good supper, and then we will see the evening performance. And then, after a good night of sleep, we will return on the noon train, which will put us back here in town before nightfall. It will be a wonderful opportunity for each of you. I spoke to most of your parents about it this past Sunday, and they have given their permission though I swore them to secrecy about it. Mr. Ledbetter, you will need to speak to your parents since we go to different churches, but make clear to them that you will need only your clothes and essentials as I will be taking care of all the expenses."

"Our parents have already agreed to let us go?" asked Peter.

"Yes, they have, Mr. Styles," the man said with a broad smile. "It will be a wonderful experience to travel with friends, and it will prepare you for when you must travel alone for college. Now, shall we dig right in?" The man opened the tome in his hands as the young men opened the smaller books they held. The rest of the session was spent reading Hamlet and stopping to discuss the story every few lines.

Later that evening, Cyril was sitting at the supper table with his parents thinking over what Mr. Bratton had told him today. "Daddy, I have a question for you."

"Yes, son, what would that be?

"Today, Mr. Bratton gave each of us a copy of the play Hamlet, and we are reading it together. And there is to be a performance in Birmingham three Saturdays from now. He would like all of us to go with him on the train to see that performance. Can you spare me from around here for one Saturday?"

"I don't see why not. That is a good play, if a bit confusing in how it tells itself."

Ida said, "A train ride into Birmingham and a play is a lot for one day."

"Well, the thing is, Mama, that we would all leave here on the first train out on Saturday, just like Daddy and I did before, but we would be staying over in a hotel after the performance and coming back on the noon train out of Birmingham."

"Overnight? In Birmingham? I do not think that is a good idea," said Ida.

"Mama, I just turned sixteen. And I have never been to a play at a theater."

William said, "He has a point, my dear; at his age, many young men are off to the Army. I remember you telling me how much you enjoyed going to plays with your father when you were a girl. You grew up in a city with theaters and companies to perform in them. He is stuck out here without those things and has never been to anything like this."

"I do not know about this, William. I am not of a mind to allow our son to get on a train and go that far away."

"Mr. Bratton says that it will be a perfect opportunity for us to travel with a group to prepare us for college. It will give us a chance to stay in a hotel. He said he always enjoyed taking his wife and daughter to the theater and has not been since his wife passed. He said he would enjoy seeing one of her favorite tragedies – and seeing it with us as we each see it for the first time. He does not wish to go to the theater alone; he says that going alone would feel like something is missing. He talked about the first time his little girl saw her first full play; he said that she called it the 'grown-up play' because it was not one of her little plays that they did in grade school."

"And how do you know the other boys will be allowed to go along on this excursion?"

"He already spoke to all of their parents at church, but since we go to the other church, he could not speak to you two about it. Please, Mama."

"I just do not think that it is a good idea. I just cannot agree to it."

William said, "Now honey, I'm not sure it would be a bad thing. Perhaps we should go on and let him see his first 'grown-up play,' as it were."

Ida gave her husband a warning look. "You can stop there, Mr. Ledbetter – you can stop right there." She turned to her son. "Your father and I will need to discuss this in private tomorrow when you are at school. We will give you an answer before you leave here Wednesday morning."

"If it is the money," Cyril started. "Mr. Bratton is taking care of everything; we are just to bring ourselves and our clothes."

"Did I say anything about money? We are not poor. I am not concerned about the expense – my concern is about the appropriateness of it all. Now that is enough about it. You go out there and start your reading, and you will have your answer soon enough."

Two days later, as usual, Cyril was the last to arrive for the after-school group. As he entered the kitchen, he saw a glass of iced tea sitting on the table for him in front of an empty chair. He saw Mr. Bratton putting something into the icebox. He sat down and noticed the other gentlemen looking at him.

Mr. Bratton turned around from the icebox and noticed Cyril. "Ah, Mr. Ledbetter. I thought it was starting to get a bit too warm for hot tea this late in the day, so iced tea is. Drink up; poor Ophelia awaits."

Cyril started to drink his tea and noticed the other gentlemen looking at him expectantly. He played it off as if he didn't see.

"Well?" asked Charlie. "What did your parents say?"

Cyril held a pained expression on his face for a moment of silence, and then he smiled and said, "Let's go to Birmingham."

"It is settled law then, gentlemen; we shall all go, the whole crew," said Mr. Bratton with a broad smile.

A couple of weeks later, the conductor's voice sounded as Cyril stepped onto the platform. "All aboard for Birmingham and all points north." In the dawn light, he could see Mr. Bratton and the other young men lined up near the last passenger car of the train as they waited to board. He hurried to join them.

Mr. Bratton looked up and saw Cyril approaching. "Ah, Mr. Ledbetter, I was growing concerned that you may not get to the train." Cyril joined the small cue of people moving onto the train.

A man approached Cyril and said, "'Scuse me, sir." Cyril turned to see a smiling Black man addressing him. The man was a porter for the railroad, and he pointed to the small carpet bag that Cyril carried. "May I take yo' bag an' show you t' a seat in one o' the cars up here toward the front o' the train?"

"No, thank you, it is a small bag, and I will just keep it with me – no need for it to go in the baggage car."

"That's fine, sir," The man continued to smile. "Can I show you to one of the forward cars?"

"No, thank you, sir; I will ride in this car."

"Well, sir. Um, see this here is the last passenger car on the train, an' it is pretty much fo' colored folks t' ride in. The white folks generally want t' ride up in the forward cars."

"Oh, I never thought about that. Is there a rule that says I cannot ride in this car? These gentlemen and I are traveling together, and I would prefer to ride with my companions. Unless, of course, there is a specific rule that dictates that I cannot do so."

"Well, sir, I know that there's a rule that says colored folks can't ride in the forward cars. But come t' think of it, I ain't heard a rule that says white folks can't ride wherever they want t' ride. Just never seen a white man who wanted t' ride back here. All right, suit yo'self, sir. Have a nice day sir." The man turned and hurried away to go and assist other passengers in getting on in the forward cars.

Cyril imagined what the morning was like at the Ledbetter house. Ida set the third plate on the table as she called, "Cyril." There was no response, so she looked at her husband.

William said, "He is probably sulking since that train that he wanted to be on is leaving the station right about now. I'll go talk to him." The man got up, left the dining room, and returned a short time later.

"Is he coming to breakfast?"

"I think that he's going to skip breakfast today – that is, unless he grabs himself something at the next stop."

There was a slow intake of breath, and the room filled with the kind of calm that comes just before a storm breaks.

The six of them got into the car, stowed their bags overhead, and were seated as the train lurched forward into motion. Cyril looked around, and he noticed that there were a few other passengers in the car – all of them Black. He tried to remember the passengers on the last train trip. He wondered if everyone in that car had been white, and he just had not noticed. After a few minutes, the door opened, and the familiar porter came in. The man moved along the aisle, speaking to everyone and taking a few minutes with each passenger or group of passengers. Cyril said, "On the trip with my father, the porter told us where to get the best lunch and pie. And I remember right where those two stops are."

"Then we will trust your memory," said Mr. Bratton.

The porter came to stand in the aisle between the seats where they sat, with four of them sitting on one side of the aisle and two of them on the other side. "I suppose all o' y'all are together then?"

"Yes," Mr. Bratton answered. We are heading into Birmingham to see a play and stay the night. I am somewhat familiar with Birmingham, but I have not traveled on this particular line before. When we arrive, we will need to find the Simmerson Hotel."

"Well, sir, we have a few stops before Birmingham, and we'll get in there just a bit after noon time. Most o' the stops are just short whistle stops, but we'll top off at two places, and we'll be there for a bit. Now at the first one of those, y'all don't want t' get off o' the train. Well, not the five of you." The man indicated the Black gentlemen. "Nothing there t' see anyway. At the ten o'clock stop, feel free t' get off and stretch y' legs as long as you stay near the station. As for food, just open a window on the platform side of the train, and the ladies will bring it right to you. You'll see 'em on the platform. Now, when you get to Birmingham, you will leave the station and go to your left, and at the next block, you take another left, which will head you right down to the Simmerson."

"We thank you for the information, sir," said Mr. Bratton as he handed the man a tip.

"You are very welcome, sir; y'all have a nice day. I will come back here from time to time if y'all need anything else." The man turned and walked back toward the front of the train and soon disappeared through the door to the car.

Cyril had a puzzled look on his face. "That is funny; when my father and I took this same trip, the porter just told us where to eat."

Isaac Jones said, "Because if you get off at the wrong stop, the worst thing that happens to you is that perhaps you miss the train."

They rode with an uncomfortable silence for a few minutes as Cyril thought about what Isaac had just said. They heard the door at the front of the car open, and they looked up to see a white man in a railroad uniform step inside the door, take a quick look around and then step back out and close the door. Then, the door opened again, and the white man took a second look and focused on Cyril. Cyril recognized Mr. Olmstead as the conductor from his previous trip and smiled at the man as he approached.

"Mr. Olmstead," Cyril said as he stuck out his hand. The man gave him a confused look. "Cyril Ledbetter, Mr. Olmstead. My father introduced us about a month and a half ago."

"Oh, now I remember you; you're William's boy. What are you doin' back here? You s'posed to be up in one of the forward cars."

"I would prefer to ride back here with my travel companions."

"Your travel companions?" The man looked at the other gentlemen. "Well, you still can't ride back here."

"I know a rule says that colored people cannot ride in forward cars. But is there a written rule that says that white people cannot ride anywhere they want?"

"There don't need to be a written rule. Why would there be? Nobody with sense would ever want to."

"Well, sir, I want to ride in this car."

"No! I am the conductor and will not have it on my train. We will make a whistle-stop here shortly – just long enough for a few folks to get on or off the train. And you are gonna do both. You will get out of this car and get in one of the forward cars where you belong. Or you can just get off of the train and stay off."

"Why? I don't understand why."

"Because that is how it is done," The man said in a clipped rhythm, "That is how it has always been done, and that is how we are doing it today. Now that's the end of it. Next stop Ledbetter." The man shook his head in disgust. "Like father, like son, I reckon." The man turned and stormed from the car.

Cyril could feel the heat as his cheeks reddened. He felt like all eyes were on him at that moment. He knew that everyone in that car had just heard him being humiliated. He glanced around and noticed that everyone was looking down – almost everyone. Actually, two sets of dark brown eyes were looking at him speculatively as if they were remeasuring him.

Mr. Bratton did not blink; he just kept gazing at the young man with the pride of a teacher in a student. The man nodded. "It will be fine. Do as he says. You have to pick your battles to win the war."

Emery Dawson quietly said, "Might even have to pick your war." Then, he looked up at Cyril for a few moments until Cyril turned away and looked out of the window, unsure of exactly why he felt so humiliated.

Twenty-Two: A Favor To Ask

It had been nearly a year since the trip to Birmingham, the storm with his mother had eventually blown over and things had returned to normal - for a time. Cyril was walking out of the trail behind the Second Baptist Church on his way to the afternoon study session. This will make three months since the young men had moved to the church and carried on the sessions without Mr. Bratton – three months since Mr. Bratton had become ill and could no longer host or lead their sessions. It was coming up on the first anniversary of the trip to Birmingham to see Hamlet. Cyril went around to the side door, which led into a large meeting room with a table the young men used for their sessions. As he entered, he saw the four other gentlemen talking at the table. "Hello, gentlemen," he said as he took his seat. "What are we talking about?"

"Hello, Cyril," Peter responded. "We were talking about the trip to Birmingham last year."

Emery added, "Specifically about how your father was waiting for that train to arrive. You looked like a man going to the gas chamber."

"I felt like a man going to the gas chamber," Cyril responded.

Isaac laughed, saying, "I still cannot believe you snuck away when your parents said no. And then you came home after. If I did that, I would have to keep going."

"Remember what his father said to him?" Charlie asked.

A chorus of four voices called out in unison. "Boy, did you want to die?" Laughter filled the room.

Cyril, his face turning red, just looked down.

"I bet that your mother nearly killed you," said Peter.

"I thought she was going to, especially when I tried to reason with her," said Cyril.

"You tried to reason with your mother after that?" asked Emery. "You are a fool."

"I know that now," said Cyril. To another chorus of laughter.

"What did you say to try and convince her?" Asked Isaac.

"I told her that it wasn't like I had run away to get married against her wishes," said Cyril. "And for some reason, that just got all over her."

"My father says that if you ever want to get to the bottom of a hole, just stop digging," said Charlie.

"What was the worst of it?" asked Peter.

Cyril looked up. "How mad Mr. Bratton was when he discovered what I had done. He said that defiant children hurt their parents in ways that he hopes I never have to understand."

Isaac said, "Yeah, we did not see you for a few weeks. I thought that maybe we just missed your funeral." Another explosion of laughter.

"That was a nice trip," said Emery. "That was the first time that I ever left Bratton."

"Birmingham was so big," added Peter.

"Wait until you get to Atlanta next year," said Charlie. "I went there once with my father to visit when he was speaking."

"Is it much bigger than Birmingham?" asked Peter.

"A lot bigger," said Charlie. "Atlanta makes Birmingham look like Bratton."

"Well, I am glad we are going there together then," said Peter. "Maybe we can stay with the same family. You know, share a room."

"Sharing a room with you in Birmingham was enough," said Charlie. "You snore too much."

"Everybody snores," Peter defended.

"Not like that; I kept waking up thinking I was getting run over by a train." More laughter.

"Alright, alright, we should get started," said Emery. "I will start with my current event."

They spent the rest of the afternoon following the schedule they had devised when they decided to continue their sessions. The four would rotate, bringing in topics from history, law, philosophy, or a current event. And Peter, the math genius, would teach the others something from that subject. In this way, they could continue helping one another prepare for college.

Later as Cyril was walking home, and just after leaving the trail onto the north side of town, he heard a familiar voice call. "Cy! Hey, Cy! wait up." Cyril stopped and turned to see his friend Billy carrying a parcel and trotting toward him.

"How y' doin'?" Billy asked. "I don't much see y' outside o' school no more."

"I'm doing well. My afternoons are still pretty busy with the college preparation classes, and the other days working on the farm helping my father."

"Well, I gotta deliver this stuff out t' Wido' Moore for Mr. Dawson over at the store. Been working for him a bit in the afternoons a couple days a week. I'll walk with y' that far."

"Okay, that would be nice." Cyril looked down at the long thin shadows stretching out on the ground in the late afternoon sun. He wondered how many times he had watched these same two shadows walking side by side over the years. He saw the toes of his shoes keep coming into view one after the other. 'I wonder if shadows know they are getting older – or if they even do get older like us.' He thought to himself.

"So y'all still having those after-school classes with that lawyer fella?" asked Billy.

"Yes and no. We still study together three times a week over at their church. But Mr. Bratton took sick a while back, so he does not participate. But we stop in and see him now and then for a few minutes."

"So, did y' git into any o' them colleges for next year?"

"I am waiting to hear back from a few more of them. I have not been accepted to any yet."

"I'm shore 'at you'll git int' one o' 'em."

"Not if that high school teacher has anything to say about it."

"Aw, he's just bitter 'cause he didn't ever git to publish a book o' his poetry. He thanks 'at he's some kina great poet, but when he reads his poems t' the class, I just sit there and thank 'at Mother Goose wrote better stuff."

"So, what about you? What are you planning for next year?"

"Well, my daddy bought both farms on either side of us. They was both owned by colored families, an' they was movin' north to work in the factories up there. He was able t' git 'em fo' a good price. The sheriff was kina pushin' them out. So, now we got the biggest farm down in the Bottoms. So after I graduate, I will work with my daddy until I take the farm over someday."

"That is not right, the way the sheriff does that to people. And the judge always helps with it too, and that makes it worse."

"Yeah, the sheriff, he condemned one house an' told 'em they gotta knock it down an' build a new one. They didn't have the money fo' a new house, but they had t' move out o' the one 'at they had. So, they sold ever'thang to my daddy and just left for Detroit. Thang is, they weren't nothin' wrong with 'at house in the first place."

"He should not be able to do that to people."

"Maybe not, but we makin' out pretty good behind it. Sheriff talked to my daddy the other day and told him 'at they's another little farm down the road from us 'at gonna come on the market pretty soon."

"Why is the sheriff helping your father so much specifically?"

"I reckon they's friends. They both go t' the Friday night meetin's o' the Society. An' I reckon 'at Society brothers is supposed t' help one another wi' thangs like this."

"I guess so."

"Hey, did yo' daddy really buy the old Moore farm and gonna let the Wido' Moore live there for the rest of her life?" asked Billy.

Cyril said, "Yes, he did."

"I reckon ever'body's doin' pretty good lately."

"Not the people that the sheriff is after."

"No, I reckon not them. But the rest of us, though, we all doin' good. Expandin' our farms an' thangs. Sheriff said 'at he gonna clean Bratton up. Welp, here is the Moore place, so I reckon I'll let you git on home. It's good to talk t' y' Cy."

"I will see you later, Billy; it was good to speak with you."

Shortly afterward, Cyril was sitting at the supper table with his parents. "I saw Billy today on my way home. He was delivering some things to Sister Moore for the storekeeper."

"The storekeeper has a name, son," said William.

"Yessir, for Brother Dawson."

"You see Billy every day at school and every Sunday at church," said Ida.

"Yes, ma'am, but we are too busy at school and church to speak with one another much."

"How are the Holsteads doing, then?" asked Ida. "Everyone has been so busy of late that we only see them in passing at church anymore."

"Billy says that they are doing well. His father has bought two of the small farms next door. He says there is a third one he might get real soon. I guess the sheriff has been helping him get them for not very much money because Mr. Holstead and the sheriff go to the same society meetings on Friday nights. I guess the sheriff has been making people give up their farms down in the bottoms and move north."

Ida got a disgusted expression. "That man is shameful."

"Yes, ma'am. Daddy, have you ever been a member of that men's society?"

"No, son I haven't. A friend of mine tried to get me to join the Odd-Fellows Lodge years ago. But I didn't like the funny hats. Pointy hats and robes just looked too silly for my taste."

Cyril noticed that his mother excused herself without finishing her supper, carried her plate to the kitchen, and started cleaning up the dishes from cooking.

Later, they sat in the parlor for their reading, and Ida casually asked. "Cyril, have you spoken to Mr. Bratton lately? How is he doing?"

"No, ma'am, not too much lately. The doctor says we have to visit him one at a time and we can't stay too long. The ladies from the church have been taking it in rotation to go over there and bring him his meals and nurse him a bit. He hired a nurse to move in and help take care of him, but the ladies from the church still send someone there every day to make sure that the nurse is doing everything correctly and that he has good food to eat. And they cover all day on Saturday so the nurse can take the day off. I will go by there in a couple of days when it is my turn. I hope that I have some good news for him."

"Well, tell him to let us know if he needs anything," said Ida.

"Yes, ma'am."

"Perhaps one Saturday soon, I will drive you over to see him, my dear. Maybe you could cook him something special, and we could take that to him. You know, just to thank him for all he has done to help get Cyril into college."

Ida sat for a few moments looking at her book. "Perhaps." Another pause. "That might be nice – just a short visit."

A couple days later, Cyril walked into the church for the regular session the same as every other day the tutoring group studied and saw the other young men waiting in the exact same places they were in each and every one of those days. "Good afternoon, gentlemen." It felt good to keep some formality with which Mr. Bratton had started the group, even though they had become so familiar with one another. The other four had been friends and gone to church and school together their whole lives. But Cyril was the new one, and he enjoyed this group and considered these gentlemen his friends. Everything went silent as he entered and sat down. He pretended not to notice the eyes on him.

"Well?" asked Charlie.

Cyril feigned confusion. "Was there a question, Mr. Scolfield?" Cyril felt a mild kick on his shin. "Mr. Scolfield, and you, the son of a minister."

"My apologies, Mr. Ledbetter. I was crossing my leg over. A simple mistake. I will try to be more careful when I uncross it – in a few seconds," said Charlie with an innocent smile.

Cyril paused momentarily before saying, "Philadelphia, I got in, and I am going to Philadelphia."

"Well, that makes three of us," Peter said. "All three of us graduating this year are accepted. And I am sure Emery and Isaac will be accepted when they graduate next year."

"Yes, but you and Charlie are both going to Atlanta," said Cyril. "I am going to be all by myself way up there in Philadelphia."

"Well, Peter and I are going to be in different colleges from one another," said Charlie, "so it is not like we will be in school together."

"But Peter said that you might room together," responded Cyril.

Charlie said, "Peter needs to stop sneaking bathtub gin into his tea. I have an older brother and a younger brother, and I want to have a room to myself finally."

Isaac said, "I will surely miss you three and these afternoon sessions next year. I don't know what Emery and I will do without you gentlemen."

"You can keep meeting, just the two of you," said Charlie.

"It will not be the same with the three of you gone," added Emery.

"I was thinking about that," said Charlie. "Last year, we stopped these sessions for school vacation over the summer. If we kept these sessions going this year over the summer until we have to leave for college, we could still help Isaac and Emery prepare."

"That is a good idea," said Peter.

All eyes turned to Cyril. He thought about it for a moment and said, "Let's do that."

Emery said, "We should tell Mr. Bratton that you three all got into college and what we are going to do over the summer; he will approve, I am sure."

"I am going to stop by today after we finish to show him my acceptance letter," Cyril said.

"Good," said Charlie. "He has already seen our acceptance letters. And you can tell him about the summer."

Peter said, "I wish we could all go over there together. But the doctor said no."

They sat silently for a moment before Charlie said, "We should probably get on with our agenda for today."

The session for that day followed the same pattern as usual, but Cyril could not think about anything other than going to see Mr. Bratton once they were through. Eventually, the boys all got up to go home. Cyril said hastened goodbyes and rushed off to Mr. Bratton's house.

When he got there, Cyril was unsure if the nurse had heard his knock, so he considered knocking again a little louder, but just as he raised his hand, the door opened. The nurse stood in the doorway, lit by the late afternoon sun. Her very dark skin contrasted with her crisp white uniform in the way that piano keys differ from one another. "Not for very long. Mr. Bratton is tired, and I will not have you exhausting him."

"Yes, ma'am," Cyril said as he entered the house. He entered the room where Mr. Bratton was sitting in his bed.

Mr. Bratton saw Cyril, and he immediately brightened up and smiled. "Cyril, so nice to see you here. Come in; come in and have a seat. Tell me everything that is happening. How is your mother?"

"Everyone is doing well, sir; my mother has been a bit quiet of late, but she gets like that sometimes. I have something to show you." Cyril pulled out an envelope, unfolded the paper inside, and handed it to the man.

Mr. Bratton looked at the paper in front of him. "Philadelphia. Congratulations, my boy, congratulations."

"Thank you, sir. I was starting to worry that all I would get were rejection letters."

"Nonsense, you were bound to get into a good school, and as I recall, this was your preferred choice."

"It was, but after two or three rejection letters, you start to fear that all you will receive are rejections. When it came, I just put it on the table, too afraid to open it for a while. Finally, my mother calmed me down enough to risk it."

"Be sure always to take care of your mother, Cyril. She is a special lady. Your father has always treated her well, but you should be prepared to ensure she is well cared for. I missed my mother very much when she passed away. Make sure that you stay close to your mother always. Promise me that."

"I will, Mr. Bratton, I promise."

"Good, good. She is a wonderful lady and should always be well cared for. I have a favor to ask of you, my boy."

"Anything, Mr. Bratton."

"I am not going to be here for much longer. I have been making lists and having the ladies organize some things I would like you to take for safekeeping, just in case my daughter ever wants them."

A sting immediately struck Cyril in his eyes, and his vision became watery. "I… I don't really want to talk about this, sir."

"It is a reality, son. You and the other young men have made my last few years wonderful. I remember that first day, when we went fishing."

"I remember that too. I wish that we had gone fishing more back then."

"Yes, I also wish we had more lazy days by the river. So many wonderful things that we did together over the years." The man had a smile. "Anyway, I have divided the books in my library between the five young men of our group, according to your interests and proclivities. You will have all of the law books. And I still have a beautiful sewing basket from my wife. Would you take that to your mother since I remember that you said she likes to quilt and is gifted with a needle? And there is my wife's chair. See if your mother has room for it in her parlor. And the quilts, all of the quilts that my wife made. My daughter helped her with a number of them. And there is a small shoe box in my closet with an old grain sack folded up in it with mothballs. It was covered in needlework by my own grandmother for my mother when she was a girl. It is the only thing I have of my grandmother – please hold on to it for me. There is a letter where I copied down everything my mother could remember about her mother."

"That is a lot to remember, Mr. Bratton."

"Oh, no need to bother. I have written out lists and instructions. Just follow the instructions and everything should work out fine. I am getting a bit tired now."

"Then, I should, perhaps, go now and let you rest."

"No, you do not need to leave. I just need to stop talking for a bit. I do have something to ask of you. That you can do for me right away."

"Whatever you want."

"Years ago, you told me about your little sister in exchange for letting me talk about my wife. And it occurs to me that we have spoken several times more about my wife, and I would like to hear more about your sister. Celene, I believe you said her name was."

"Yes, that was her name. I guess that I can tell you more about her. Let me see. Well, Mother was always fussing about her getting tanned by the sun. She always had to have long sleeves and a bonnet. She looked so much like Mother and always seemed to tan so easily. Mother always kept her hair up in a bun because she said it would get too tangled if she wore it down like the other little girls. Mother spent half her time making pretty dresses for Celene with lace and ribbons. Mother would get so angry with her because she would kick off her little shoes and run around in her stockings. Mother had darned every stocking that Celene had at least twice. And she would snuggle up in our father's lap, lay her head against him, and drop right off to sleep." Cyril looked over at Mr. Bratton.

"Please, go on. I am still listening."

"And she had these big eyes just like mother – they looked like chocolates they were so brown. And when she got mad, her eyes would crinkle up, and she would stamp her foot. And she had these thin little lips, but she could still pout with the best of them. But she was sneaky too – one time, she slipped around and ate a whole peach cobbler and got herself so sick. And she was always singing these little songs that she made up. Some days she would sing everything instead of saying it. And there was this little rug in the bedroom that she used to sit on to play. And she would sit there playing with the rag-dolls Mother made for her. I used to get jealous because my mother never made me any rag-dolls. And she would never eat a biscuit until it was covered in butter and molasses."

Cyril felt a touch on his shoulder, and he looked up to see the nurse, who nodded toward the bed. Mr. Bratton had fallen asleep with a peaceful smile, breathing slowly and deeply. Cyril stood to leave, and he noticed that his college acceptance letter was still lying on the bed, so he quietly picked it up.

That evening, Cyril sat with his book in the parlor. "I went by to see Mr. Bratton today. That was why I was so late getting home. I showed him my letter, and we talked for a while."

"What did you talk about?" Asked Ida.

"A little bit about you."

"Oh, what about me?"

"He just asked how you are doing. And he made me promise to always take care of you, no matter what. Kind of strange, but I think he is just missing his mother. He even has an old grain sack that his grandmother decorated for his mother when she was a little girl."

"Oh, did you see that?"

"No, ma'am, he has it in a box, but he told me about it. And he divided up his library among the five students, and all of the law books were for me. And the quilts that his wife made, in case his daughter ever comes here and wants them because she helped her mother make many of them. And there is a sewing basket that belonged to his wife. And her favorite chair too. Do you think that we have room in here for that chair?"

"I am sure we can find a good place for it here in the parlor," said William.

"And then he said that he has told me so much about his wife and daughter from time to time that I should tell him about my sister, so I

232

told him all about Celene." He immediately regretted mentioning that last part.

Ida gently closed her book and took a deep breath. "I think that I will turn in early it has been a – it has been a tiring day." She gently placed her book in her chair, walked over to Cyril, bent and kissed him goodnight on his head, and slowly glided from the room with her usual grace.

William watched her go, then stood and said, "I think I will join her; you go ahead and finish your reading, son." He stood up and quietly walked after his wife.

Cyril continued to sit for a while before he went to his room. It was quiet in the house, and he could hear his mother quietly crying just beyond the door. And he knew that his father would be holding her and gently rocking her in his arms. 'Why did I have to say anything about Celene?' he asked himself.

The following week, the young men were having their usual Wednesday session at the church. They were finishing up an impromptu debate about the love life of Alexander of Macedon and getting ready to finish their day when the door opened. Dr. Barnes walked in, and the room fell silent – a tense silence wherein the room was alive with dread. "I see that you are all still here. I have just come from seeing Brother Cyril. I wanted to say that you young men are the closest thing to family he has around here, so you should all be sure to visit him sometime in the next four or five days and tell him anything you need to say. And more importantly, listen to anything that he needs to say."

The session came to a close for that day, and one by one, the young men left the room, each one feeling a mountain of sadness fall on him, stealing his breath. Cyril didn't exit through the side door as usual; another door led into the church's sanctuary. He sat in a back pew in the darkening church, watching dust motes drift through the shafts of afternoon sunlight streaming through the window. They would appear as if from nowhere as they floated from shadow into the light and then would slowly dance their way across until they would suddenly vanish again into shadow. His eyes began to sting, and his vision wavered. It felt so hard to breathe. After a time, he felt another presence in the room, and a man sat silently next to him. He turned, and through his watery vision, he saw Reverend Scolfield sitting quietly beside him. The man said nothing; he just sat there looking toward the front of the church. It was mostly dark in the church except for a few thin shafts of sunlight, but the man's brown eyes seemed to shine with a gentleness that could examine the soul. He just sat with Cyril for a while without speaking, and eventually, he placed his hand on Cyril's hand for a few moments, gave a soft smile, and stood and left as quietly as he had arrived.

Twenty-Three: A Visit

Cyril hopped down from the back of the truck as his father brought it to a stop beside the road in front of the white picket fence. He went around to his mother's side of the truck to open her door for her. She handed him a basket with a cloth draped over it, and he backed up so that his father could help his mother from the automobile. It was a Saturday morning, but his parents had dressed as if it were a Sunday. His mother was in one of her lovely dresses, and she had her hair pulled into a tight bun and a nice hat pinned in place. She had gloves and a small handbag. She was wearing a lace shawl on her shoulders, which she said belonged to her mother.

Cyril led the way up to the house and knocked. A few moments later, the familiar face of Peaches Jones appeared at the door. "Hello," said Cyril. "We are here to visit with Mr. Bratton, these are my parents, and my mother cooked some food for him."

Then, Mrs. Jones smiled at Cyril. "I know your parents, child – I've known your father since he was a boy. Then, she looked at Mrs. Ledbetter and addressed her directly. "He is having a very good day today, so he is sitting up in bed wishing someone would come to visit. I was just about to make some lunch for him, but if you brought something, he might eat without fuss. He has been trying to live off of lemonade and iced tea – doesn't want to eat anything much lately."

She stepped back to let the family enter. "He will be glad you are here," she said to Cyril. "He had been asking for you, wondering when you would stop by."

"Does he have a nurse to care for him?" asked Ida.

"Yes, ma'am," answered Mrs. Jones. "But she leaves on the first train Saturday morning for her day off, and she will return on the evening train. The sisters from the church take it in rotation to come and care for him. I will be here until about two o'clock with him."

Cyril led the way to the room where Mr. Bratton was sitting in bed. As he walked in, he heard that familiar voice. "Cyril, my boy, come in. I was hoping I might see you today."

"Hello, Mr. Bratton. How are you feeling today?"

"Today is a good day; I am feeling much improved." The man saw Ida walk in, and he paused. "Oh, Mrs. Ledbetter, I did not expect to see you here. This is a pleasant surprise." The man seemed a bit taken aback.

"Good morning, Mr. Bratton," she said with a polite smile as she turned slightly to look over her shoulder. "You will remember my husband, William."

As William walked into the room, Mr. Bratton said, "Yes, certainly. Come in, Mr. Ledbetter; I am pleased to see you all." He motioned toward a rocking chair to one side of the bed. "Please, Mrs. Ledbetter, have a seat. You gentlemen, feel free to get yourselves a couple of chairs from the kitchen if you wish."

As she sat, Ida said, "Mrs. Jones tells me you are not eating as much as you should. We brought some things for which I hope you can muster up an appetite." She motioned for Cyril to place the basket on the floor beside her.

Cyril said, "It is one of my favorites. She takes a skillet and puts a beef stew in it, and then she pours a cornbread batter over it and bakes it in the oven until the cornbread is done."

"It was my mother's recipe," Ida added. "And, I remember, was a particular favorite of my father."

Mr. Bratton sniffed the air. "It smells lovely. I am sure that I will enjoy it this afternoon."

"And there is a pie also," added Cyril.

"Yes, let me see," said Mr. Bratton as he sniffed the air again. "I would say apple – no, pear pie but baked like an apple pie. My wife always made those. I have not had one for years now."

"Mother makes them that way too; she learned it from her mother," Cyril said, "I am going to get one of those chairs from the kitchen. Do you want one, Daddy?"

"No, thank you, son; used to being on my feet this time of day."

Mr. Bratton and William Ledbetter began chatting about the weather, the crops, and a few points of local news. Ida sat and quietly watched the two men socialize. Cyril returned and sat at the foot of the bed.

After a few minutes, William said, "Well, I think I am going to leave you all to talk and go sit on the porch for a bit and give everybody some room. I wanted to thank you for all you have done for Cyril over the years, teaching him to drive and helping him prepare for college."

"It was always a pleasure to work with him. He was raised very well and by good parents. You have been a good father and should be proud of him." He held his hand out.

William stepped over to shake the offered hand as he said, "I am; I am very proud of him." He nodded toward Mr. Bratton, turned, and walked out of the room to wait outside.

Mr. Bratton watched the man leave, and then, he turned toward Ida. "I am told that you enjoy sewing and especially quilt making, so there are a few things that belonged to my wife that I wish for you to have. Cyril already knows what they are."

A sad smile crossed her face as she whispered, "Thank you."

The man continued. "There are a few other things that I will send with you for safekeeping if you don't mind – family pictures, a couple of Bibles, things like that. If you could hold them for me in case anyone ever wants them."

Ida quietly said, "Gladly, I am certain they will be wanted and treasured."

"We are going to hold all that stuff for your daughter to come and get when she is ready," added Cyril.

Mr. Bratton turned and looked at Cyril, "Thank you for that." He turned to Ida. "And thank you."

Ida said, "William is serious; we thank you for all you have done for Cyril. I could not have asked anyone to treat him better or show more care and understanding – even when he was difficult."

Mr. Bratton said, "He was never any more difficult than my daughter, so I was well prepared."

Ida paused and then continued. "I am certain she regrets any difficulty she ever caused you."

"Oh, I know that; I have always known that," Mr. Bratton said.

Mrs. Jones entered the room quietly with two glasses of lemonade which she sat on the bedside table within reach of Mr. Bratton and Mrs. Ledbetter.

"Thank you, Sister Jones," said Mr. Bratton as Mrs. Jones quietly moved away to stand nearby in case she was needed for anything. Mr. Bratton looked up and saw that Cyril was starting to shed a few tears. "Ah, son, there is no need for that. Do not feel sadness for me. I have had a wonderful life; these last seven years living here have been excellent. I have truly enjoyed our time together."

Cyril said, "I know you never met your grandchildren, but I will hold on to every memory I have of you. I will hold on to every fishing trip and everything we have ever done. And someday, I will tell your grandchildren about you. When they come to get this stuff, I will tell them about every memory. I will sit down with your grandson and tell him about your wife and the things that I learned from you. See, I never got to meet my grandfathers, but if I had ever met one, I always hoped he would be just like you. When I was a little boy, and I would get home after us going fishing or something like that, I pretended that I had spent the day with my grandfather." By this point, Cyril knelt down beside the bed, took Mr. Bratton's hand, put his head on it, and cried. He felt Mr. Bratton's other hand come to rest on his head. He stayed there until he finally felt hands settle on his shoulders, gently guiding him to his feet.

"Come on with me," Mrs. Jones said. Let's go out to the kitchen, get you a glass of lemonade, and get you cleaned up. Brother Cyril is getting tired, and you must let him rest soon."

The young man let the woman guide him toward the door. As he stood, he noticed tears in his mother's eyes. He saw her give him a gentle nod and smile. In protest, Cyril balked at the door and said, "You should stay, Mrs. Jones, in case he needs something."

Ida said, "I will sit with him. You two go on out to the kitchen and catch your breath. I will call if he needs anything."

Cyril let himself be guided from the room, and he heard Mrs. Jones close the door behind them before guiding him out to the kitchen. "You sit down right there, and I will get you some lemonade, and you can gather your thoughts." She sat a glass down in front of him, then went over to the sink and started cleaning up as she quietly sang to herself.

The sound of the singing calmed Cyril, and after about five minutes, he drained his glass and started to stand up. "I think that I am ready to go back in there."

"You might be ready, but you need to sit right back down. You are not going back in there this quick. You need to give him a bit of time to rest. Just let him sit quietly with your mother to watch him for a few more minutes."

Reluctantly, Cyril complied with the woman, and he sat back down as she refilled his glass. "Drink this one slower," said Mrs. Jones. Cyril nodded and sipped his lemonade.

After another ten minutes, Cyril looked at Mrs. Jones. "Now?" He saw her nod, and he headed for the bedroom. As he opened the door, he saw that his mother was standing beside the bed and had removed one of her gloves. Her bare hand gently rested on Mr. Bratton's temple against his hairline. Cyril was a bit surprised to see this.

Ida noticed her son walking into the room, so she slowly drew her hand back and began to put her white glove back on. "No, sir, I do not think you have a fever; it is just becoming a warm day." She stepped back and looked at the man for a short while, and then, she continued. "I will hold on to these things as you wish, and you should try to eat something if you can."

"Oh, I intend on eating it, every bite of it. You were thoughtful enough to make your family favorites. How could I not enjoy that?"

"Sister Jones, please see that he eats at least some of it."

Mrs. Jones went over and picked up the basket and said, "Oh, I will make sure that he eats something."

"Thank you," said Ida. "Thank you and the ladies for taking such good care of him." She took out a lace handkerchief and dabbed at her cheeks and eyes. Then, she walked over to the bureau on the other side of the room and picked up a photo album and a shoe box. "I will take these things with me now, as you asked, Mr. Bratton."

The man said, "Thank you, Mrs. Lebetter. And thank Mr. Ledbetter for me."

Ida stopped at the bedroom door and turned back to take a moment and look at the man as he sat in the bed looking at her. He looked at her, smiled, nodded, and said, "Thank you for visiting." Then, she turned and glided from the room.

Cyril stood for another moment. Then, he walked over to the bed. He bent and hugged Mr. Bratton. After a few moments, Mr. Bratton said, "You run along, I am getting tired and I still need to eat something, and your mother is waiting."

Cyril walked slowly toward the door, then turned back to look at the man. "I will be back to visit with you some more." He saw the man smile and nod to him just before he turned to walk out.

That evening at supper, Cyril said, "Mother, I noticed you brought home a couple of things today."

"Yes, I did. Mr. Bratton asked me to bring those with me for safekeeping."

"Well, I was wondering if I could see that album of photographs that you brought home. I have seen some of the pictures from his wedding and back when he met his wife and when his little girl was small. But I have never seen the book's last few pages, and I wanted to see what his daughter looked like as she got older."

"Oh, perhaps another time. I have already put those things away, and I do not wish to go and get them right back out.

"Yes, ma'am. Well, I would like to see them sometime if I could."

Soon it was Monday afternoon, and Cyril opened the side door to the Second Baptist church, and his four compatriots were sitting at the table waiting for him. He saw his mother's basket sitting beside the only empty chair. The other gentlemen looked up, and he saw the tears in their eyes, and he felt his own eyes sting and the whole world seemed to be drowning underwater. He made his way to the empty chair and sat down. "When?"

"This morning," Charlie said quietly. "While we were in school."

"Won't see us graduate next week," said Peter.

"Yes, he will," answered Emery.

Isaac said, "My mother sent that basket, Cyril. She said everything belongs to Mrs. Ledbetter and wants you to carry it home with you. She said to tell your mother that he ate every bit of it and finished the last of it for his supper last night."

"There is going to be a wake at his house this evening," said Charlie. "The undertaker, Brother Peabody, is already over there getting him ready. There will be a lot of folks there tonight for it. And the funeral is tomorrow, just a little before noon. My father said Mr. Bratton's niece is on her way down from Birmingham on the train. I guess she is the only family he has living close enough to be here."

"I do not much feel like doing anything today," said Cyril.

"None of us do," said Emery.

Peter said, "Maybe we should all just go home now and get ready to return for the wake later." The rest of the young men agreed. After the five young men left the church, they walked silently toward the main street. Cyril had his head down and watched the five shadows walking with one another. He watched as they arrived at the street and four of the shadows turned toward the south, leaving one lone shadow standing there looking as if it were as alone as Cyril felt.

Cyril was the only one who did not live on the south side of town, and rather than take the long way through the woods, he headed north on the main street. As he reached the familiar white picket fence, he saw the front door open, and a tall light brown man in a dark suit stepped out, placed a wreath with black ribbons onto the door, and stepped back to ensure it was perfect. Cyril vaguely recognized the man from around town and assumed that this must be the undertaker for the south side of town. Cyril opened the gate and headed toward the porch.

"May I assist you?" asked the well-dressed man.

"Is he ready and all laid out for this evening?" Cyril asked.

"Yes, he is. Everything is prepared for this evening. I know you were close to Brother Cyril, so if you want to go in and sit with him for a while, you may. His niece is expected on the train shortly, but she is not here just yet."

"Thank you, I think that I would like that."

The man smiled and quietly opened the door so Cyril could enter. Cyril set his basket down on the porch and walked in. He heard the door close behind him, and then, he was alone in the room. The furniture had been rearranged, and Cyril could see the wooden coffin on a table against the far wall. Some wooden folding chairs were scattered around the room's edges, waiting for the visitors coming by to show their respects. Cyril walked up to the coffin and looked down at Mr. Bratton, who was impeccably dressed as if he were on his way to the court. He looked like he was happily sleeping. "I told you that I would come back and visit with you some more, and here I am."

Cyril sat in Mrs. Bratton's favorite Victorian chair, sitting near Mr. Bratton. He sat quietly for a while and then heard a train whistle down at the station. He figured that Mr. Bratton's niece must be getting off the train, and since the station was only a five-minute walk from the house, she would be here soon. After another ten or so minutes, he heard voices on the porch, and then the door opened, and he heard footsteps behind him.

A woman's voice sounded behind him. "Thank you, I'm sure that we can find everything and would like to clean up before guests arrive." There was the sound of the door closing.

"Violet, you take these bags and see if you can find a spare room."

"Mama, look, somebody is sitting over there."

"Hello?" came the sound of the first voice.

Cyril stood up and looked around and saw a Black woman with a medium skin tone, and beside her stood a young woman who looked to be about his age and had a darker skin tone. "Hello, Ma'am; I was just sitting with him briefly before everything started. You must be his niece from Birmingham. I will get out of your way. But let me show you where everything is." He walked over and picked up the two bags the women had placed on the floor beside them. "The spare room is right here, off of the kitchen." He led the way and put the bags in their room for them. Then, he returned to the front room where Mr. Bratton was laid out.

The woman followed him. "Thank you, young man. You seem to know where everything is. Were you here visiting Uncle Cyril often? Did you know him well?"

"Yes, ma'am. He moved here when I was ten, and we got to know one another pretty well over the years. We had a college preparatory study group that met here three times a week. Did you know your uncle very well?"

"Well, his wife was my mother's sister, so we were pretty close when I was a kid, but we had not seen him after Auntie passed." The younger woman came into the room. "This is my daughter, Violet." The young woman smiled.

Cyril smiled at the young woman. "Nice to meet you."

"We always wondered why Uncle Cyril moved here after Auntie passed. But I guess that he must have liked this town. Or maybe he just liked living in a town with his name on it."

"He told me that he was born here or on the plantation near here, before the Civil War."

"Oh, we didn't know that. I guess that he was just coming home then.

"I suppose that you know his daughter, or did." Cyril moved on to a new subject.

"Yes, we were close as children, but she moved away and married many years ago."

"I do not suppose that she is coming, is she?"

The woman took a deep breath. "I doubt that she will be here. She eloped with a man, and Uncle Cyril said she moved far away."

"Well, if you ever hear from her, you let her know that he asked my mother and me to hold on to some of the family things for her in case she ever wants them. Pictures and family bibles and things like that."

"I will be sure to let her know. May I ask your name so I know who to tell her to see?"

"That was how we got to know one another. He was the only other person I met with the name Cyril. That is also my name."

"Your name is Cyril?"

"Yes, ma'am, Cyril Ledbetter. If she comes to town and asks for Ida or Cyril Ledbetter, we will have that stuff for her."

The woman sat down. "Cyril Ledbetter, and your mother is named Ida?"

"Yes, ma'am. I should leave and let you all get ready. I will see you later this evening."

"Cyril, wait a moment; I want to ask you some questions."

"Yes, ma'am?"

"Your mother is holding on to that stuff for him. Did she know him well?

"She met him a few times. Once, when I broke my leg, and he carried me to the doctor. And we had a nice visit with him just Saturday, and she cooked him some of her mother's special recipes. He seemed to like that a lot."

"Was he happy?"

"Yes, ma'am, as far as I could tell, he was very happy – other than missing his wife and his daughter."

"Good, I'm glad."

"I will see you again in a couple of hours." Cyril hurried for the door as he felt his eyes begin to water up again. He opened the door to see two figures standing in front of him. He put his head down and backed up so that they could enter. "Ma'am, the Reverend and Mrs. Scolfield are here to see you." He hurried through the door, picked up his basket, and started walking.

"Mr. Ledbetter," called a voice from behind.

"Yes, Reverend?" answered Cyril as he stopped and turned.

"I have asked the other four gentlemen from the college preparatory group to act as pallbearers tomorrow, and I would like to ask you to join them."

"Yes, sir," Cyril said quietly. He nodded to the preacher and turned back toward home. "I will see you later."

Twenty-Four: Partings

The truck stopped outside the Second Baptist Church in a small area set aside for a few automobiles to park. Cyril climbed down from the back and looked at the church. He saw a steady line of people slowly entering the building. Most of the people who were here for the funeral were Black but there were a few non-Black faces here and there. Cyril started toward the church.

"Cyril," Ida quietly called to stop him. "Wait for us."

Cyril paused for a few moments while he waited for his parents. Then, the three joined the line of people going into the church.

As they entered the church, Ida looked around and led the way to an empty pew in the back, where the three took their seats. As they sat watching the church prepare for the service, Cyril noticed Mr. Bratton's niece speaking to a few people near the front of the church. He leaned toward his mother and said, "That is his niece who came in from Birmingham for the services. Her mother was his wife's sister."

"Is that so?" Ida asked as her eyes followed the other women with a sad expression.

"Yes, ma'am. I asked her to tell his daughter we have some of his things for her. She said she would pass that along if she ever hears from her cousin."

247

Ida nodded and said. "I will be sure to thank her. I will ensure she has our name and address if she wants it."

"Would you like me to give her all that information, Mother?"

"No, I will do it after the service."

Reverend Scolfield stepped up to the lectern and waited a moment as everyone found their seats and the room quieted down. "Friends, we are here today to celebrate the home-going of Brother Cyril Bratton."

A deacon did a reading from the Bible; then, three ladies sang a song. The preacher spoke, and the choir sang a few songs with the whole church joining in, and then, a few different people stood and shared memories of Brother Cyril alternating with more music. Some of the songs were familiar to Cyril as ones that he knew from church, and he sang along. But other songs were new to him though everyone around him seemed to know them well. Even his mother knew the unfamiliar songs.

The service flowed well and seamlessly moved from songs to speakers peppered here and there with Bible verses. The atmosphere expressed the loss and conveyed a sense of celebration and hope. Cyril experienced a lot of different emotions, and he was even able to laugh along with everyone else a few times. The service felt very cathartic to the young man.

Cyril felt a tap on his shoulder, and he looked back to see Charlie Scolfield standing behind him. Charlie motioned for Cyril to follow him. Soon, Cyril was standing beside his four friends and Mr. Fletcher as they lifted the coffin onto their shoulders and began the walk through the church as the people continued singing. They slowly negotiated the few steps down to the ground, carried the coffin out, and placed it in an old-style hearse carriage. They silently accompanied the hearse to the nearby graveyard, with the congregation following along behind. The graveside part of the service was brief, and it was not long before the funeral-goers returned to Mr. Bratton's house. After speaking to his friends, Cyril stood with his father to one side in the front room as folks milled about carrying plates of food and talking with one another.

Cyril wondered for a moment where his mother had gotten off to when he saw her through a doorway. He saw her standing in Mr. Bratton's room, speaking to his niece. Cyril started to head in that direction when he heard his father's voice behind him. "Wait here, your Mama is fine. Let them speak alone."

"Yes, sir," Cyril answered. He could see them speaking, but he could not hear the conversation. He remembered how much he always hated feeling excluded from a conversation. After a few minutes, Mrs. Scolfield walked over to the room, and it appeared that she was invited in, and as she went into the room, Cyril saw his mother look up and notice him watching her. Cyril saw his mother as she stepped over and closed the door so that only the three women were in the room, and he could not see what was happening.

After several minutes he saw Mrs. Scolfield open the door and step out, and for the few moments that the door was open, he could see over her shoulder into the room where the other two women were still talking. Mrs. Scolfield returned a few minutes later with the Reverend, and she paused to knock on the door, and then, the couple went in. The door remained closed for another ten minutes, and when it opened back up, Cyril saw his mother come out and head in his direction. Mr. Bratton's niece exited next, and her eyes followed Ida for a few moments before she stepped out to begin mingling with the other folks. Reverend and Mrs. Scolfield came out of the room last.

Ida looked at her husband. "William, I am ready to leave now."

"Okay, my love, I will get the truck from the church. Are you riding along with us, Cyril?"

"No, sir, I want to stay here longer and walk home later this afternoon."

"We will see you at home then."

"I will walk with you over to the church," said Ida. "Be sure that you do not become a nuisance to the family, Cyril. She has much to do since she will also take some things with her. So do not get in her way or overstay your welcome, and come on along home before too much longer."

"Yes, ma'am."

Cyril remained inside after his parents left. He could see them through the window as they walked across the yard. Then, he saw the Reverend follow them out. "Mrs. Ledbetter," the preacher's voice sounded as the door closed. Cyril saw his parents turn and wait for the man. Moments later, Mrs. Scolfield followed her husband through the door. He saw first Rev. Scolfield and then Mrs. Scolfield walk up to his parents and begin to speak with his mother. He could not imagine what they would be talking to his parents about since they really only knew one another in passing. 'Maybe they are talking about Jimmy Scolfield, he thought to himself. Probably thanking my father for hiring Jimmy.' He watched through the window for the next couple of minutes until Mrs. Scolfield stepped forward and hugged his mother – that particularly comforting hug that only a preacher's wife can give. He saw his father and the Reverend shake hands, and then his parents turned and continued on their way as the Scolfields returned to the house.

As Cyril looked away, he noticed another person also watching from inside the house through another window. He watched as Mr. Bratton's niece turned, and he caught her eye. They looked at one another for a few seconds, and she gave him a sad smile. Then, she motioned him over, and he followed her to the kitchen where many ladies were gathered, and a few men and children were milling around a heavily laden table. "I didn't tell you my name yesterday when we met. I am Sarah Batson, and my daughter is Violet."

"Yes, ma'am, I remembered her name from you calling her yesterday. But it is nice to officially meet you. And I want you to know how sorry I am for your family."

"Thank you, Cyril. And I am very sorry for you and your loss as well – and all of the young men he tutored. You carry a wonderful name; always be proud of it."

"I will."

She paused and looked closely at him for a moment; she smiled as she laid a hand on his shoulder. "You do favor your mother just a bit. Now, get a plate and get started on that food, people brought so much, and I can't take it back to Birmingham." She gave him a slight push toward the table.

"Yes, ma'am."

The following Saturday, Cyril drove the truck into town to pick up everything Mr. Bratton had listed for him and his family to have or hold on to. When he brought the things home, he put the chair in the parlor for his mother. The quilts went into the linen closet except for two, one for each bed in the house. There were a few boxes and some chip tins. Cyril set up some bookshelves in his room to hold all the law books he hoped would someday grace his law office.

A letter came for Cyril a few days later. He opened it just before supper after getting home from the afternoon study group. Later as he sat at supper, he told his parents about the letter. "That letter I received today was from an attorney settling the Bratton Estate. He will be in town next week for a reading of the will and asks that I be there along with the other four gentlemen from the group." Cyril's parents were comfortable with this and there was not much discussion about it.

It was a Wednesday afternoon, and the five gentlemen walked into the side room of the church. They were just returning from the reading of the will. "Well, we all already got the books and things that he left for us, so we don't have to do that," said Peter.

"It will seem strange for someone else to live in that house now. But I guess they will sell it and send the money to his family," said Emery.

"Does he have much family?" asked Peter.

"He has a daughter he has not seen in many years," said Cyril.

"A daughter?" asked Isaac. "Why was she not at his funeral? We all met his niece, but we didn't see a daughter."

"I guess that she lives too far away to make it for the funeral, or maybe she just did not want to come," said Cyril.

"Still, it does not seem right for her not to be here," said Isaac. The other gentlemen nodded in agreement.

After a few moments of silence, Charlie changed the subject. "I cannot believe that he did that for all of us. I knew he had saved a lot of money from his work as a lawyer, but I had no idea he would do that."

"I know," said Peter. "College was going to be a stretch to pay for, but not now."

"All of us, he left money in that fund to pay for all of us to go to college," said Emery.

"I still miss him, though," said Charlie.

"We all do," Cyril agreed.

"But still," said Charlie. "I wonder why he did that."

"Just a good man, I guess," said Peter.

Cyril looked up. "He once told me how some people did a lot for him when he started college."

Later that day, Cyril was sitting at the supper table with his parents. "Well, we all went to hear what the lawyer had to say about the will. He said that Mr. Bratton left some money in a fund to pay for college for all five of us who have been in the afternoon study group."

Ida got a surprised look on her face. "Why would he leave you money? He had no reason to leave you money for anything. We cannot accept that sort of thing. We will pay for your college ourselves."

"He didn't leave money to me or even just for me. He established a fund to pay for all five of us to attend college."

"Well, you are not going to accept it. Let the other boys have all of it to pay for their school."

"But Mama, he wanted it to pay for all five of us. He told me a story once when we were fishing. I asked him about how it felt when he left his family to go to college. I was worried about how you two would get along without me helping around here. He told me his stepfather was a minister and his mother was a seamstress. He said that a bunch of the people from their church saved up money, just a lot of folks saving up a little bit each. He said that they saved up a big part of his college money that way since he was the first one from their church to be able to go to college. And he said everyone from the whole church came down to see him off when he left. The men all got together and bought him some nice shoes and a good hat. And every lady in his church had sewed him something to wear. And his mother made him a new suit. He said he had plenty of nice clothes, a good suit, good shoes, and a good hat when he showed up at the college. He said that it made him feel like he belonged there and had as nice clothes as anybody in that college and way better than some. All those folks did that so that he could go to college for all of them. Some of them could not even read, but they worked and saved up so he could study. I think that when he helped those people in the Bottoms keep their farms, he was paying those folks back for what the others did for him years ago. I think that this is him trying to pay those folks back. They all worked together to send one person to college, and he worked all of his life, and now he can send five people to college."

Ida sat there listening to her son. And after he finished, she continued to sit there as if she were still listening. William slowly got up, walked around the table to stand behind his wife, and put his hands on her shoulders. She reached one hand up and laid it on top of his. He bent down and put his cheek next to hers as if he were going to whisper in her ear, but he stayed silent. She leaned her head toward him, pressing herself against him, and he breathed deeply the scent of her hair. Her eyes puddled up, but they did not spill over. She looked up at her son, and he could see her eyes sparkle from the tears they held back. She slowly nodded as she pulled herself back up to her usual proper posture and composed herself. "Then, you must do well and make him proud."

"Yes, ma'am."

The summer flew by with Cyril keeping himself very busy. Even though school was finished and three of them had graduated, the gentlemen continued to have their sessions together every Monday, Wednesday, and Friday afternoon. The rest of the time, Cyril was working hard around the farm. Sister Moore passed in late summer, and Jimmy Scolfield and his wife moved into the old Moore house to be closer to his job and to have a house for his new family. The sheriff had been by to talk to William about it, and they had argued a bit, but in the end, Jimmy stayed put. Part of why Cyril was working so hard on the farm was that he was nervous and excited at the same time about leaving this little town and everyone to go to a place as big as Philadelphia.

"I cannot believe that we are getting on a train tomorrow and going away to college," said Peter.

"I know," said Emery. "We are going to miss you."

"Hey, Emery, are you still writing letters to that girl?" asked Isaac. "What was her name again?"

"Violet," said Cyril. "Her name is Violet."

Emery looked down and blushed. "Yes, we are still writing to one another."

"Well, make sure you keep up with your studies and do not get distracted," said Charles.

"No way that I would let that happen. She said that she is going to marry a man who has been to college, and she has no interest in any man who does not go to college," responded Emery.

"Oh, so you are already planning your wedding," laughed Peter.

Poor Emery looked even more bashful. "Can we just change the subject?"

Isaac said, "You are just jealous, Peter. I saw you trying to talk to her after the funeral."

"You did not see anything," snapped Peter.

Laughter filled the room.

"At least you two will be in Atlanta together," Cyril told Peter and Charlie. "I am going to be all alone up there in Philadelphia. I am going to miss all of you."

Later that evening, William asked over supper. "Are you all packed, son? There won't be much time for you to get ready in the morning. You'll have time for breakfast and to get to the early train."

"Yes, sir."

Ida said, "I will pack a paper sack of food for you to take on the train."

"Thank you, Mother."

"I think he has his heart set on a pie and some fried chicken along the way," William said.

"Or he can save his money."

"That will be nice, Mother. I am sure I will start missing your cooking when I am up there."

"I bet you will," said William. "I couldn't imagine being away from your Mama's cooking."

"When you finish eating, I want you to get a good bath and get to bed early," Ida said. "That new haircut looks good, but you must be clean and smelling like soap when you get on that train. It is going to be a long trip to Philadelphia."

"Yes, ma'am."

"Now, did you pack that new bottle of hair oil?" She asked. "I will not have you coming home with anything living in your hair."

"Yes, ma'am, it is all packed."

"Since you will be around so many people in the city, you must use that hair oil at least once a week."

"Yes, ma'am, right after my hair is dry from my bath every week."

"And you make sure to keep your hair cut close. I am not having my son walk around looking shaggy. And I know that you are prone to forget."

"Yes, ma'am, regular haircuts."

"And you make sure to find a laundry there to keep your clothes clean. And you brush that suit from time to time too."

"Yes, ma'am."

"I doubt that he is going to forget, what with you reminding him in every letter." William smiled sweetly at his wife.

"You can say too much, Mr. Ledbetter. You are all grown up now, so trying to be cute will not get you out of trouble."

The following morning, Cyril saw his shadow as it crept ahead of him in the first light of dawn. It had a bag in each hand to take on the shadow train to college. His shadow beat him to the platform stairs and began to fold itself as it ascended the stairs ahead of him. He reached the top stair and noticed that his shadow had flattened back out and was resting on the platform. He could hear his parents as they came up the stairs behind him.

"Do you have your ticket in your pocket?" asked Ida.

"Yes, ma'am."

"You take your bags over to the train and let a porter help you with them."

"Yes, ma'am."

"Do you have any money to tip the porter?"

"Yes, ma'am."

Cyril looked down the platform toward the last passenger car of the train, and he saw a small crowd of Black folks gathered, and he knew that most of them were the families of his friends who were also leaving on the early train to Birmingham. He headed toward one of the front passenger cars and put his bags on the platform. He turned to his parents and said, "I want to go and speak to Peter and Charlie before the train leaves."

"Alright, son, you go talk to your friends, and I will take care of the porter for you," said William.

Cyril quickly walked to the other end of the platform and joined the crowd of folks gathered there. He could see his four friends standing at the heart of the little crowd.

He heard Charlie call to him. "Cyril." Charlie waved him over, and the people parted and let him through.

"Are you all packed and ready?" asked Charlie.

"Yes, I've got my ticket and everything," answered Cyril.

"Peter and I must go to Birmingham first and then get another train to Atlanta."

"I stay on this one passed Birmingham and switch later to a train going to Philadelphia," said Cyril.

Peter said, "We are doing it, Cyril – we are all going to college." The young man had a big smile, which made Cyril smile, too, even though he felt a little sick to his stomach.

"I wish I could ride back here with you two," Cyril smiled.

"Don't try that again," said Peter.

"Yes, last time you nearly got us all thrown off the train," added Charlie

Isaac and Emery were there to see their friends off. Emery said, "That conductor did not know what to do with you." The young men laughed.

"I didn't know what to do with myself riding up there alone. I brought a book to read this time."

"All aboard," came the call of the conductor.

"I need to get back to my parents," Cyril said as he held his hand out to Charlie, who shook it quickly as Mrs. Scolfield wrapped her son in an embrace. Cyril managed to shake hands with each of his friends and with Reverend Scolfield as the crowd moved toward the door of the last passenger car. He then turned and quickly returned to the front of the train, where his parents were waiting. And he could see another familiar face waiting to say bye.

Billy reached out his hand as Cyril approached and, as they shook hands, said, "Known you all o' my life, Cy. I hope 'at you do good up there in college, an' 'en, you come back."

"I'll be back occasionally to visit, so I will see you soon enough," answered Cyril.

"All right," said Billy. "We always been friends, an' just 'cause you goin' t' college don't change nuthin' 'tween us."

"Not a thing, Billy – not a thing."

"Boy, you best get on the train. The porter just took your bags on, and he is waitin' for you," said William.

"Yes, sir." Cyril shook his father's outstretched hand. The handshake felt somehow different, and then, his father pulled him into a hug.

"You're a man now," smiled William as he pushed his son back to arm's length to look at him; then, he turned the young man toward the train.

Cyril turned and saw his mother standing between him and the train. Her eyes glistened, and she smiled. He took a step toward her and put his arms around her. "I am going to miss you, Mama."

"You will be too busy to miss me."

"No, ma'am. I already do miss you."

"You are going to be fine. And you are going to make us proud. Now, you get on that train."

Cyril stepped back and saw his mother pointing to a bag on the platform beside her. "Take that and save your money," Ida said.

The train heaved as it started to move. Cyril quickly kissed his mother on the cheek, picked up the bag, and jumped onto the train as it lurched forward. Moments later, he sat in his seat and looked out the window as the town slowly slipped by. He watched the shadow of the train as it moved along and picked up speed. Soon, the shadow of the train was quickly skimming across the landscape. He thought how strange it looked, almost like a snake slithering across the ground as it moved effortlessly over and across all obstacles. His shadow was the only one going away to college with him – going into his future with him.

Part Three

Twenty-Five:
Who Do You Think You Are?

The shadow of the motor car leaped along beside the road as it slid over the land, dipping down into the ditches or standing up for fences and walls. C.W. Ledbetter Esq. occasionally glanced at his shadow as he drove through the Alabama countryside heading for his hometown. He was alone and thinking about home and childhood as he listened to the radio. "That was Frank Sinatra with Five Minutes More, the number five selling song of nineteen forty-six; next, we will be hearing The Gypsy from the Ink Spots as we count down to the number one song of last year."

It was only a week since the funeral, and he was on his way back to settle his mother's affairs and make arrangements for the family farm. Last week, after the funeral, he returned his wife and two children to Pensacola and took a few days to clear the schedule of his law office to come right back to Bratton and take care of everything. It was not a long drive from Pensacola to Bratton, and he certainly knew it by heart after so many trips bringing his family up to visit the farm and their grandparents and then only their grandmother. And now, she was gone – she had waited a while to join her husband, but C. W. knew she had missed her William very much for those three years. He thought how glad he was that his children were old enough to have plenty of good memories of their grandparents. They could remember their grandfather's jokes and their grandmother's cooking. C.W. had never known his own grandparents, and he had always felt a hole where memories of them should be.

He passed an old overgrown dirt road that turned off the road – so overgrown that he would not even notice it if he didn't already know where it was. He thought about the day he had broken his leg and how Mr. Bratton had tried to drive so carefully on that little dirt road while bringing C.W. out of there. In a few minutes, he was in Bratton, driving up through the south side of town. He passed the houses of the folks who lived on the south side of the tracks, and when he reached Second Baptist Church, he slowed down as he remembered all those afternoons studying there with his friends. A few moments later, he drove slowly by the house where he had spent so much of his childhood visiting Mr. Bratton. He thought about how he had resolved to study law in that house. It was twenty years since Mr. Bratton died, but C.W. could still hear the man's voice speaking to him in that clear, unaccented manner that attorneys often use – teaching him to drive or debating the importance of Aristotle.

He watched the shadow of the car as it slipped by the train station, and he remembered many trips in and out of that station – but mostly, he remembered the fried chicken lunches that he liked to get there when he had a little extra pocket money as a boy. He parked in front of the post office to run in, see if there was any mail for his mother, and mail the letter in his pocket. He had the habit of stopping at the post office to pick up any mail headed out to the farm – a habit developed over the last dozen years. He got out of the car and, as usual, looked at the clock on the nearby train station and checked his watch. It was a habit that he had learned from his father, even down to adjusting all of the clocks in the house on Sunday after church. Catching sight of himself reflected in the glass of the large window, he felt a pang because, for a moment, it looked like his father was there wearing a suit. He opened the door and heard the little bell jingle.

"Brother Cy Ledbetter," came a familiar voice.

"Hello there, Billy. Or should I say, Reverend Holstead? How are you doing today?

"Doin' well. I guess you are back to take care of your Mama's affairs."

"Yes, lots of things to do. I wanted to thank you again for the funeral service last week. And thank Mrs. Holstead for the food."

The preacher nodded. "I'll tell her. Everybody in town was at that funeral. People shore are gonna miss Sister Ida. Your mother was quite a woman."

"That she was."

"Have you decided what you are gonna do with the farm?"

"I am going to keep it for now. I have no heart to sell it. The kids love it so much. When my father got sick, he sold the old Moore place to James Scolfield. And Mr. Scolfiled has been taking care of things for my mother since my father died. So, I will offer him a business deal where he continues to manage our farm along with his. Then, our farm stays as a working farm, and we will have the house to visit on weekends."

"Jimmy has a bunch of sons, so he should be happy to keep managing everything," said Reverend Holstead. "Sounds like a good plan, an' 'at way your kids can still get out t' the country."

The two old friends exchanged a glance, wishing their children could grow to have friends as great as the friendship they shared.

Reverend Holstead then continued, "You stoppin' in here to get your Mama's mail, I reckon."

"That and drop a letter in the mail for my wife."

"A letter for your wife? Didn't you just see your wife this mornin' before you left Pensacola?"

C.W. smiled and said, "Yes, I do it whenever I am away from home for a couple of days. A good way to keep your wife – maybe you should try it sometime."

"Walk down to the post office to mail a letter to a woman I see every day?"

"Yep, to ensure that you keep her."

"I don't have any trouble keeping my wife."

"Did you ever wonder if she has trouble wanting to keep you?" C.W. grinned.

"Never thought of it that way."

"Maybe you should."

Reverend Holstead laughed and held out his hand. "I have to git back. Takes a lot runnin' a farm and a church. You gonna be in town for a few days, I imagine, s' I want you t' come out t' the house for supper tomorrow."

As they shook hands, C.W. said, "Thank you, I will be there."

C.W. pulled into the farm and parked. Getting out of his car, he noticed a familiar woman walking around from the back of the house. She was every bit as beautiful as had been her mother, Helen Powell. 'Jimmy is a lucky man,' C.W. thought to himself. "Hello, Mrs. Scolfield. How are you today."

"I am doing well, Mr. Ledbetter. How are you doing this afternoon?"

"I am doing well, thank you. I was wondering if your husband got a letter from me."

"Yes, he did, and he looked it over and said that he likes your proposal if you want to stop by and talk to him about it."

"Well, I will spend the rest of the day going through things here. Would tomorrow sometime be good for me to stop by?"

"Yes, tomorrow will be fine. I tell you what, you come by at lunchtime, and you and he can discuss business over the table."

"That would be very nice, Mrs. Scolfield. I also want to thank you for all that you did helping my mother over these last few years."

"Oh, it was a pleasure. Mostly, we sat and talked. She liked to reminisce about her parents and her childhood. Told me all kinds of stories about the candy store. And how she met your father and when they eloped. She was full of stories about her parents."

"Well then, you probably know more about her early life than I do – she never spoke much about it to me."

"Well, you start going through things, and then later, if you want me to tell you any of her stories, just let me know."

"I will definitely take you up on that offer. I know absolutely nothing about my grandparents."

"About a week before she passed, she asked me to help her start going through lots of her papers and everything because she said there were many old things that you would have no use for and that she didn't need anymore. We never did get to throw any of it out like she wanted. It is all sitting in the front room. A few boxes of letters and some old photographs and things. If you want just to leave it all there, I will have one of the boys come over and get it tomorrow."

"That will not be necessary; I will take care of everything myself. Thank you."

"Well, I need to get home to get supper on the table."

"Yes, ma'am. Thank you. And let your husband know that I will be by to see him tomorrow and maybe even listen to one of those stories about my grandparents."

"Bye now."

C.W. watched the woman for a moment and then turned and looked at the farm. He decided to walk around and look at the barn and the land before going into the house to settle down for the evening.

He spent an hour looking through the barn and taking his time. Really, he was just putting off the inevitable – walking into an empty house. No sound of his mother singing. No smells coming from the kitchen. He dreaded walking into that house where he knew memories would haunt him like ghosts. Finally, he turned toward the house and headed for the back door. As he neared the porch, he saw a young man walking out through the door. He was about ten years old, and C.W. could not remember the child's name but recognized him as one of the Scolfield children.

"Hello, Mr. Ledbetter. My Mama sent a plate over for you. She said you were out here with no supper and nothing in the kitchen to cook, and she would not have you go hungry."

"Bless her; my stomach was starting to complain. That is very welcome. Be sure to thank your mother for me."

"Yes, sir. I set it in there on the stove, but it is still warm if you want it now. I'll see you later."

"Thank you."

C.W. felt a bit of relief since this gave him a reason to finally go inside and something to do when he got in there. He braced himself and went in the back door through to the kitchen. He could smell the plate of food, and that was nice since he had never walked into that kitchen and not smelled cooking or baking. The screen door closed behind him; the sound echoed through the empty house. There was an eerie feeling with the windows closed because nobody had been there for a week, so the usual sounds outside were not filtering in. Something else seemed off, but it took him a few moments to realize what it was. There was no ticking anywhere in the house. The clocks had not been wound for over a week, and every clock had stopped. This left an unusually hollow silence in the place. 'Well, that is something to do before I sit down to eat,' he thought. So, he went through the house and wound every clock and set them all according to his watch, just like he had seen his father do every Sunday for eighteen years.

After the clocks were all set and ticking away again, C.W. pulled a fork out of a drawer, carried the plate of food over to the sink, and pulled the cloth cover off it. The food was no longer warm, but the smell of fresh biscuits filled the air. Just as he was trying to take his first bite, he heard his mother's voice calling from a memory of his teenage years, sounding like she was standing right behind him. 'You will not stand over my sink and eat. I do not care if it is late and you are eating alone; you will carry your plate to the dining room and have a seat.'

"Yes, ma'am," he whispered as he turned toward the dining room. He could not help but glance toward her bedroom door where she had stood so long ago. He began to eat silently as he listened to the clocks ticking, and the afternoon began to rush toward evening. The daylight streamed in, so the house was still well-lit, making it seem all the more empty.

After finishing his meal, he took his plate to the sink to wash. The pump needed priming, so he reached for the pot of water he knew would be sitting there. He remembered how his mother would fill that pot with water as her last duty in the kitchen so it would be ready to prime the pump first thing in the morning. He stopped momentarily as he realized that the pot of water in his hand was the last water she ever pumped over her sink. He grabbed a glass and poured a bit of the water into it, and took a drink. Then, he poured the rest into the pump and got the water flowing, and he refilled the pot before returning it to the stove. He then proceeded to wash up his plate and fork.

C.W. turned away from the sink after he finished and looked into his parent's room. He saw the bed sitting there, awaiting its passengers' nightly journeys. He saw the beautiful quilt – one that Mrs. Bratton had made. He saw his mother's pillow and he slowly walked toward the bed. He picked up the pillow and hugged it to him very closely, and he buried his face into it the way he used to bury his face into her neck and hair as a little boy. His mother's familiar smell soothed his ache – or perhaps made it worse, he could not be sure. He stood and rocked himself and the pillow for several minutes; then, returned the pillow to the bed and plumped it so that it would sit just right – the way his mother always placed it.

He looked around the room for a few moments and made his way through the kitchen and the dining room to the parlor once he felt he had looked around enough. He saw that recently his mother must have had Jimmy come in and move a few things around for her. Her rocking chair was now in a corner, and Mrs. Bratton's old Victorian chair was sitting in front of the window where the rocking chair had been for as long as he could remember. It sat at just the right angle to catch the late afternoon sun just over a shoulder for reading and still be able to see the whole room. 'Mother must have wanted to sit in the softer chair; it was most likely easier on her back,' he thought. He noticed the shawl that his mother had always treasured from her mother. He thought about his mother sitting there reading.

He spied the boxes and photo album that his mother intended to get rid of. 'Well, they are already out, so I might as well start there. He picked up the photo album with three shoe boxes sitting on it. He started to carry them over to the settee, which had always been his place. But he thought better since the chair in front of the window would have the best light for reading this late in the day. He sat in the old Victorian chair and felt himself sink back. As he leaned back, he caught the scent of his mother's perfume from the shawl draped right behind his shoulders. He smiled as he looked down at the objects in front of him. 'Let's get you opened up and see what you are,' he said as he opened a shoe box. It looked like the box was full of letters, carefully folded and returned to their paper sleeves, and there was one longer envelope inside with the shorter letters. He picked up the long envelope and pulled out the paper inside. He lifted the top fold of the paper to see what was on it. 'Certificate of Marriage,' was at the top and C.W. could see a date and his father's name just above the fold.

He closed the paper and returned it to its envelope, and for a moment, he wondered why his mother would want to get rid of that or if maybe it was just a mistake. 'We will keep that,' he thought as he tucked it down next to his leg to keep it separate from the other things. He lifted one of the smaller envelopes to one side to see that the letter was addressed to. Mrs. Ida B. Ledbetter. 'Oh, these were to Mother,' he thought to himself. He slipped the letter out and opened it to find three pages.

My Dearest Ida,

Your mother and I hope that…

'From her father,' he thought. 'I will definitely keep these for reading later.' He pulled another letter out for a quick scan and saw that it was also to his mother and from her mother. He quickly checked and few more of the letters – just their openings. Most were from her father, with a few from her mother. One of the envelopes slipped onto the floor. 'I will grab that in a bit,' he thought as he closed that shoe box and set it aside. He looked down and saw the envelope on the floor resting in his shadow. He smiled and thought about how he would watch his mother's shadow as it slowly crept across the floor with the setting sun every afternoon when he was a boy. And now his own shadow was the sundial as it crept along the floor. The head of his shadow had not even made it to the edge of the braided rug, so he had plenty of time left.

He put that shoe box to the side of his lap as he opened another one. The strong smell of mothballs filled the air. He lifted a piece of rough cloth out of the box – actually, it was an old cloth grain sack. Beautiful embroidery covered the sack with animals and flowers and even a few scenes of people. There were a couple of embroidered faces of women on the cloth of the sack. He remembered Mr. Bratton telling him about this. He carefully folded the old cloth and returned it to its box, which he also set to the side. He glanced to see how his shadow was progressing and saw that it had moved to the edge of the rug.

He opened the last shoe box and saw that it, too, was full of letters. He lifted one and saw the recipient's name. 'Mr. Cyril Bratton, Esq.' He opened that envelope and looked at the top of the first page.

Dearest Father,

Please, I beg you. Do not do this. You cannot, under any circumstances, come here. These are rigid people who would never understand should there be even the slightest mistake. The county sheriff here is not a man with which to trifle in any way, and he is, by nature, a deeply suspicious man.

'That was unexpected,' he thought as he folded that letter and returned it to its envelope. 'I will have to get back to that one later.' He put the envelope back, closed the box, and set it aside. He looked at the photo album that was left sitting in his lap. He noticed that the top of the head of his shadow had already reached the middle of the rug. 'Never seen it move so fast,' he thought. He wondered at the photo album, and it took him a moment to recognize it as having once belonged to Mr. Bratton. 'I guess that no one ever wanted this after all. But she kept it safe just in case.' He smiled to himself. 'I always wanted to see the last few pages of this one and see what his daughter looked like. I will have to go through this later.' He started to put the album to one side but then felt the urge to see that familiar face, so he placed the album back in his lap, and he opened the front cover to the first page to the smiling face of a young Cyril Bratton with his brand new wife. C.W. sat there for a moment and then turned the page to see the pictures of the new baby and the young family. He caught a glimpse of his shadow, which had already rushed to the other end of the rug and was starting to march steadily toward the wall. The room was getting a bit less bright as the sun dropped more and more behind him. 'I should put these aside and find another bunch of papers to start going through while I still have some daylight.'

He closed the album, then bent forward to retrieve the dropped letter, and as he sat back up, he looked at the address again as he inserted the letter back into its box. 'Mrs. William Ledbetter. 'Oh, he changed it from Ida B. to Mrs. William Ledbetter. I wonder why.' He thought for a moment and realized that he never knew his mother's middle initial. He had always known her as Ida Ledbetter, but he had never seen her use the B. He wondered what her maiden name had been. He pulled the letter back out and looked at the sender's address.

C. Bratton
2 Harcourt Ave.
Memphis Tenn.

C.W. could no longer hear the clocks ticking because of the rushing wind as the sudden storm wind battered against the house – no, not the house – his ears. His pulse was pounding in his ears. He looked up and saw that his shadow was moving steadily up the far wall as the room grew a little bit darker. 'The wall, when did it reach the damned wall? Find that marriage certificate!' He wrestled the marriage certificate from under his leg where it had slipped. He tore open the envelope and completely unfolded the paper.

Miss Ida Bratton of Memphis Tenn.

'Miss Ida Bratton of Memphis Tenn.'

'Miss Ida Bratton …'

C.W. felt his eyes sting, and now the room was getting dark, or maybe it was his eyes he could not be sure. He looked across the room. His shadow was already a good way up the wall. 'How is it moving so fast?'

He grabbed the photo album and opened it to the last page. He leaned forward to try to get a clear look. The light was dying, everyone in these pictures was Black, and he was having trouble seeing through his tears. Then, he got a clear look at a picture of a young woman – a familiar woman, much younger than he could ever remember. He took a pained breath, and he felt shaken.

He started opening letters and trying to see them in the fading light, but he could not make out anything on the pages, but he still kept pulling them out and trying. Even if he could not see the words, he knew they were there. A box fell, and he instinctively reached for it to find himself holding a rough cloth. He squeezed the cloth as he sat back against the chair. He could smell his mother, or he thought that he could. 'Is that why she started sitting in this chair, to be near her mother?' With his free hand, he caressed the cloth arm of the chair as he tried to recall everything Mr. Bratton ever told him about his wife.

He sat very still now. It was too dark to read. 'Where are those lamps? Damned Alabama is not going to electrify out here for years.' Profound darkness was dissolving everything around him. He looked across at his shadow, which was now sitting even with him but also almost gone. "Who are you?" He asked his shadow in a whisper. It just silently vanished into the rolling tide of darkness.

Epilogue:

... then they lay trembling in the night.
Quietly awaiting dawn, when they see their edges.
And perhaps remember who they are.

www.ingramcontent.com/pod-product-compliance
Lightning Source LLC
Chambersburg PA
CBHW060305260626

47160CB00007B/2514